THE BUFFALO TRACE

BOOKS BY VIRGINIA S. EIFERT

Three Rivers South: A Story of Young Abe Lincoln

The Buffalo Trace

STILL THE PEOPLE CLIMBED. THE ROCKS HURT THEIR FEET. THE HORSES
STRUGGLED UPWARD, SLIPPED, FELL, PACKS SLID OFF . . .

THE
BUFFALO TRACE

by

VIRGINIA S. EIFERT

ILLUSTRATED BY MANNING de V. LEE

WILDSIDE PRESS

THIS BOOK IS DEDICATED
TO MY MOTHER

*In a larger sense, I also dedicate it to Bathsheba
Lincoln, who made a home in the wilderness*

ACKNOWLEDGMENTS

MY THANKS to all those people who helped me in gathering together the material which became THE BUFFALO TRACE. My gratitude in particular goes to Mr. and Mrs. Siegfried R. Weng, Evansville, Indiana; to Miss Margaret Flint of the Illinois State Historical Library; to Mrs. Audrey Major and Miss Lucille Fritz, reference librarians at Lincoln Library, Springfield, Illinois; to Larry and Herman Eifert who explored with me portions of the Wilderness Road and the Buffalo Trace; and to Miss Dorothy M. Bryan, Dodd, Mead & Company, who spent many hours over my manuscript, hammering it into shape.

V. S. E.

FOREWORD

This is the story of Abraham Lincoln, Esquire, President Lincoln's grandfather, as it may have happened in the turbulent days of Daniel Boone, the Wilderness, Road, and the settling of Kentucky. Young Abe never knew his grandfather, but perhaps it was the force of that first Abraham's character and the weight of his decisions which, in a large measure, influenced the destiny of the grandson he did not live to see.

The general situation and many of the events described in this book are based upon historical facts. However, the fictional characters are wholly imaginative: they do not portray and are not intended to portray any actual persons.

ILLUSTRATIONS

xi

THE BUFFALO TRACE

CHAPTER ONE

He stood in the sweet dusk of a night in spring, in the year 1780, and listened with yearning to the sounds of wild geese flying north. Swelling flower buds on his peach trees glimmered pallidly in the twilight, and the mockingbird which always nested in a big lilac bush beside the front door broke into a crazy medley of tinkling tunes, full of the fine feeling of springtime.

As he stood there, Abraham Lincoln, Esquire, was thinking once again of Kentucky and of the man who had told him so much about that green wilderness. Ever since Dan Boone, riding up the Valley of Virginia in the summer of 1779, had stopped his horse to let it graze beside the Lincoln fence, and talked so earnestly about Kentucky, Abraham had been in a fever of inner impatience to follow the lure of the Wilderness Road to the land Boone loved.

For nine years Abraham and Bathsheba Lincoln had lived prosperously on their two hundred and fifty-two acres of fine red Virginia land along Linville Creek. By 1779 their peach trees were bearing well; every year the apple orchard held heavy crimson fruit; the Lincoln horses were keen of line and swift of foot. Abraham and Bathsheba had four children to further anchor them to this lovely land below the Shenandoahs. Mordecai, at eight, was growing tall with the lengthiness of leg which marked most Lincoln men. Mord was fond of horses, just as his father was, and helped train some of the yearlings to the saddle. Little Tommy, the baby, at seventeen months was already deeply in love with horseflesh. Whenever Mary, who was four, a slender, serious little girl and Tommy's guardian, lost sight of the toddler, she could find him at the stables. And usually Mord was not far away.

Josiah, at six, was small-boned and fair like his mother; he was more interested in planting things than in working with creatures which snorted and kicked. He had a little garden of wildflowers and ferns which he had brought from the big woods down the creek. His father and the slaves always said admiringly that Jo could make a dead twig shoot leaves merely by sticking it into the clay. It hurt Jo Lincoln to see a dying tree, and none of his own trees and flowers were permitted to do so much as wilt for lack of water. It was Jo who, the year he was five, had planted a vegetable garden and with pride brought his early lettuce and onions and new peas to the big, brick-floored kitchen.

"My, my, how dat chile do make things grow!" cried Leah, the Negro cook who was six feet tall and wore a neatly wrapped turban which only increased her height. Jo beamed shyly, and then ran out with Mary and Mord to build a dam across the little rivulet tumbling into the creek.

Standing quietly and alone in the dark spring orchard, Abraham remembered how eagerly he had listened to what Dan was saying the summer before. He had listened, even though he knew that a man with four children and a fifth one on the way had no business to go chasing off with a footloose rascal like Dan Boone, whose own family had had to fend unhappily for itself during his long absences. Dan had moved them at last to his new fort at Boonesborough because his wife, Rebecca, had put her foot down and said she wouldn't stay behind another time. But Rebecca Boone was used to living in wild places, and one wilderness or another mattered little to her as long as she was with Dan. Bathsheba was different, and Abraham wondered if she would like as wild a land as Kentucky must be.

While he had listened to Dan that summer day, Boone had talked with such deadly urgency that it ate steadily into Abraham's resistance.

"It's a fair land, I tell you!" Daniel Boone had said. "A right purty

place and it ain't over-run with folk like it's gettin' to be round about.
I *cain't stand* folk a-crowdin' me, and if you know what's good for
you, you won't stand for it neither! 'Tain't right for a man to have
no elbow room, not when he can live in the wilderness with space
to breathe!"

Abraham had looked around him at his green acres, at his fat
cattle and his lean-flanked, glossy horses, at his orchards where the
slaves were picking peaches and laying them carefully in leaf-lined
baskets, at his brick house with the big windows, set on the slope
above the spreading lawns. Crowded . . . well, you couldn't say
he was exactly pinched for room. But there was something in what
Dan was saying which got into his blood.

Daniel Boone went away on his errand to try to persuade the
Virginia Legislature to send more men and arms into Kentucky.
Unsuccessful in his mission, he came back down the Valley of Vir-
ginia in October of that year and stayed overnight with the Lincolns.
Abraham had another chance to ask him a little more about Ken-
tucky. Not that you had to *ask* Dan Boone to talk about Kentucky.
He was so full of it that it almost spouted from his long, thin ears,
Bathsheba thought wryly, and it was the only thing he seemed to
know or talk about, or that he figured was worth telling.

"*Land* in *Kaintuck?*" Boone exploded, sitting back in his chair.
"*Land?* Why, man, there's miles of it, hundreds of miles of it, the
purtiest grazing land you ever did see and the best timber and the
finest water. And there for the taking, at forty cents the acre, mind
you! Why, Abe, you couldn't do better if you went to the ends of
the earth!"

"It's pretty nice here in Virginia," commented Bathsheba mildly
from where she sat sewing. In the last of the autumn daylight the
younger children were playing cat's cradle on the doorstep. Mord
was studying by the fire, with one ear cocked toward the conversation and his mind rambling far from his sums to the sweet land of
Kaintuck somewhere beyond the mountains. Now and again he
cast an admiring glance at Mr. Boone, his hero. Mord didn't think

3

that the great Daniel Boone looked so important—he wasn't as tall as Pa, nor at all fierce-looking, with that pink-cheeked, mild face of his and those ice-blue eyes that could look right through a fellow. But Dan Boone's stained buckskin clothes showed he'd been out in the great wilderness and had been fighting Indians. And Mord Lincoln would have given anything he owned to be allowed to go off and fight Indians with Mr. Boone.

Bathsheba, sitting quietly in her low rocking chair, let her eyes move from one man to the other and across to Mord and back again to Daniel Boone. She made a pretty picture, with her blue skirts spread neatly around her ankles, her quick fingers working steadily at her sewing. Her pale hair was fastened loosely enough for some of the irrepressible little curling tendrils to escape around her oval face, and beneath the cap she wore, her eyes were level and thoughtful.

"Yes, it is, it's truly beautiful in Virginia, I'm not denying," Abraham agreed hastily, but his lean face held secrets and there was a far-away yearning in his gray eyes. Always, always, within him was the restlessness of the Lincolns who were impelled to move on, ever searching for some grail none ever quite attained. "Virginia is a fair land, and we have a right nice piece of it here on Linville Creek, Dan, but it would pleasure me to go up into your Kaintuck and see what it's like. What is the road? Is it a hard way to travel, and long?" Quietly, Bathsheba watched the two men.

Dan Boone did not smile. He took a long drink of his ale. "Abe," he began, licking the foam off his lips, "when you go to Kaintuck you leave comfort behind. There *ain't* no road. It's as hard a trail and one as full of dangers and besot with Injuns as any in this whole land. They killed Jamie, my oldest boy, along that trail. It's a far piece and a bad one in spots, and I make no bones of hidin' that fact from anyone, but it won't be like that always. Even though it's tough goin', it's worth it, Abe. Because when you git yourself to that there big high mountain that's a-standin' afront of the path, and you wonder how any man could ever git over to the other side, and then you find the place where the buffalo been goin' that way since the

4

Year One, you begin to know what Kaintuck's goin' to be like, and maybe it frights you some.

"It's a tough trail, Abe, but a horse'll get over it if you walk alongside the critter on the steep places. The buffalo been climbin' it for a long time and I guess a horse ought to. At the top of the Cumberland Gap, Abe—" He paused, turning to where Bathsheba sat listening. She had put down her sewing and was watching the two men. She knew what was happening to her husband. Abraham Lincoln was going to go to Kentucky.

"At the top of Cumberland Gap," Boone went on, a far-off look in his eyes, "with the Pinnacle towerin' higher still—and thankful you be that you don't have to climb over *that*, too—there's Kaintuck lyin' down there, green and full of forest, and Yellow Creek sparklin' in the valley. Abe, *that's* when it begins to be worth the pain of it. I told you I ain't disguisin' that it's hard work to go to where I built me my fort. But when you cross the ford of the Cumberland and then the fords of the Rock Castle, and git through all them there thickets we call 'laurel hells,' because that's just what they are, you begin to see why the buffalo been goin' that way for so many years. They found the easiest way, after all, and a man uses good sense in a-followin' them. The buffalo've beat out a track in some places that's big enough for a wagon and team, that they have. Only trouble is, there's no way to *get* a wagon and team over the Gap and through the rest of the trail—not yet, anyway, but some day we will. Well, bye and bye you come to the Kaintuck River, and up there is my town, Boonesborough. I named it fer me. 'Twould have been the first town in Kaintuck, if Jim Harrod, the old buzzard, hadn't of slipped in ahead of me and built his fort at Harrodstown! Not that we don't need all the forts we can build, I'm not denyin' that.

"The land is good around there, deep and rich," Boone went on, his face clearing, "and the meadows been feedin' the buffalo and deer for nigh on to a thousand years, I guess likely, and they'd feed your horses and cattle equal as well."

Dan Boone went to bed in the spare bedroom that night. Bathsheba hoped he would take off his boots when he retired, and wouldn't muddy her best sheets. Some frontiersmen slept in their boots and sometimes they even forgot to take off their spurs—most disastrous to the linens!

When Boone was bedded down and Bathsheba and Abraham were preparing for sleep, too, she spoke. Abraham had been very quiet all evening. Too quiet.

Deftly and neatly plaiting her pale hair in two long braids, a candle casting a soft glow over her earnest face, Bathsheba said gently:

"Abraham, if you want so bad to go to Kentucky, why don't you go along with Mr. Boone tomorrow? It's better to do it than to always wish you *had* gone, and then be unhappy all of your days. Mord is big enough to help me in many ways, and Jo is getting to be right smart of a worker, too. And I've got Leah and Demaris. We could manage."

Abraham looked wonderingly at his wife. Her slim fingers flew down the shining lengths of hair, laying them back and forth, back and forth, until they were fastened in a thick braid. Bathsheba, at twenty-nine, still looked as young and pretty as she had when he had married her nine years past, Abraham was thinking, watching her. He paused as he took off his boots and let one drop with a thud to the floor.

"Basheby," he said reproachfully, "I'm mightily surprised at you, I am that. And you with a new young-one on the way. Much as I wish I could go to Kaintuck with Dan, I won't go till I know it's all well with you and the baby. I'll wait, Basheby, and when the time comes, might be I'll even change my mind and stay. But I have my doubts!" He grinned sheepishly. "To tell you the truth, I can hardly wait!"

Bathsheba smiled, too. "I still say we could manage all right, Abraham," she said, relief in her gentle face, with the steadfast blue eyes and the firm, sweet mouth. "However, if you can see fit to wait until next March, when the new baby is born, then . . . then maybe all of us can go with you. If Rebecca Boone could manage the trip with eight children, I should certainly be able to manage it with five!"

Her husband would never know how much effort and courage it cost her to tell him that, for Bathsheba Lincoln loved Virginia and she loved their fine big house with the polished doorknobs and the glass panes in the windows. She loved the way her braided rugs looked on the well-oiled floors, and how pleasant it was to have a cook like Leah in the kitchen and Negroes like Angeline and Demaris. Abraham would miss his slaves to work in the fields and orchards of Kentucky, but he would not take them into such a wild and unknown situation; and he could never in this world transport his best horses and cattle over the mountains. To leave all this and go off into the wilderness . . . to follow the trace of the buffalo and the Indians and that wild man, Dan Boone . . . but Bathsheba Lincoln knew she would do even that if Abraham was set on it. She could see that he was.

All this had happened in October, and Dan Boone had gone on his way. Winter came and went, and it was March at last. In 1780, spring moved early into the Valley of Virginia. Blue mists hung low in the Shenandoahs and the first white puffs of shadbush flowers sparkled against the dark mountainsides, like little clouds that had come too low. The peach buds were showing pink and the new grass in the pastures along the creek was lush and green and delicious to the horses' mouths; drifts of sky-colored bluets blossomed above the glowing red wet earth of the Virginia roadsides. All winter Abraham had waited, and in the waiting he had inwardly grown more certain of what he would do and more impatient to be on his way.

In February he had arranged to sell the farm. It had been a wrench, after all, to part with it. His father, John Lincoln, had given him most of the land and he had bought more, had improved it, had built the house. But Kentucky was calling and the siren voice of the wilderness overrode his better judgment and his sadness at losing his home place. Later he would sell his cattle and his pigs and his horses, all but the few he would take along on the journey into the new country. He did not tell Bathsheba of the sale. He was ashamed to keep it a secret from her, yet somehow he could not bear to tell her yet. It was the first time he had held back anything so momentous from his wife. Time enough later, he thought, time enough when the young-one is born and she feels more equable.

And so he came at last to the soft night of March 24, 1780, when the new baby was about to be born. With Leah to tend Bathsheba, there was nothing Abraham could do, so he walked up and down restlessly in the peach orchard, waiting, waiting. He looked toward the dark, star-sprinkled sky, straining to see the geese whose wild calls came down to him. They called to something deep within him which answered and might have followed them if only he had had wings.

When Leah finally came to the door, it was after midnight. The geese had gone, but the mockingbird, drunk with springtime, was singing madly in the darkness. Abraham could see the huge form of Leah silhouetted darkly against the dim glow of the room.

"Mistah Lincoln," her deep voice called. "Mistah Lincoln! God is good—you have a daughter!" Nancy Lincoln had been born in the plantation house above Linville Creek, in the green Valley of Virginia.

When Leah brought the little morsel wrapped in flannels to her father, and Abraham looked at the red face of his youngest child, he knew that here was his release. The baby had given him leave to go . . . to follow Daniel Boone over the heights of Cumberland Gap and travel the Wilderness Road to the meadows and valleys of Kentucky.

CHAPTER TWO

"HANANIAH WAS here today, Abraham," said Bathsheba from her couch. She had not regained her strength very quickly after Nancy's birth, and Abraham had delayed his departure. "He wouldn't stay. He said he'd come back tomorrow because he had important business to transact with you."

"Hananiah!" exclaimed Abraham, pausing on his way to the barn. "What on earth—I thought he was still in Carolina." Cousin Hananiah Lincoln, twelve years younger than Abraham, was a flighty character whose whereabouts and activities always left his less dashing kinfolk somewhat breathless when they contemplated him. Hananiah Lincoln believed that the best money you could make was the easy kind, and easy money could be had if you knew how to manage men and divert them in the way you wanted them to go. With Abraham, he had served a spell in the militia during the Cherokee Wars, and had fought with George Washington in the defeat at Brandywine creek in '77. Hananiah and Abraham had both come out of the American Revolution with the rank of captain, but Hananiah had money in his pocket far and above that usual for a captain in Washington's army.

'Niah Lincoln was jaunty and always wore the latest fashion in clothes. His knee breeches were sleek and smooth fitting; his shoe buckles were polished brightly; his wig, when he wore one, was always well powdered and queued. He was handsome and he was tall, and well he knew the fine appearance he made. Women looked adoringly at him when he swaggered boldly past, smiling, and when

9

he bowed from the waist to kiss a lady's hand at a ball, there was no man in the assembly who would not gladly have thrust him through and through with his sword, nor any lady who would not willingly have gone off with him to the ends of the earth. His kinfolk put up with Hananiah; perhaps they were a little proud of him; certainly few of the Lincolns were so darkly handsome or so well fixed with ready money.

"He said he had ideas about how you could invest your money from the sale of the farm," said Bathsheba in a studiedly quiet voice.

Trust Hananiah to mess matters! Abraham had wanted to tell his wife in his own way that he had sold the farm; but he was slow to act, slow to bring about changes, and now 'Niah had told her, and from the way Bathsheba was acting, he must have told it to her all wrong. Abraham went over and sat rather awkwardly on the edge of her couch and took her cold hands in his two big warm ones. He bent and laid his lips on hers before he spoke.

"Listen, Basheby," he began, groping for the right way to say it, "I know I should have told you long ago, but you were so weak, I hadn't the heart. And when Michael Shanks offered me such a good price, and gave us our own time to vacate—he'll wait years if need be, Basheby—I couldn't let it pass. He'll pay me five thousand pounds; in fact, I have it now."

"Yes, I know," said Bathsheba distantly, taking her hands away from his, her eyes fixed on the far blue mountains beyond the window. "Hananiah told me."

That Hananiah! Kin or not, the man was an interfering meddler.

"Yes, I do have it now, and part of it'll buy us plenty of land in Kentucky and the rest will be savings—savings for when we're old, education for the children, too. They'll have schooling, more than we ever had; they'll never know want. We couldn't manage so well if we lived in Virginia. Land is cheap in the wilderness, if we get it now, and Dan says it's twice as fertile as it is here."

"And what shall we do if you do not come back from this Kentucky?" asked Bathsheba in a coldly level voice which she hardly recognized as her own, carefully spacing the words so that each stood out in clarity and full meaning. "You may not, you know. The Indians are very bad there now."

All that had occurred to Abraham, especially at night when he had lain awake thinking about it.

"If you are killed," she went on bitterly in a rush of words, "and you have the money with you and are robbed, our farm will be lost, we shall have no place to go, no means, no shelter! Abraham Lincoln—*why* did you do it—why did you sell the farm without telling me?"

There were tears in her eyes now, and still she would not look at him.

"Listen to me, Basheby!" he said fiercely, angry at her and at himself. "I sold the farm because I thought it was the best thing to do, and I still think so! If I did it, then it's done, and you've got to accept it the best you can. I'll not take the money with me," he went on impatiently, "only the treasury warrants I bought in March. They cost only five hundred pounds. If I don't come back, you'll still have the rest—I've thought it all out, more than you might suspect. I'll leave it with you, and by disposing of some of the stock you could easily repay Michael Shanks, and he'll give you back the farm, just as it is now. But before I do, you'll have to sign papers releasing your dower rights so it's all square and proper. I've been waiting till you felt stronger and could ride the eight miles into town."

Tears came easily to Bathsheba nowadays. She had never been one to weep very much, so that she was furious at her inability to control her emotions, furious at the weakness which made her say all the things she should not say and did not really mean. She pulled her hands away from his and covered her face.

"I can't—I can't—ride all that way—on a jouncing horse—to sign away—my dower rights! Not now—not now." She sobbed jerkily, her thin body shaking. "Oh, I can't! I'm not able."

"Then I'll bring Michael Shanks and John Owens, the notary, and you can sign it here," he said quietly and went out to the barn.

And that is what they did. Her weakness conquered, Bathsheba Lincoln calmly signed the papers, and the deal was completed.

Hananiah Lincoln galloped up the red earth road just as she was finishing her painful signature.

"Well, well, if it's not Cousin Basheby, looking as good as new and prettier than ever! How are you, Cousin, and how's little Nan?" Hananiah cried jovially. "Signed everything nicely?" He beamed. "That's the girl. I knew you would! Now Abe," he said in a different voice, turning to his cousin, "I got some plans for us that you might be interested in hearing. A thousand pardons, Basheby—if you'll please to excuse us!" He bowed and smiled at her—that charming, flashing smile—and Bathsheba nodded wordlessly. Hananiah turned back to Abraham and took his arm.

Bathsheba almost wept again when she saw the two men going off up the pasture, talking earnestly; Hananiah was waving his slender white hands to emphasize whatever he was saying. He had borrowed money from Abraham several times and was not always as swift to repay the loan as he was urgent in demanding it. If he had his eye on that 4500 pounds—then Abraham had better be alert if he wanted to save it for his old age!

Abraham did not tell his wife what the conversation in the pasture was about. And Hananiah did not stay to dinner as he usually did, even though Bathsheba promised him batter-fried chicken with some of Leah's famous biscuits. He had business which must be attended to in Charlottesville, on the other side of the mountains, he said hastily, and he would be gone a week. Bathsheba, in spite of her cordiality, was thankful to see him go.

There was little more for Abraham to do in completing his preparations for the journey. When he set off a few days later, he took with him only the five hundred pounds in treasury warrants. He left the remainder of the money with Bathsheba.

"No matter what Hananiah says," he warned her again as he was ready to depart, his loaded saddlebags fastened securely, Duchess stamping impatiently to be off, "don't let him have a penny of it until I come back!"

It would have taken tigers to make Bathsheba part with that money, and he knew it. He kissed her lingeringly, kissed each of the children. He waved to Leah and Demaris and Angeline and the field hands, who had gathered to see him off and were all weeping.

"Can't we go with you, Pa?" begged Mord for the hundredth time. *"Can't* we, Pa?"

"Not now, boys," answered Abraham, as he had answered all their urgent pleas to be allowed to go. "But when I come back, then we'll pack up and off we'll ride, even Nancy, and we'll travel the way Dan Boone says to the new farm I'm going to buy. Take care of things, boys—Mord, you watch out for your mother and for the horses. Jo, see that the gardens are cared for and tell the hands to mind the weeds. Mary, honey, I count on you to help Mother with the little ones—I know you'll be my big girl. Tommy—hey you, boy, get down from that stirrup!" And Tommy, letting go, rolled under the horse. If Duchess had been a nervous mare, and not so steady, she might have shied at the sudden racket and trampled the youngster. But Duchess only twitched her expressive ears and tail, and did not move a hoof.

Tommy just kept on rolling until he was safe. Mary ran and picked him up. Angeline came with Nancy on her arm and flapped the baby's small fist in the general direction of Abraham and Duchess. He slapped the mare on the flank and they were off down the red earth road.

There was a great bond of friendship and understanding between the red mare and Abraham. He had bred her mother, Felicity Belle, with Colonel Colson's red stallion, Firebrand, and the colt, Duchess, had her father's magnificent coloring and her mother's slender legs. Her feet, which fairly seemed to dance as they stepped along, were almost the color of her satin hide. Her beautiful head had all of Felicity Belle's feminine charm and Firebrand's strength. Abraham supposed that he was as much in love with Duchess as a man could be who is also in love with his wife. Duchess was sure footed and level-headed. She would get him safely to Kentucky and back again if any horse could, and he could no more have chosen another mount to take him there than he would have given up the trip itself.

Steadily, Duchess' hoofs beat along the road south, down the

Valley of Virginia. Even so early in the season there was enough dryness to push up little puffs of ruddy dust which hid the mare's galloping heels. At the bend of the road, Abraham turned his head to look back and saw his household all standing at the gate where he had left them. There was a sudden hurting in his throat. He had never before gone off like this and left his loved ones. He found it hard to swallow, and the blurring in his eyes wasn't because of the dust, and he knew it.

Around the bend, and he had left them all behind. He looked ahead, down the red earth road which was as much a part of Virginia as the blue mountains rimming the distance, and a splendid feeling of ex-hilaration, like a bright bubble, rose inside him. He was on his way at last. "I'm coming, Kentucky," cried Abraham Lincoln, not aloud; only he and Duchess knew what his heart was singing. "I'm coming!" Suddenly he felt as free as a boy and as lighthearted as any colt.

CHAPTER THREE

ALTHOUGH DANIEL BOONE took a good deal of credit for the Wilderness Road, it was the buffalo and the Indians who were responsible for the original laying out of the great trail from the Valley of Virginia to the meadowlands of Kentucky and beyond.

Long before there were red men or white men in America, the great herds of bison traveled their ancestral routes from the south to the north and back again. Going and coming with the changing of the seasons, with the winter's browning and the spring's greening of the grazing places, the huge creatures trod out roads. Eventually the Buffalo Trace became one of the oldest roads in America, and until the late nineteenth century it was one of the most heavily traveled highways—a road beaten out by the feet of animals and the feet of men.

In their migration journeys, and in their wanderings in search of salt licks, wallows, and grazing places, the buffalo broke out great roads which lasted long after the herds themselves were gone. They liked to follow the uplands; their trails hit the high places and shunned the lowlands, except where there were wallows, because in the marshes the vast tonnage of thousands of buffalo could sink and be lost in the morass, just as the mastodons had been lost in the salt licks long before. The buffalo traveled fast, and as they went their cloven hoofs trampled the trail so hard that its earth stayed trampled in winter and summer, through rains and snows.

Side trails led to the salt licks. Salt, left over from ancient oceans and imprisoned in limestone, leached out in the water of slow springs so that the mud was impregnated with it. Here the buffalo came eagerly to lick the delightful confection which their big tongues found in the mud, until, in well-used licks, the earth was channeled so deeply that a buffalo bull could stand on the bottom and not be able to see over the top, while he continued to lick salt. The herds were constantly coming and going around the licks; these were social gathering places, the spots where Indians could creep up and kill as much meat as they needed.

The side trails went to the licks, and they went to two other important places in the lives of the buffalo—to the wallows and to the stamping grounds. When the herd rested to chew the cud, the great shaggy bulls arranged themselves in a dark circle around the young with their mothers. But because the creatures were constantly moving about, shoving, crowding from the outside toward the inside to get away from the hordes of flies and other biting insects which tormented them, they trampled a clear space which became known as a stamping ground. When a herd had stamped long enough in such a circle, the mark was left as a permanent scar on the face of the green meadowlands of Kentucky.

In pools of water and in marshy places without quicksands or too thin mud, the old males came to wallow. They lowered themselves with rumbles of satisfaction on one knee and then on the other, lay on their backs, finally, and twisted and gouged with their heavy heads and horns until there was an excavation into which muddy water seeped. By and by there was a cool, oozy place into which each bull, cow, and calf came by turn. They arose coated with mud, which dried to form a protective armor through which few insects could penetrate until the casing at last cracked and fell off.

When the Indians came into the hidden hunting ground which was Kentucky, they found it easier to follow the buffalo roads than to blaze trails of their own through an almost impenetrable wilderness. When the tribes moved from place to place, or when warriors set out on a raid, it was convenient to travel in the footprints of the great herds. Sometimes, too, Indians found they could lure their enemy to a certain doom by feigning buffalo tracks. There was a time, old stories related, when a party of Shawanese lay in ambush along an animal road which was old and beaten flat under the hoofs of thousands of mighty beasts. There had been a rain and the Trace was softened; no animals had been over it lately to leave fresh tracks. So the Shawanese fastened buffalo hoofs to their moccasins and ran and cavorted with silent laughter along the muddy road, then leaped off to hide in the underbrush.

Along the convenience of this highway came the innocent Piankeshaw hunters, intent only on following the fresh footprints of bulls which they were sure had gone that way. Wild yells broke the spring stillness and the hunters fell under tomahawk blows—fooled by the footprints of false buffalo.

But the Buffalo Trace had a mightier destiny than luring unwary hunters to their deaths. Where the present states of Kentucky, Virginia, and Tennessee come together at a point at the base of the Cumberlands, there is a lower place in the tremendous wall of mountains which, on the west side of the Valley of Virginia, parallels the Shenandoahs. At no other spot have men and animals been able to cross as easily as they could at Cumberland Gap, but this is not to say that it was easy, because the climb over the Gap was enough to kill the weak and discourage the strong. The buffalo had found it, however, and in dark hordes had climbed up and up over the rocks, had paused, panting and blowing through their big wet nostrils when they reached the top, and, with the smell of water coming to them from the valley, started on the more gentle slant down into Kentucky where Yellow Creek and the Cumberland River lay waiting for them.

Indians entering Kentucky followed the buffalo trail over Cumberland Gap and along the Cumberland Valley in Kentucky. Later, the hunting trail became the Warriors' Path from the villages of the Shawnee on the Ohio and Scioto to the Cherokee settlements in Tennessee and North Carolina. The Buffalo Trace and the Warriors' Path went as one over the Gap and moved for fifty miles or more north through Kentucky. Then the Indian trail went directly northward while the Buffalo Trace meandered, seeking the licks and wallows northeast of where Lexington and Louisville later were built. The Buffalo Trace crossed the Ohio between Louisville and New Albany, into Indiana, and went in a fairly direct route slant-wise across Indiana and over the ancient crossing at Vincennes, thence into the level lands of Illinois.

Buffalo . . . Indians . . . pioneers. Of them all, there were perhaps no travelers on the Buffalo Trace more determined than the pioneers, nor any others more beset with dangers undaunting to their bullheaded determination. Dr. Thomas Walker, in 1750, was one of the first white men to enter Kentucky, and it wasn't long after this that Daniel Boone and John Finley followed and fell so deeply in love with its wilderness that Boone, at least, was never quite the same again. A man can scarcely fight his way into and through and out of a wilderness as tremendous as that which lay in Kentucky without being changed by it. Some men hated it and never went back. Some men died and left their bones in the Kentucky earth. But Dan Boone couldn't stay away. When he came dutifully back to the cabin on the Yadkin and tried to live decently with his family, he couldn't lose that far-away look in his eyes. He would sit musing near the fire and Rebecca would have to speak sharply to him several times before he could bring himself back to the room in which he sat. Rebecca gave it up after a while. When a man is as far gone on a piece of country as Dan was, you just had to accept it along with him and make the best of the situation.

"I'm not goin' to sit home year after year, Dan Boone," Rebecca finally told him crisply, her black eyes snapping, "and wait for word of you, not knowin' if you'll ever come back alive or if them red varmits'll git you at last. I'd rather we came along with you, man, so's at least I could see where they killed you and could bury your body decent!" Rebecca Boone was always plain-spoken and she was that now.

Dan brought his attention back to the room. He blinked, and Kentucky reluctantly receded a little way.

"Becky," he said gently, "Kaintuck ain't no place for a woman

"LAND IN KAINTUCK?" BOONE EXPLODED. "LAND? WHY, MAN, THERE'S
MILES OF IT, HUNDREDS OF MILES OF IT

ABRAHAM TURNED HIS HEAD TO LOOK BACK. . . . HE HAD NEVER BEFORE
GONE OFF LIKE THIS AND LEFT HIS LOVED ONES

yet, nor for childern. But it will be. Mark you my words, some day there'll be plenty of women. When I git me that fort built up on the Kaintuck and there's a proper place for women and younguns, then you kin come. But you got to possess yourself in patience, Becky, because it may be a right smart long time."

But the time came sooner than he calculated. When the Transylvania Company, under Colonel Richard Henderson, hired Boone to help hew a trail through the wilderness into Kentucky—which in those days was still a back-country county of Virginia—he worked toward a plan to bring his family to the land he loved. He and thirty men chopped through laurel thickets and through cane tangles; they located the best fords, though none were very good except that which lay below Pine Mountain on the Cumberland; and, whenever they could, they followed the buffalo road. For fifty miles they followed the Warriors' Path and the Buffalo Trace, then found a buffalo trail which took them westward to the Rock Castle River, up Roundstone Creek, through the gap in Big Hill, and down along Otter Creek to meet the yellow waters of the Kentucky River. It was true that part of Boone's Trace was well known to other hunters and explorers, but it was he who actually marked it for others to follow. That same year, 1775, another trail-blazer followed Boone, but at the point on the Rock Castle where Boone's trail went to the right, Ben Logan continued on in a northwesterly direction. Logan built a fort called St. Asaph, and helped to continue the trail all the way to the Falls of the Ohio at Louisville. Eventually it was Logan's Trace which became known in its entirety as the Wilderness Road. Nevertheless, it was always known as *Boone's* Wilderness Road, even though the majority of people followed the left-hand fork to Harrodstown and the Ohio, instead of the right-hand fork which led to Dan Boone's fort called Boonesborough.

For twenty years the Wilderness Road wasn't wide enough in most places for a wagon, yet during that time a hundred thousand people—men, women, children—traveled the trail and brought household goods, printing presses, livestock, everything they could carry on horseback or on human backs, to build the settlements of

Kentucky.

Some went only a little way. If a horse broke a leg or a member of the family fell ill, or died along the trail, the others stayed at that spot, built a cabin, and they and their descendants became the hill people of Kentucky. Some went on and founded the early settlements at Danville, Louisville, Boonesborough, Harrodstown. Still others went farther on and settled in the green meadowlands which later became the Bluegrass. They laid out beautiful towns, they laid out great farms, they built fine houses, they brought culture and civilization to Kentucky. It became a proud place to live in—the Bluegrass Region of Kentucky. But in the days of Daniel Boone, and until the middle of the nineteenth century, no one ever called it that, for the bluegrass itself was a native of Asia and did not come to Kentucky until many years after Daniel Boone had lived there and built Boonesborough.

Kentucky. There it lay, with the Wilderness Road and Boone's Trace marking a great forking path through it. For many years it was not safe to go alone to Kentucky. Only men like Boone dared to do that, and even he preferred at least a small party to go along for company and safety. Usually, travelers gathered at various block houses and way stations in Tennessee and Virginia, where they waited until sufficient numbers had arrived with ample arms and ammunition to make a safe journey into the Indian country.

Abraham Lincoln rode his mare Duchess for several days until he reached the block house on the Holston River. From there he rode to Captain Martin's fort, the jumping off place to Kentucky, where he joined a group preparing for the trip into the Wilderness.

" 'Light and rest, friend," was stout Captain Martin's welcome when Abraham's weary Duchess stopped at the long hitching rail outside the log fort. "We're about to eat supper and trust that you'll join us."

"This is where the party leaves for Cumberland Gap—they've not gone yet?" asked Abraham before he got down. He had ridden so long and so far over the red dirt roads that he felt as if the saddle were part of him and he of it. But he didn't want to dismount until he was sure that this was the place, and that the party hadn't gone.

"This is it!" cried Captain Martin, slapping Duchess on the rump. Her dusty hide twitched and she blew suddenly through her dust-rimmed nostrils. "You go in and I'll take care of your mare; good blood in her, I can see that. Come far?"

"Far enough, and I'm hungry and tired," Abraham explained wearily. "Maybe I better come along and see that she's fed proper; ought to rub her down, too. . . ."

"You go in and set down," Captain Martin said firmly. "I got a boy'll take as good care of your mare as you would, if not better, seein' you're about done in and she, too."

Abraham had heard a good deal about Captain Martin, and he knew that if the worthy captain said that Duchess would be cared for properly, that's the way it would be. Saddle and saddlebags would be safe. Abraham opened the big door and walked into the square room where people sat at two long tables.

He met the stares of a compact group of people who looked at him briefly and then returned to their food. It was not considered manners to stare long at a stranger, nor to ask his name and business. If he wanted to tell you, that was all right. But until he was ready to talk, you were polite and not prying.

Abraham found an empty place and sat down on the puncheon bench. A young fellow moved over to make more room.

"I bid you welcome, suh," he said in a soft voice. Abraham turned to look into the friendly brown eyes of a youth in his early twenties. "Jesse Hamilton, lately come from Savannah, at your service, suh!"

"And I, too, say howdy." The man on Abraham's right grinned at him. "Glad to have you join our select little party. I see you got you a rifle gun; goin' to need all we can get, that we will. Ahab Littleford is the name, and this is my wife, Mary Fay, beside me. We make you welcome!"

The warmth in these kind voices revived Abraham even more than the food. Mary Fay Littleford looked shyly at him and smiled, then turned her eyes again to her plate. She looked frightened and pale, he thought, though you never knew about women; the pallor could be natural, and any right-minded woman ought to be frightened at the prospect of going to the wilderness of Kentucky. Now the woman sitting opposite him—there was a female fit to travel the roughest road! No Indian would possibly be brave enough or maybe rash enough to stand up to that forbidding, ruddy visage. The woman talked loudly, in a deep voice, while she ate, and dominated the group around her. She shed a glance in Abraham's direction, and between forkfuls of beans, paused long enough to boom, "Mrs. Parmeaneas Jellico, sir; glad to have you in our group," before she turned her snapping black eyes to the little man at her right. "Mr. Jellico, welcome the man! Don't you have any manners?"

Little Mr. Parmeaneas Jellico looked up briefly from his plate. Abraham saved him the embarrassment of speaking.

"Thanks, all of you, for your kind welcome. I beg to present Abraham Lincoln from up near Harrisonburg!" He looked at the group and they looked at him, and that was that. He saw a thin pretty young woman holding a little baby on her lap and trying to keep it quiet while she ate, but the baby was fretful and Mrs. Jellico was growing annoyed.

"Why don't you put that child down on a pallet with a sugar tit to keep him quiet? Then you can eat in peace!" And Abraham heard the acid inference in the woman's loud voice that the rest of them could eat in peace, too.

The young woman looked with hunted eyes at Mrs. Jellico and without a word she got up and went over to a dusky corner of the big room, where she rocked back and forth in an effort to soothe the child.

"That's Margaret Jenkins," whispered Mary Fay Littleford to Abraham. "Her little boy's been sick and she's so worried. She thinks they ought to go back home till he's all right, but John Jenkins won't hear of it. He's set on going to Boonesborough and buying a farm somewhere near there."

"Come, Mr. Jellico!" Amy Jellico's deep voice drowned out Mary Fay's whisper, and the husband and wife left the table and went over to sit on a settle near the fire.

"She always does that so they'll get the best seats," audibly whispered a round-faced woman farther down the table.

"Oh, Delphia Ann, she just eats faster than we do." Rhuhama Randall giggled. "She just *shovels* it in so's to be finished early and always get the best seat and the best bed. Some day I'm going to beat her to it and there I'll sit and she can plump herself down on the floor for all of me!"

"I dread traveling a month with that woman, I do for a fact," murmured Jesse Hamilton in Abraham's ear. "Look how she's got that meek little husband of hers jumping when she cracks the whip. We'd better look lively or we'll be doing it, too! Come along, Mr. Lincoln," young Hamilton said, getting off the bench, "and I'll show you where you're to sleep. If we're to get off to an early start, we'll all need to turn in early."

The men slept in the big loft; the women were quartered downstairs, in the big room. Abraham, from a distance, could still hear the fretful Jenkins baby wailing, could hear Mrs. Jellico booming advice. Before he fell asleep, Abraham thought of Bathsheba and wondered what she was doing, and if Hananiah had come back—but he wasn't worried about Hananiah getting that money. Not from Bathsheba. Might be he could find a good way to worm it from Abraham himself—and Abraham Lincoln smiled wryly in the darkness when he thought of how easily 'Niah could persuade him to do something when Bathsheba wasn't near to hold him firmly back.

CHAPTER FOUR

B LUE AND TALL in the distance, silent and frightening in its awful immensity, its determined stance blocking the route of the travelers from Virginia, stood Cumberland Mountain, with the Gap lying in the saddle.

"May heaven preserve us all!" cried Mrs. Jellico loudly. As her horse plodded over the stony trail, she clasped her red hands with the reins in them. The big woman rode her mount capably and solidly, yet she had complained of everything all along the way. Abraham had grown tired of her irritating voice and her eternal worries and complaints. "Oh, dear me, how we'll get over that horrible mountain *I* do not know!" she went on nasally, in the voice Abraham had grown to dislike thoroughly. "Mr. Jellico, *what* have you brought me into, I'd like to inquire? To expect a lady to climb over that mountain—Mr. Jellico, answer me!"

"You just set tight and Daisy'll haul you from here to t'other side of the Gap. It's no matter of trouble. I've rid over it myself once before and I ought to know!" Parmeaneas Jellico, with his thin lips set in a tight line, having delivered himself of more words than Abraham had ever heard him utter before, moved his horse ahead with the other men and left his wife to continue her horrors to the women.

Most of them were silent, not listening to her, eyeing with foreboding and inward dread the grim blue wall of the Cumberlands lying athwart the trail. There was no doubt of it, each one was thinking. You *had* to climb Cumberland Gap before you got to Kentucky; and then your troubles, said the old-timers who had traveled it with Boone and Finley and Harrod, had only just begun.

Adam Marlow, a burly giant of a man, as tall as Abraham but, as he said, laughing, twice as thick, broke the silence. His resonant voice, the voice he had used to preach with when he was a minister of the gospel back in New England, started a song:

> "Oh, Cumberland Gap is a noted place
> Cumberland Gap is a noted place
> Cumberland Gap is a noted place
> Three kinds of water to wash your face!"

Jesse Hamilton, grinning, added his own fine tenor to the tune, and Abraham joined in. Maybe if they could get the group to singing, they'd feel cheerier. Goodness knew they looked glum enough with that big blue mountain always ahead of them, and Mrs. Jellico worrying out loud all the time. The three Randall boys got into fights on the horse which they shared, and had to be spanked; and Mrs. McAllister, a spare, tall woman with a beautiful, withdrawn face which held secrets, kept lagging behind on foot to look for herbs. Women and children! Abraham was beginning to lose patience with both of them.

But not so Adam. Beating time with one big hand, he led the song:

> "The first white man in Cumberland Gap
> The first white man in Cumberland Gap
> The first white man in Cumberland Gap
> Was Doctor Walker, an English chap!"

"How much farther do we have to go today?" Delphia Ann Reynolds queried. "It don't seem to me's if we're getting any nearer that mountain. We just ride and ride, and it never comes any closer!"

> "Lay down, boys, and take a little nap
> Lay down, boys, and take a little nap
> Lay down, boys, and take a little nap
> It's five more miles to Cumberland Gap!"

"Five miles!" groaned Amy Jellico. "Mr. Jellico, tell our leader that we simply must stop before we get there. We don't *have* to reach the Gap tonight!"

"Now, Amy," murmured little Mr. Jellico, "we got to do what the whole group wants."

"Don't be puny, Mrs. Jellico," Meg McAllister remarked acidly, pausing to look at a shrub she hadn't seen before. "We're *all* tired but *you're* the only one who complains!"

The procession moved on at a brisker pace, its tension broken so that no longer was there only the sound of horses' hoofs on the gravel, only the clank of metal on leather, the breathing of the animals and the fussing of the children. Amy Jellico, however, grumbled pointedly about the unseemly racket the singers were making, but Adam Marlow continued his ballad, resoundingly, with all fifteen verses and some he made up as he rode, and when they were finished, the caravan had reached the base of the Gap. There they set up camp for the night.

Mary Fay Littleford was a deft hand with a skillet, and she, with the help of Margaret Jenkins, Delphia Ann Reynolds, and Rhuhama Randall, cooked the evening meal for the party. Meg McAllister strolled about, looking for plants, and pulled up several and put them in a bag she carried. The men fed and watered the horses and took off saddles and packs.

As the firelight illuminated the faces of the sober people who gathered around, lit the dark forms of the horses that grazed placidly on the outskirts, there was a comforting sense of oneness. The aroma of frying pork rose into the cold spring air. Corn dodgers browned in the three big spiders, while Delphia Ann superintended the brewing of the coffee, which sent its own rich, comforting fragrance into the dusk.

Abraham, sitting with the other men, waiting for supper, was still humming under his breath that tune he had almost forgotten since his troop under Washington sang as they marched—"Cumberland Gap with its cliffs and rocks . . . Home of the panther, bear, and fox . . ." And now he was sitting below Cumberland Gap itself. He stretched out, with his head against his saddle there on the stony ground, and luxuriated in doing nothing. Horses fed, tents put up for the women, gear stowed away . . . he felt immensely satisfied and content. Danger seemed far and remote. Maybe Dan Boone had exaggerated about the trials of traveling the Wilderness Road.

Spring was not as far advanced at the Gap as it was up in the Valley of Virginia where the altitude was not so great, and when a sudden chill wind blew down off the mountains it scattered the embers of the fires in all directions. Abraham and Adam Marlow leaped to stamp them out, then carefully rebuilt the fires for warmth.

When supper was over Adam suggested, "Better get settled for the night. Looks like it's turning down colder; no stars out. Wrap up good and get some sleep. We've got a heavy day ahead of us tomorrow."

The women and children went to their tents. The men made a tour of inspection around the camp, saw that the horses were hobbled so that they could not wander far, and then the men, too, rolled up in their blankets. No one said very much. The ominous presence of the Gap looming darkly against the cold, cloudy sky oppressed their spirits again, silenced their tongues. The sense of security which the fire, the strong leadership, the songs, and the food had given them seemed to have melted away in the dread of the unknown and the fear of what the blackness all about them might hold before morning came.

Rain began slatting down in the night and by morning the wind shifted to the northeast and snow was blowing down from the heights. It lay white on the horses' backs, on the frail tents where the women and children slept, lay melted around the blackened remains of the campfires, covered the men in their blankets. It was cold, bitterly cold, in the gray light of early morning when Mary Fay Littleford, rubbing her hands, came out of her tent.

She poked around in the damp embers and caught a spark at last. She worked until she had a fire going, and the coffee pots were steaming before she roused the children and the other women. The men rolled yawning out of their snow-caked blankets and shuddered in the cold.

"Hey, look you here!" cried Enoch Lambert, tending the horses. "Two've wandered off—my black mare and the sorrel. Broke their hobbles . . . can't be far. We can follow their tracks all right in this snow. Help me look, boys!" In a moment the camp was astir and the women were surmising how and when the horses had broken loose. Delphia Ann Reynolds leaned over to look at the broken hobbles on the ground, and straightened her back suddenly with quick alarm in her round blue eyes.

"Those hobbles weren't *broken*, they were *cut!*" she cried, and put her hands to her face as the impact of the words came to life in her mind. "Cut! Somebody crept in amongst us in the night and cut those horses loose. It *could* have been our throats! Tom—Tom Reynolds, come back here! Those horses didn't wander off, they were stolen. Tom! *Tom!*"

The men turned back at her cries. The women gathered in a frightened huddle. The baby cried. Everyone tried, then, to find human footprints which would lead them to the identity of the thieves, but by that time too many people of the camp had trampled the light snow and there was nothing to discover there.

Sudden panic swept over the group of people who were terribly lone and helpless in the shadow of the wild peaks.

"Let's go on!" cried little Mr. Jellico, beginning to saddle up in a hurry. "Let them horses go! We're lucky we got our lives!" His alarm infected the others. There was a wild flurry of packing and saddling.

"Wait!" cried Mary Fay Littleford loudly, clapping her cold hands to get their attention. When this did not do it, she reached for a spider-lid and a big spoon and beat with the spoon upon the iron until the racket made everyone stop in his tracks. "Wait! We've got to eat to keep our strength up. Land only knows what trials we'll meet this day and we've got to eat while we've a chance! If we were going to be killed by the varmints who took the horses, they'd have done so by this time. Now come and eat." Adam grinned

28

approvingly at her, and Abraham wondered at the strength of will in that frail-appearing figure of the woman who cut and handed out pieces of pone and smoking-hot pork, while Meg McAllister quietly poured mugs of coffee. Docilely, now, like children who have been relieved of panic by a wise parent, the people gathered around to eat.

When they had finished, short, dark-browed Enoch Lambert stood up.

"I'm a-goin' after them horses," he said with determination. "Don't wait for me. . . . I may not get back. But I aim to find my horses or die huntin'. They were my two best mares and I can't afford to lose them."

"Wait, I'll go with you," spoke up mild Tom Reynolds.

"Oh, no, Tom—*no!*" cried his wife hysterically. Tom gave her a long, quiet look and she subsided. Mary Fay put her arms around her.

"Don't wait for us," said Enoch Lambert, as serenely as if he and Tom were about to head for the barn to milk the cows. The two men started off along the thin trail which the missing horses had left in the light snow. It was already melting as the morning moved on, and if they were going to follow that trail at all, they would have to do it fast. "We'll try to catch up with you," Enoch turned to call back, "and likely we can, because we can travel faster alone than the whole lot of you. And if we don't get back—" Delphia Ann sobbed into her hands and would not look at the two men as they went off through the laurel and dogwood tangles of the mountain-side where the trail of hoofs led them.

Sobered, quieter than ever, the rest of the party looked westward to the heights of Cumberland Gap, above which towered the Pin-nacle. "And glad you be that you don't have to climb that, too," Dan Boone had said, Abraham remembered. He tightened his saddle, helped Delphia Ann on her horse, saw that her saddle would not slip. The group was ready to go.

The procession went single file along the trampled road the buffalo had made. The going grew steadily harder, steeper, more rocky.

The horses were struggling; their nostrils flared red and foam flecked their mouths. Silently, one by one, the men dismounted and walked beside their horses. The women still rode, until Mary Fay Littleford suddenly pulled her bay to a halt on a level spot and jumped lightly down.

"It's not fair to the beast to have to haul me up those cruel rocks," she said simply. The other women got down, too, even Amy Jellico, who muttered things under her breath but loudly enough for no one to mistake what she said; Margaret Jenkins dismounted with her sick baby. Everyone toiled on foot up the steep trail. The three little Randall boys were overjoyed at the chance. They scampered like woodchucks over the rocks and threw stones until Adam Marlow sternly forbade them—a bouncing pebble had startled a pack horse which had nearly fallen as it shied.

Silently, for they had no breath left to talk, the men and women and children and their animals climbed the trail. There was no surplus strength to be wasted in speech. The top seemed as remote as it had appeared from the floor of the valley. Brightly in the young-flowered redbud trees the Carolina wrens sang their ringing, rollicking songs. The gray clouds tore apart and the sun came through, then was hidden again, and there was another brief spit of snow. Violets were in bloom beside the terrible trail, but Meg McAllister was the only person in the party who could notice flowers.

"That woman would pick flowers off her own grave," remarked Amy Jellico, panting as she heaved her bulk up the steep grade. Mrs. McAllister cast a single disdainful look at red-faced Mrs. Jellico.

"Undoubtedly *you* would complain at the gates of Heaven, madam," she said icily, and paused to pull up a bit of wild ginger root which she added to her bag.

Still the people climbed. The rocks hurt their feet. The horses struggled upward, slipped, fell, packs slid off, children cried. The Jenkins baby screamed. He began at a point about halfway up the long trail to the top of the Gap, and he continued screaming until they had reached the summit, when he abruptly stopped.

Abraham and Adam were busy making sure that all the horses

managed the ascent. They helped the women and saw to it that the Randall boys killed neither themselves nor anyone else. It was almost noon when they arrived at the top. As if at a signal, the clouds had risen and now floated white and gay in a bright sky lit by spring sunshine. The remnants of fog and cloud drifted down the valley below the Gap, climbed on air currents, joined their brothers in the sky. The snow had vanished as if it had never been.

> "Daniel Boone stood on Pinnacle Rock,
> Daniel Boone stood on Pinnacle Rock,
> Daniel Boone stood on Pinnacle Rock,
> *He* killed Indians with his old flint-lock!"

roared Adam Marlow's incredibly loud baritone when he reached the level top of Cumberland Gap, a mighty figure of triumph, singing powerfully as if he had never been out of breath in all the long climb. Then he helped the almost exhausted women, saw that the entire party—with the exception of the two men who were horse-hunting—at last stood safe in the saddle of Cumberland Mountain.

On that high point of the Wilderness Road, Abraham Lincoln felt a vast, swelling sense of exultation in his breast. Below him, to the west, lay the springtime forests of the Kentucky wilderness, where the golden-green glow of sugar maple trees in bloom contrasted brightly with the burning color of the scarlet fruits of red maples, and the elms were already in leaf. He could see the sparkle of Yellow Creek down there, saw a shadow pass across the Gap as a buzzard on set wings floated on an updraft. It was all beautiful, and it was all dangerous. But he could begin to understand how it could possess Dan Boone, how the very struggle for attainment could make this land below him all the more desirable to win. He could see how it was beginning to possess him, too.

CHAPTER FIVE

ABRAHAM'S PARTY paused to rest on Cumberland Gap and eat their noonday meal on this lofty spot. Most of them felt better when it was time to start down the slanting trail on the other side, a longer way but far less abrupt than the direct route up from Virginia. But it was steep enough to need to rein in the horses now and then, to prevent accidents. Everyone had mounted again and they all felt that some of the worst was surely past. Mr. Jellico assured everyone that at no other place ahead was it as steep as the place they had just climbed.

"Don't talk so much, Mr. Jellico!" snapped his wife.

Then, suddenly, trouble struck.

Abraham, who had been bringing up the rear, had dropped back a little way, and as he rode forward he was just in time to see three Shawanese burst out of the laurel thickets and attempt to snatch the three well-loaded pack horses at the end of the procession. The attack took place so fast and so silently that no one knew what was happening until Abraham yelled and galloped up to defend the party.

An Indian slashed at him with his tomahawk, but Abraham dodged, wheeled, fired. Ahab Littleford and Adam Marlow fired, too, and one Indian dropped, spurting blood from his chest and kicking in agony before he died. The horses were plunging and snorting and two packs fell off and were badly trampled. Jesse Hamilton closed in. Abraham, who had reloaded, shot again, and another savage lay dead in the trail, just as Jesse's horse, terrified at the nearness of the shot, wheeled, reared, pawed the air and plunged backward with its rider still frantically trying to get free of the stirrups, down the rocky, laurel covered slope.

The third Shawanese vanished. He did not run, Mary Fay Littleford thought, watching petrified with horror at what was happening. The dark-skinned man of the forest simply melted into the laurels, so that they parted without a rustle, and he was gone as completely as if he had never been there at all. But the others lay dead in the trail, and down the slope Jesse Hamilton's horse was snorting and whinnying in terror, threshing about and trying to get to its feet. The men rushed down the mountainside to Jesse, who was still pinned under the struggling horse.

With his fine way with horses, Abraham somehow got the rider free and persuaded the animal to his feet. But Jesse groaned and sank back. He was pale as the shadblow above his head and Abraham thought the boy was going to faint.

"It's my—leg!" was wrenched from Jesse's pallid lips. Abraham hastily examined the leg, which was doubled up all wrong under Jesse. It was, as he suspected, broken. A broken leg on the Wilderness Road—well, that could spell your doom as surely as a Shawnee's tomahawk or a lead bullet in your brain.

"Don't move him till I can put on splints," ordered Abraham as the others crowded around to help. They wanted to carry the suffering man to the trail. Adam and several others were out scouting for more Indians who might be lurking near by. "Wait! You want to kill him? Go bury those Indians if you want to do something!"

Somehow, after hunting around impatiently over what seemed like half the mountainside, Abraham found some sticks which, with some flattening from his big hunting knife, would do for splints. He ripped off the canvas cover of his pack and made wide bandages which served to secure the splints around the broken leg. As carefully as if he were tending little Nancy at home, Abraham straightened the leg. Then, while Adam and Enoch held Jesse's shoulders and arms, and he writhed in spite of himself with the excruciating, wrenching pain, Abraham pulled strongly, gritting his teeth, until the bones in the leg grated and lay at last in a straight line. Jesse conveniently fainted just then and when he awoke Abraham had finished. The leg lay well splinted and bandaged. Now they would be able to move him, groaning a little in spite of himself, up to the trail again.

"We'll have to camp here for the night," said Abraham in a low tone to Adam. "Jesse could never travel now. Land only knows how we're going to carry him along on horseback with a leg like that, but maybe I'll think of something. Anyway, it's getting late and this is a fairly level place for a camp. I doubt if the Indians will come back, but we'll keep a careful watch, just to be sure."

Adam nodded. "This is only the beginning, Abe," he said soberly. "We've got a long way to go and anything can happen. And I don't like the look of this attack by only three Shawanese. They generally travel in bigger packs. Unless I misjudge 'em, we'll meet 'em again!"

Jesse was delirious all that night, a night filled with apprehension for the travelers, to whom every rustling in the forest suggested stealthy footsteps. Abraham kept constantly awake, watching over the suffering young man and listening, always listening.

He heard the snarling cough of a bobcat somewhere down in the forest. He heard the young sound of motion in the new leaves on the trees and the *squeak-squeak-rasp* of two branches rubbing together whenever a breeze moved them. It was quiet for a time until the baby started to wail again. Margaret, her face drawn and her hair bedraggled, came out of her tent to warm some water to put in a flask and lay on the baby's stomach. Abraham Lincoln said nothing and she did not speak. He nodded, and she looked with bleak eyes toward him. . . . When the water was warm, she poured it with shaking hands that spilled half of it, until the flask was filled, and then she went back into her tent. The baby cried and cried. Jesse Hamilton stirred and moaned, and then everything was still again.

Abraham sat with his loaded rifle. He heard the sudden, faintly ominous crunch of a dead twig breaking and was instantly alert. Slowly he got to his feet, facing the sound, his rifle cocked, his heart hammering.

And a deer came placidly stepping along on slim, pointed hoofs, curiously stared at the campfire and the man standing tall behind it, paused a long moment, and then walked on.

Abraham smiled at himself for being so alarmed over nothing. He sat down again. It was all right to be alert to all these small noises, the natural sounds which came with any night in spring on the side of the wild Cumberlands, but if there were Indians near by, no one would hear them until it was too late.

Not many white men could estimate what the Indians would do next. Some could—Dan Boone, for instance. He thought like an Indian; could anticipate what they would do before they did it; could think "now where would I hide if I was an Injun?" And there he'd go, and there they'd be, surprised as anything, but old Dan was never surprised. Not at what Indians were likely to do, anyway. Abraham wished Dan were with them now on this trip along the trail, could tell him what on earth to do about the wounded traveler, Jesse Hamilton, who groaned again and began to talk wildly in delirium.

It was a long night. Some time before daylight, when only the faintest change had come in the darkness, Abraham heard a quiet movement among the sleeping people and saw Mary Fay Littleford, dressed and smiling at him in the firelight.

"What are you doing up at this hour?" he whispered. "It's nowhere near time to be up. Go get your sleep; you'll need it!"

"*Sshhh!*" she whispered back. "I've had my sleep. I'm wide awake. It's you who've been up all night with poor Jesse. Now you go roll up in a blanket and sleep. I'll stay with him and I can wake you fast if there's any danger—I've got good ears and if there're Indians around, I'll hear them as soon as you would. Now go!" She smiled again as she ordered him off—just like Bathsheba, he thought, firm but sweet about it.

Mary Fay endlessly amazed Abraham with her quiet intelligence, her ability to absorb hard work, to take over responsibility, to travel a difficult trail without outward fear when the other women sometimes gave way to worries and lamentations. She might be small and

frail-looking—she was like Bathsheba in that, too, he suddenly re-
alized—but her capacity for meeting peril and discomfort was magnificent. Like Bathsheba Lincoln, certainly, he thought drowsily,
and as he shut his eyes he knew that if a woman like Mary Fay Littleford could travel the Wilderness Road, he need have no qualms about
how his wife could manage it. Women, he thought—*some* women
—were truly amazing.

On the morning of the third day after the accident, when the
party had kept vigil night and day for further attack by Indians,
they heard voices and horses coming up the Wilderness Road from
the valley of the Cumberland in Kentucky. Alerted, the men stood,
guns ready, waiting, anxious to see who it was.

"If they're Indians," commented Abraham so that everyone could
hear him, "we'd not hear *them* until they attacked . . ."

Around a bend in the trail came a party of travelers with horses
and dogs and two cows which had to be prodded from the rear to
make the climb. The two parties met.

"If you're a-goin' to Kaintuck, you might as well turn around
now while you have a chance," cried the stout man who had been
prodding the cows. "*We've* had enough, I tell you!"

"What happened?" asked Adam guardedly, standing huge above
the others.

"Happened? Plenty happened," snapped a woman. "We been
attacked by Injuns twice and that's twice too much for me! I aim
to go back to Virginia where I can die peaceful when my time
comes."

Everyone talked at once; some of the women in Abraham's party
cried out at the dreadful things the others told—about how Tom
Agnew went off the trail to shoot a buffalo for meat, and the Shawanese got him and scalped him, and left his body hung up on a tree
limb, his mouth stuffed with dirt.

Adam Marlow was grim. "I've heard of them doing that. The
Shawanese say the white men are so hungry for land, they can have
it—stuffed down their dead throats and pushed into their gaping

dead mouths! Go on, tell us all of it. Might as well know the worst."

But that was the worst—the killing of Tom Agnew, the burning of the camp, the theft of three valuable horses with loaded packs. In a panic the people had turned about, determined to have no more of Kentucky, now or ever again.

"It ain't worth the risk," muttered one of the men, who wore a rough, blood-stained bandage around his head. "Kentucky may be a fair land, but it ain't no good to a corpse, and that's what we're all a-goin' to be if we keep on. The Injuns are dead set against us, I tell you, and they ain't goin' to stop till they kill us all and git back their huntin' grounds. Dark and Bloody Ground, they call it: well, I guess likely!"

The parties joined for noon dinner around the campfires. John Jenkins brought in a deer he had shot near the camp, and the women broiled steaks for everyone. There was a good deal of talk, subdued talk, sudden outbursts of excited conversation. Abraham heard snatches of it and he was not surprised when Mrs. Jellico stood up, shook her skirts and pushed back her hair. Her ruddy face was set in determined, grim lines; there was a dribble of venison juice from the corner of her mouth and on the front of her dress.

"I speak for Mr. Jellico and myself," she said loudly, "when I say that this journey is too dangerous and we propose that we join this returning party and go back. I, for one, don't care if I *never* see Kentucky as long as I live, if this is the way it is! It's no place for civilized people," she added righteously. "Isn't that so, Mr. Jellico?"

"Yes, dear," murmured little Mr. Jellico, staring moodily into the fire.

"*I* say that we join this other party," the large woman went on with satisfaction, "so we can get back safely to the settlements!"

"No!" shouted Adam Marlow, leaping to his feet. "Be still, woman! You've been nothing but a plague and a trouble ever since we started out. Go back if you want, but don't try to break up the determination of the rest of us to make homes in this new land. Kentucky is a good place and a safe one when we make it so. Fear won't do it, and running back because we're afraid of Indians and catamounts and our own shadows won't build farms and settle towns and get rid of the dangers. Go back, if you want; Kentucky doesn't need cowards! But let those of us who have the courage go ahead—"

The woman broke in with, "You—" He glared at her. She flushed a deeper scarlet and worked her mouth around the words she was wanting to say, but Adam's glare froze her tongue.

"I said be still!" he roared. "We're going up to Boonesborough and Harrodstown and we'll go out around there and buy us land while it's there waiting for us, fresh and new and unspoiled by other men. This is a virgin paradise; *we're* the ones who are going to be privileged to see it and take it while it's still beautiful and new. Dangerous, yes," he said scornfully, his eyes flashing. "The East was too tame; that was one reason why we all started out like this to the wilderness. So what do we do but cower at the first hint of danger and want to run home like whipped dogs!" Adam Marlow, his long legs wide apart and his big hands on his hips, stood there like a thundering Jove and glowered at the people, who looked down at their hands or into the fire and were ashamed, like children caught in a misdeed.

"All those who have the stamina to travel the Wilderness Road with me, come along. Those who want to go back—go! Go back to your nice, easy, settled lives in the East. Go back to your old ways and your safe little towns; be little and be fearful. But go, and go now, get out of our sight! You don't belong on the Wilderness Road. Kentucky doesn't want you!"

Adam Marlow knew how to talk, knew how to lay his tongue into a sentence and make a man feel it clear down inside himself, could make him think as he never thought before. Abraham applauded Adam's speech and stood up beside him to watch the division of the party. There was a good deal of argument. Some of the women were still terrified from listening to the tales brought by the fleeing party, and begged their husbands to return with them. Margaret Jenkins had still another reason.

"John, we've just got to go back," she pleaded, her worn face pale and haggard after her sleepless night with the sick child. "Danny isn't getting any better and I'm feared he'll die 'less we get a doctor soon!"

John Jenkins looked at his wife and Abraham could see the tumbled emotions chasing across his face as the man fought with himself.

"Margaret," John Jenkins said in a low voice, just for his wife to hear. "I know the baby's sick and I know you want to go back. But Margaret—this is our chance. We've come this far, and if we turn back now, we'll never come here again. We'll settle down where our folks settled, and there we'll live and there we'll die, grubbing away in land that's already worked to death. We named Danny for Mr. Boone because we figured our son would grow up in the country Dan Boone opened up to us. We can't go back now, we just can't!"

"All right, John," Margaret whispered through her gray lips, and stumbled to her tent where the baby was crying again. Abraham, seeing the tragedy on the young woman's aging face, put his hand on Adam's elbow, suddenly, as if he wanted to tell him something, as if he would like to help these people do the right thing. If a man only knew *what* was the best—if he only knew. What would *he* do if it was *his* baby, little Nancy, crying and crying and growing weaker each day on this frightful journey—what would he do if, in desperation, Bathsheba begged him to go back? He didn't know. Perhaps a man never knew until the time came to act, and then trusted in God to lead him aright.

Parmeaneas Jellico was like a man who had terrible decisions to make, too. He didn't say much when the time came for the returning party to go on. He walked up to Adam and Abraham and shook their hands, quickly, briefly, and looked up into their sober faces where lines of responsibility were etched deeply.

"I bid you good-by, gentlemen," little Mr. Jellico said thinly. "It hurts me to have to go back, it really does, but Mrs. Jellico's too much frightened to go on, and it's a husband's duty—" His eyes wandered vaguely away from the faces sympathizing wordlessly with him, and he glanced off toward the dark forest where new spring leaves sent a glitter of sunlight to the earth. Then his eyes came back to Adam and Abraham, and he smiled quickly. "Good-by," he said again.

"Mr. Jellico, do come," cried his wife in stentorian tones. "We're all waiting for you and you're delaying the party. Hurry, Mr. Jellico! You *talk* too much!"

The party which set out on the upgrade to the crest of Cumberland Gap had been increased by six members of Abraham's group. With them, unwillingly, went Jesse Hamilton. He would have given anything he owned if he could have gone on, but he knew that with a broken leg he could never expect to travel the Wilderness Road. He would be a constant care to the others, and in time of danger he would be of no help, but only a hindrance who could endanger the entire party. So they propped the young man on his horse and walked the beast up the trail. Jesse looked back and waved to Abraham and Adam, but especially to the former, who had saved his life and the use of his leg.

"Good-by, Mr. Lincoln," he called brokenly. "Good-by! When I get well I'll come back to Kentucky and look for you there. I'll repay you—somehow—for all you've done for me!"

Abraham silently raised his hand in farewell and watched until the caravan was out of sight.

The silence was broken by Rhuhama Randall's high-pitched laugh.

"Well, I guess there's *some* good in everything!" She giggled. "At least we're rid of that woman, though I can't say I envy the folk who'll have her on their hands all the way back East!"

"I do feel sorry for that poor little man," said Mary Fay softly. "He looked like a lost soul when he got on that bony horse of his and followed along after she roared at him."

The Kentucky-bound party assembled its gear and set off down the trail. At the bottom there was a halt while the horses drank from the cold waters of Yellow Creek. When everyone had mounted once more and the caravan was on its way through the cane-grown valley, the sounds of hoofbeats were heard approaching along the creek.

Wheeling, the men faced east, fearing anything now. Three horsemen came forward at a gallop, shouting and waving their hats—and

Delphia Ann screamed and slid out of her saddle in a faint on the ground.

Abraham squinted in the sunshine to try to make out who the riders were. He soon recognized Enoch Lambert and Tom Reynolds, right enough—but who was the third rider on a bony horse, pounding along the trail behind them, with loud whoops and much hat waving?

"By thunder, it's Parmeaneas Jellico!" exclaimed Price Randall. "How in the tarnal gracious did he get away from that woman of his?"

Rhuhama Randall giggled. "Must've broke his traces and then cut and run!" she exclaimed. The Randall boys tore off to meet the riders.

By now little Mr. Jellico was ahead of Enoch and Tom. He was grinning broadly.

"Howdy, folks, I'm back!" he cried, beaming all over his narrow little face. "I just decided I didn't *want* to go back to Smithsburg, and I up and told Amy so. But she said, no, I must go with her 'cause she was afeared to go back without me. Hoh! That woman ain't been feared o' naught since *I* knowed her. I rid on with them a spell, though, and when we met Enoch and Tom with their horses which they'd found, I just turned my horse around, and off I went without even a by-your-leave. I reckon Amy's fair angered, but she'll manage. Me, I aim to settle in Kentucky and there ain't no one, man *nor* woman, who's goin' to stop me now!"

Meanwhile, Delphia Ann was being quickly revived by Tom's whiskery kisses, and everyone was talking at once.

"Where'd you find the horses?" the men cried, crowding around Enoch, since Tom Reynolds was so busy with his wife, who by now was sitting up and crying down his neck, she was so relieved to have him back.

"Well," began Enoch, "we thought for a while we'd never catch up with them before the snow went off; it was meltin' fast, I tell you! Time we got halfway up that there mountain, 'twas all we could do to see where them horses'd gone. Then suddenly we heard sounds, and we slid into the laurels—there was a mighty bad tangle of laurels on that mountain, thick enough to hide a herd of buffalo and not show sign of one. Pretty soon as we crep' along in the direction of the voices, we seen two Injuns. They was a-sittin' down by a little fire where they was roastin' a partridge, and the horses was grazin' quiet not far away.

"Well, Tom and me, we got the same idea at once. We looked at each other, then crep' closer so we got a good bead on each of them varmints, and we fired mighty nigh at the same moment, and by Harry, we got 'em both, right through the heads. We was feared there might be a camp near by, so we didn't linger none, but started back with the horses. And then we lost our way. The snow was gone and we couldn't find a sign o' our tracks nor those the horses had made. I don't know *how* we could have missed that trail!"

"Well," he went on, looking over at Tom and wishing he'd come and help him out on the telling. "Well, it took us till now to catch up with you folks. Met that other party on the trail, and to hear 'em talk, you was all headin' to your certain *de*-struction, like as if the Angel Gabriel was just a-waitin' till the Shawanese got through with you afore he took you up to Heaven. But Tom and me, we allowed we'd take our chances, and then Mr. Jellico he decided to come along, too. Glad to be back. Got any cold pone or somewhat to eat? We're a mite hungry!"

The women fluttered in a flurry of sympathy around the hungry men and then hurried to build a fire. Since it was mid-afternoon, the group decided to camp there for the night, and soon the savory odors of supper mingled with the late-afternoon scents of the lowlands—the creek, the plum trees all in bloom, the wild, splendid aroma which was Kentucky.

Meg McAllister, a rapt expression on her serenely beautiful face, wandered about picking flowers and now and then pulling a root to add to her herb bag. Her husband helped the men get the horses fed and watered, but Meg seldom troubled herself to join the other women in preparing the meals; she walked about like a queen while the others worked. She never seemed aware that they whispered about her and wondered why she acted as she did, always wandering, every chance she had, into the forest.

"Ain't you feared o' wolves and catamounts?" Rhuhama Randall asked her one day, trying to egg her on to talking. "You're like to walk in there some day and not come out again!"

"No, I'm not afraid," said Meg calmly, and that was all she would say.

CHAPTER SIX

T HE VALLEY narrowed as it neared Pine Gap and the mountains stood darkly menacing. There seemed to be only enough room for the Cumberland's rushing green waters to pass through; but there was a way through the Gap, and the north-bound party—as so many hunters, explorers, settlers, Indians, and buffalo had done before them—followed the slippery trail along the river. They came to the ancient ford where animals and men for thousands of years had found a sure-footed crossing.

Beyond the ford of the Cumberland the valley grew a little wider, but the tangles of cane in the bottoms were sometimes almost impenetrable, where old and new growth intermingled in a jungle which tripped the horses when they went down to the river to drink. There was a trail; the Buffalo Trace itself was easy to follow, but often it deviated toward the licks and then the travelers took a smaller, man-made path. Dan Boone hadn't troubled to clear it enough to keep out the overgrowth of vines and cane and laurel. On some of the mountain slopes where the trail was thin, the blaze-marks on trees showed the travelers which way to go, but the laurels encroached on the meager track. If a man got off the Trace, he could wander in a laurel wilderness and lose his way for days in the deadly sameness of those evergreen bushes, whose leaves were poisonous to a horse if it ate one of them, and whose tough stems slashed back as man and rider pushed through, and cut flesh until the blood ran. Laurels were a menace, and yet they had blossoms which were among the

44

most beautiful in America.

Abraham, easing Duchess along some of the worst parts of the path, didn't think kindly of the so-called Wilderness Road. It was there all right—Boone and Logan and the other hunters and explorers had marked it well enough—but it seemed to Abraham that if *he* were laying out a track through country like this, he would see to it that it was not only well marked, but that it was more easily followed than parts of this one. Except where it lay on the broad, hard buffalo roads, it was only a footpath. No wonder Indians could lie in wait for travelers. If *he* were doing it, fumed Abraham Lincoln, leaning forward to rub Duchess' glossy neck, he'd bring a gang of men with axes and *really* cut out a trail that *was* a trail, broad enough for wagons, safe enough for women and children. He couldn't see how he and Bathsheba were going to transport many of their household goods over this miserable excuse for a road; certainly they could manage none of their furniture. Road indeed! He'd give Dan a piece of his mind when they got to Boonesborough. Luring men, and women, too—and some with babies like that pitiful little scrap Margaret Jenkins was having such a bad time with—into a horror like this, where even a starving catamount would scratch his flanks going through! He marveled at how the gently-bred Duchess, who had never ventured into a deep forest in her life, had adapted herself to the Wilderness Road. Her slender feet still danced a little as they picked a safe way along the rocky trail. Her bright eyes were alert, her ears pricked forward, constantly listening, her nostrils testing the air for new smells, in a land in which such a beautiful horse doubtless had never been seen before. But it would see many fine horses after this, vowed Abraham, planning even now the Kentucky horses he would breed and would admire as they grazed on the green pastures Dan was always talking about. Then his mind came back to the very real present of the Wilderness Road. That thin wailing sound —it was the Jenkins baby again.

The baby cried. It cried most of the time now, and Abraham began to feel he couldn't stand it much longer. The unhappy shrieking sounded so far through the quiet woods, too, and he could never seem to escape it. The baby constantly brought into his mind the memory of Nancy, the tiny daughter he'd left behind. If things went wrong with him, Nancy would never know her father. Maybe he had better go home to Virginia and behave himself, instead of trying to struggle toward a goal which he might not even recognize when he got to it. If only he could be sure what was the right thing to do; if there were only some way to tell, some way to know. The baby gave a sharp little scream and began to gasp in a strange way which turned Abraham cold. He rode forward.

Margaret, in a panic, reined in her horse. "Mary Fay!" she cried out in a shrill voice. "Oh, come quick, something's wrong!"

Mary Fay urged her horse to Margaret's side and reached over to take the baby from her. The terrified mother relinquished the little bundle and, dropping her face into her hands, began to weep in heavy, jolting sobs which shook her thin body. Margaret Jenkins was almost exhausted.

John Jenkins was up ahead, helping to cut through some laurels to make the way easier for the women, and he was not aware of what was happening. The party paused uneasily in the trail.

Mary Fay, balancing the baby carefully, slid off her horse. Delphia Ann helped Margaret down. She put her arms around the sobbing woman.

"Honey," said Mary Fay tenderly, "honey, he's dead. He's been so sick—it's a wonder he lasted till now. Don't take on so, Margaret, you'll hurt yourself," she urged pityingly, her own eyes filling as the mother dropped to the soft earth and let her hysterical tears pour into the fragrant leaf mold of the Kentucky forest.

The women with the dead baby stood weeping in the wilderness. Abraham and Tom Randall didn't know what to do.

"I'll go get John Jenkins," Abraham said. Action was better than standing about doing nothing. He rode after Jenkins who, pale and tense, came back fast.

"It's my fault, it's all my fault," he muttered over and over. "If I'd gone back when she wanted to, maybe it wouldn't have happened. It's all my fault . . . she'll never forgive me . . . I'll never forgive myself . . ."

Abraham reached a big hand across and gave the bereaved father a brief pat on the shoulder. But he had no words which would have mattered just then, or would have consoled.

Even the wild little Randall boys were quiet, standing about with big eyes as the women wrapped the baby neatly in the knitted blanket Margaret had made months before the child was born, and laid him on a bank of soft bright moss where white violets blossomed in a delicate drifting of flowers and leaves. Meg McAllister, looking strangely pale and drawn and almost ill, went off alone among the great trees. Abraham caught a glimpse of her skirts before she vanished in the gloom of the forest, and he hoped she would find her way back before it was time to leave.

Mary Fay whispered to her husband, "Ahab, we can't just bury that poor little thing here in the forest without a coffin or anything. It'll just kill Margaret to do it. Can't we fix up some kind of little coffin-box for him?"

Ahab shook his head. "Out here in the wilderness? Woman, you don't know what you're asking. Miles from a settlement, surrounded by savages, for all we know . . ."

Abraham broke in. "If we can delay the trip again, just a little, I think I can fix a coffin, something that would do, maybe." And he opened one of his saddle packs and took out his carpenter tools, which he had brought along for another purpose in Kentucky.

Abraham Lincoln scouted around a bit and when he found a not-too-stout fallen hemlock log which was hollow inside, he worked until the perspiration rolled off his face as he sawed through the section of log. It was a little longer than the baby's body. He cleared out the inside of the log until it was smooth and neat. He cut two rounds of wood which fitted each end tightly, and one end he fastened in with wooden pegs. The men stood around and watched. The women sat with Margaret, who had ceased her wild weeping and was now white and drawn and limp. Around them lay the deep forest, scented with springtime and the damp, rich odors of a land which had never known the ax. Rosettes of gray-green lichens

47

brightened dead wood, embroidered the great trunks of tulip trees and beeches. It was very quiet, except for the soft sounds of Abraham's tools on wood, and no birds sang. Then a high, delicate, music-box tinkling performed a magic sort of song that was like nothing else in the whole world—a winter wren was singing. Margaret became more calm, listening.

When Abraham was finished, Mary Fay Littleford gently slid the little swathed body into the coffin, and he sealed the opening with the other piece of wood.

Adam Marlow had scooped a grave in the loose earth of the forest where mosses were thick and lush, and there, silently, they placed the little coffin and heaped the primeval forest earth over it. Adam Marlow prayed. Enoch Lambert, Price Randall, and Tom Reynolds brought logs which they piled neatly over the grave so that wolves or bears could not dig into it, and before the party moved heavily on again, Mary Fay carefully placed a handful of white violets and arbutus on the topmost log.

The days went on and the party went on, and sometimes it seemed that the journey would never end, but that they would go on forever over a trail through the wilderness. To people on foot, the Kentucky hills were as mountains, and the rivers and creeks, when rains filled them bankful, were almost insurmountable barriers. Yet the people and the horses climbed those mountains and forded those streams, and when a river did not recede soon enough, the party camped on the shores and waited.. Sometimes the men shot wild turkeys, which they roasted for dinner, but daily the supplies of corn meal, salt and pork brought from the settlements grew smaller, shortened still more by accidents—as when Enoch Lambert's horse, in a sudden panic at the sight of a bear crossing the trail ahead, ran away and threw down the saddle bags. Enoch's powder gourd was shattered and much valuable powder was lost, and a wallet of corn meal was broken and a good deal was spilled. The party could ill afford to lose either powder or meal.

There was rain; day after day it rained. The only advantage Abraham Lincoln could see in so much water which swelled the streams and wet clothing and powder, was the fact that there was mud in which the secret tracks of moccasined feet would be easily discovered. Nightly, watch was kept for Indians, but none were seen, only their footprints in the mud. Day after day, slowly, painfully, the people and the horses moved north through Kentucky. They felt lucky if they could travel twenty miles between dawn and dusk.

Always, however, they could see the valley growing broader, the mountains less high. They were only hills now, hills becoming greener as springtime came on at a faster pace than it had in the higher places. Dogwood was beginning to splash its masses of white flowers against every slope. The countryside was growing more alive, more beautiful, more gentle, more reassuring.

One day fresh buffalo tracks cut the mud of the trail. Buffalo tracks! Lots of them! Abraham's skin prickled at the excitement of discovering them, for he had never seen buffalo and he felt the imminence of their primal majesty. The fresh tracks led him to a salt lick not far from the trail.

He had gone ahead of the others to find out whether there were any deer at this lick—which Parmeaneas Jellico remembered from having stopped by it in '78—and left Duchess on the trail while he went on foot to follow the buffalo tracks. The creatures he saw at the lick were so large and there were so many of them, that at first his eyes did not focus clearly. He wasn't sure just what he was seeing; no animals could be so massive, so unbelievably huge! His heart was pounding with excitement and his hands shook as he lifted his rifle. The great dark beasts became aware of something alien close by. The bulls began to mutter sonorously down in their shaggy throats, and moved around so that their rumps shoved the cows and calves to the rear. Abraham was suddenly confronted with a solid wall of wild dark eyes and whuffling wet nostrils as the bulls tested the air for the source of that foreign odor. Then a little wind blew past Abraham and ruffled the back of his hair, and as his scent was carried strongly to those big nostrils, the buffalo charged off to the east in a sudden stampede, as if wolves were at their heels. Abraham involuntarily stepped back a pace and caught his balance again. The thunder of hard hoofs on the packed earth of the east trail rattled in his ears and dust filled the air. He put down his rifle. He felt a little weak in the knees as he walked back down the animal trail to where he had left Duchess quietly waiting, her nostrils flared and her ears pricked forward at the commotion up ahead, but she had not panicked as many another horse might have done in a like situation. The rest of the party caught up with him and he had to confess that he'd shot no meat.

"But forty buffalo!" cried Ahab Littleford, his eyes shining. "I'd have given a lot to have seen 'em!"

"Oh, you'll see more up around Boonesborough," Enoch Lambert assured him. "I've heard tell of 'em, hundreds of buffalo grazin' in the meadowlands!"

At the fork in the Wilderness Road where Boone's Trace went north and Logan's Trail went northwest to Harrodstown and eventually to Louisville, the party halted.

Adam spoke up. "I'd planned it to go on to Harrodstown. I promised Jim Harrod I'd settle up near his fort. But with Indians like they are, I guess we'd all better stick together now and go to Boone's place first. When we get there and see how the land lies and what the Indian situation is, we can go cross-country to Harrodstown on a buffalo road I've heard of, and we might all be safer. I don't know . . . but we'll be a whole lot better off if we don't divide now, small as our party is."

So they all turned right on Boone's Trace.

One bright morning in May, when the cardinals were whistling in the thickets and the buzzards floated serene and black against a bright Kentucky sky, Abraham, riding ahead on the faithful Duchess, saw the stockade which was Boonesborough. The mare saw it, too. Her ears pricked forward and she whiffled under her breath, as if she sensed the presence of other horses somewhere not far away.

The yellow waters of the Kentucky River curved to the right around the fort, and the sycamores on the bank and the forest on the limestone bluffs across the river formed a green background for the

JESSE'S HORSE, TERRIFIED AT THE NEARNESS OF THE SHOT, WHEELED,
REARED, PAWED THE AIR AND PLUNGED BACKWARD

BATHSHEBA BEGAN HER PREPARATIONS TO LEAVE THE FARM IN VIRGINIA
FOR THE UNKNOWN HOUSE AND LAND IN KENTUCKY

weathered logs which comprised the stockade and fort. Sharpened logs—whole trees, they were, shorn of branches—fifteen feet high, were thrust into the earth to form a square stockade inside which were log houses whose roofs Abraham could see from the rise of ground up which he rode Duchess. There was a blockhouse at each corner of the square, with loopholes to fire through in case of attack. Snug inside this sturdy stockade, which followed the pattern of most forts in the wilderness, lay Boonesborough, staunch settlement in the heart of Kentucky.

Abraham yelled, and the men in the party yelled, and they threw their hats into the air and fired a volley of shots, though they could ill afford to waste their powder in jollity. After a moment of silence in the fort, there was an answering volley and the big double gates flew open as men and women poured out to welcome the newcomers. Bringing up the rear was Daniel Boone himself.

Abraham urged Duchess forward to meet the man of the wilderness country.

"Dan Boone!" cried Abraham. "We got here, we really did, but I thought sometimes we'd never make it! Why don't you do something about that road you're always so proud to talk about? Be ashamed of it if I were you!" And laughing, Abraham leaped down from Duchess and pumped Boone's hard, calloused hand. He and the trail blazer danced and cavorted, still gripping hands wildly—as if they were Indians, Delphia Ann commented, smiling at her husband. He was grinning all over his broad, tanned face. The Randall boys were running circles around everyone and whooping like Shawanese. Everyone felt like dancing with Daniel Boone, they were so glad to have got here at last.

Boonesborough was not the end of the trail for Abraham Lincoln and Adam Marlow and the Littlefords. In several days' time the Littlefords and Adam set off on a buffalo road in the direction of Harrodstown, a party of Boonesborough men with plenty of arms accompanying them, but Abraham stayed a little longer. He wanted to talk to Dan. It was good to be able to see first hand what it was the trail-blazer was always talking about.

"It's gettin' too blamed *crowded* hereabouts, Abe," Boone complained one evening as they sat before the fire in the Boone cabin within the stockade. "Kaintuck ain't what she used to be, that I'm tellin' you. People comin' up here all the time now, pushin' in, yappin' for this and that, buildin' houses, plowin' land for corn, cuttin' down the trees. I got to have me more room, Abe, and I'm not findin' it here in Kaintuck any more. Now across the Mississippi, they say . . ."

But Abraham only laughed at him. Abraham had come to Kentucky on Boone's advice, but he wasn't going to stir a step to follow him in the direction of the Mississippi, or across it, either. Kentucky was good enough for him. And from what he saw of it, barring the grim wilderness southward on the trail, he had fallen in love with the country and its lush meadowlands.

Rested and refreshed, Abraham set out toward the west and he and Duchess traveled the wild country for several months. He was comparing land. He wanted rolling meadows for pastures and level lands for fields, a good supply of sweet water for his stock and an unfailing pure spring near the house. The water ought surely to be good hereabouts, he concluded, because of the limestone underpinning, whose presence was revealed in rocky outcroppings on hillsides and along the streams. He found several places which took his fancy.

He made his choice at last. He bought four hundred acres on Long Run of Floyd's Fork, in Jefferson County northwest of Harrodstown; and in Lincoln County, to the south, he purchased eight hundred acres lying six miles below Green River Lick, "beginning at a buckeye at A on the river bank . . . and running thence down the river with the meanders as is laid down in the platt to a sugar tree and buckeye at B on the river bank at a bend of the river . . ." as his deed was written.

At first he had felt satisfied with the four hundred acres on Long Run. He rode up to Louisville on the Ohio and at the log courthouse he registered his deed and paid his treasury warrants. But land at forty cents an acre—Dan Boone hadn't lied about that—was too cheap to let pass, and since he still had two of his treasury warrants left, Abraham decided to buy that other piece of land he'd admired down by the Green River. So a few days later he rode back to Louisville and registered eight hundred more acres of land in his name. It was more property than he'd ever owned in his life, yet he had spent only five hundred pounds. Beautiful country, fine land all of it. He could see his sleek horses and cattle grazing on that deep green grass, could begin to visualize his house and his barns as he would one day build them. With empty pockets but a wonderful feeling of satisfaction and elation in his heart, Abraham Lincoln, Esquire, went back to the Green River farm and there he camped in an old cabin a hunter had put up a few years before.

CHAPTER SEVEN

During that long, hot Kentucky summer, Abraham Lincoln cleared his land, and the carpenter's tools which he had brought with him in his saddle packs from Virginia met their intended use at last. All summer his bright ax bit into the great tree trunks. As the white chips fell in heaps on the ground, the vast leafy boughs shivered, the birds flew out and the squirrels leaped to safety, and, groaning, each tree came down to crash mightily upon the earth.

From the first fine logs Abraham built a cabin. Adam Marlow came over one day to help him lift them into place, with the notches firmly in each saddle that had been cut to fit the size of the log which was to be laid into it. Adam was as big and strong as Abraham and they worked well together. After so many lonely weeks clearing his land, with only the trees and the beasts to talk to, it was good to feel the companionship of another man. They didn't talk a great deal, but when they did say something it was to savor the sound of each other's voices. No matter, really, what they said, be it politics or Indian trouble or about their families, waiting to come out. It was satisfying just to talk to a human being again.

Sometimes afterward Abraham thought a good deal about what he and Adam had discussed, as when they had spent a large part of a day in arguing about this union of the states which had come from the Revolution. Oh, yes, Abraham Lincoln had fought in the Revolution and had been mustered out as Captain Lincoln; he knew what war was about, and he believed he had been fighting for a good thing, but he never thought very deeply about the matter. He'd enlisted when Washington wanted men, and he'd fought as well as he could, and led his ill-trained men to the best of his and their ability, and that was all any man could do. The Revolution would have made sense, he remarked to Adam one day, as they strained to lift a high log and then eased their muscles to let it slide into place, if it had been only the British fighting the Americans because of taxes and such-like which the Americans wanted to be rid of. He could see why he and other Americans wanted to be a separate country when they were the ones who were cutting forests and grubbing brush so they could plant and build in the new land. If it had ended at that—but it hadn't. When the British got the Indians into it, that made the war something else.

"It's every man for himself, I guess," Abraham said bitterly, wiping the sweat from his brow. "We're not fighting for the colonies or the states," he went on, "we're fighting for our homes and our lives because the Indians have been urged on by the British and that Hamilton, which they call the Hair-Buyer—or were till Clark sent him off to gaol. The government isn't doing anything to help us. Look at Virginia: Kentucky's a county of Virginia, yet *she* won't send money and ammunition when we need it so desperate—" Abraham already was thinking as a Kentuckian, not as a Virginian—"even though they say Kentucky is beholden to pay taxes to Richmond. I tell you I don't see the sense to it!"

"Well, no, I can't rightly say I see it, either," Adam said cautiously, resting a moment on a log. "But it takes time, Abe, it takes time. You can't develop a land as big as this without some injustice being done and some blood shed. I can't say it was right for the British to send the Indians against us, when they were plenty set against us already; they always did feel no white man had a right to Kentucky. And paying for our scalps hasn't helped. But when I get to feeling all the heavy hates and discouragements that a time like this can bring on, I get to thinking what Governor Henry said that time," Adam paused a moment to collect his words, and then flung them forth in his magnificent oratory that made Abraham's spine fairly tingle; as if Patrick

Henry himself in the First Continental Congress at Philadelphia were there instead, in the Kentucky Wilderness, talking to him:

"We are in a state of nature! All distinctions are thrown down. All America is thrown into one mass. The distinctions between Virginians, Pennsylvanians, New Yorkers, and New Englanders are no more. I am not a Virginian, *but an American!"* And Adam Marlow, flushed with the fervor he felt when he spoke those flaming words, went on in a lower tone, "That's what I mean, Abe—we aren't fighting as Virginians or as Kentuckians, but as *Americans* to build America! And if it's hard, then maybe we'll make America all the better and stronger because of how much we've suffered. Mark you my words, Abraham Lincoln, you'll see the day when all this trial and trouble are over, and it won't matter then about who sent supplies to a handful of Kentuckians off in the wilderness!"

Well, they talked, yes, but they got the rafters up, too, and then Adam had to go back to his own place, close to Harrodstown, where Abraham had promised to follow the next week to help him raise his own cabin. Abraham was sorry to see Adam Marlow go, but that was the way of things in the wilderness. Men were glad to help each other when they needed helping, but always they must go on to their own places, always live aloof from the crowds, until at last the wilderness melted away and there were adjoining farms and towns full of people instead.

Abraham had to smile, sometimes, thinking of what Dan Boone had said, so piteous-like that you'd half believe him if you didn't know the old scoundrel better, that things were "gettin' too crowded hereabouts in Kaintucky—no elbowroom!" Crowded! Unless a man went to the forts and stations and to the few little settlements and beginnings of towns, he had to hunt long and patiently to find a white man.

Abraham was at his labor as soon as the sun was up and he worked until night moved blue and cool across the Kentucky hills and the whippoorwills were loud in the sycamores along the river. Then for days at a time he took his frow and split clapboards to lay across the joists to make a loft, and he built a strong ladder for the going up and the coming down. Mord, Jo, and Tom would love it up there, a snug, cozy space for their beds, and a place up under the eaves, besides, to dry the walnuts and hickory nuts and beechnuts which they'd gather every autumn from the forest close by. And the family down below, sleeping in the great room, would hear the mice and squirrels rolling the nuts over the floor and stealing some, like as not, to store away in hideyholes of their own up under the roof somewhere. The roof he finished, too, with the overlapping rows of clapboards, shingling it tightly against snows and storms. He got the big stick-and-clay chimney up and the fireplace built—a fireplace that would take six-foot logs—and set in it a strong iron trammel to regulate the height of the pothooks on which Bathsheba would hang her kettles. He got Adam once again, to help him bring in a smooth, broad slab of limestone for a hearth, for want of bricks, and the two men laid it tightly so that no corner would rock.

As he worked, Abraham thought a great deal about Bathsheba and wondered what would be her opinion of this home he was building for her. It would not be like the fine brick house she was leaving behind forever in the Valley of Virginia. Later on he planned to build a better place, because he didn't want to live in a log cabin for the rest of his days, but for a while this would have to do as their home. The boys would like it, he knew. He hoped Bathsheba would take kindly to it, too. At least he would give her more comforts than most wilderness women had in their first cabins, for this house of his had a puncheon floor, tight and as smooth as he could plane it, not tamped earth, and there would be windows.

Yes, windows. He would have to cut some because she liked light and she wanted to see out of her house; and he, too, rather enjoyed it himself when he could stand with his feet apart and his hands under his coattails, and see the horses grazing on the green slopes, or watch the children playing in the dooryard. He had set the cabin so that it faced the long slope down to the river. There were some dogwood trees on the hillside which would be pretty in spring and bright red in fall; already he could see the beginnings of scarlet beads as the berries ripened and splashes of red came into the green of the oval leaves. There was a right good spring flowing out of the hillside not too far from the house. So he cut two fine windows; Bathsheba could look out and see the dogwood flowering and could see the spring, too. Most cabins in the wilderness, if they had any windows, which many didn't, boasted only one, but his would have two and maybe later he'd cut another. He had no glass panes to put in them. No matter. Shutters would have to do until another day, when perhaps he could get some glass from Virginia. A piece of paper greased with bear oil would let in the light, and so would a thin hog membrane, taken with care from leaf lard and fastened to the frame.

He planed the big planks for the door so that they were smooth and wouldn't give off splinters to small hands pushing eagerly to get in or out, and built stout hickory hinges to swing it. He fixed a deer-hide latchstring so that it could be fastened from the inside and keep out intruders. For real intruders—Indians, maybe—he cut a large, strong hickory bar which could be slid across the door and dropped into slots so that no one could ever get in without the consent of those inside. He made heavy shutters for the windows, too.

Wet weather did not keep Abraham from working. During a spell of autumn rain he sat in the cabin and made three-legged stools and benches, a puncheon table, and a corner cupboard for Bathsheba's dishes, built a chest for clothing—*his* family needn't hang clothing from wall pegs, along with powder horns, bear-traps, harnesses, and such gear—and he worked on a bedstead which would be lashed with ropes to support the featherticks. Those ticks at first would have to be stuffed with straw or corn shucks or with dry oak leaves, he was sure, until Bathsheba had geese which could multiply enough to produce feathers for a proper ticking. The children would have to sleep on leaf-beds on the floor. Might be Bathsheba would object, but she must realize she was a wilderness woman now and her children would have to learn wilderness ways. Later they would get comforts and conveniences. Just now he could provide only the needful things. When the family was together again, there would be plenty of time for fripperies.

Abraham worked hard, but he worked with satisfaction. This

was his own land, his own house, his own building for the future. It had been good in Virginia, but his father had *given* him that land and he had had slaves to help with the house-building and the barn-raising—slaves to make all the bricks and set them neatly with mortar, to build the fireplaces and lay the hearthstones. The cabin in Kentucky was his own handiwork and he felt a deep and enduring pride in the results. The lines of his lean face were set in a certain peace and inner content he had not known before.

When the house at last was finished and the logs were chinked with chips and a mortar of stiff clay from the river bed, he set to work at clearing his fields. Duchess got callouses and took on a rough, unkempt look as she served as a draft horse to haul out stumps and drag brush and logs to the burning place. One by one the ancient trees went down in the forest that had never before known the touch of an ax, and what Abraham didn't need he piled in great heaps for burning. And the glow of his fires leaped to the autumn stars and sent fountains of sparks high into the night sky. Indians on the far hills saw his flames, but no visitors came near. Not then.

Autumn moved with a golden light over Kentucky. The tulip poplars, always early with their coloring, stood bright yellow against the green oaks. Sugar maple colors dazzled the eyes. Gum trees along the river turned all manner of harlequin colors, from creamy white to gold and purple and all the hues between, Abraham vowed as he saw the star-shaped leaves fairly twinkling with color in the wind. The red maples blazed scarlet and finally the oaks fired up with rich and kingly colors. From yellowed hickories came the sounds of falling nuts as they dropped with small thuds to the leaf-strewn earth, an earth that was being brightly buried under millions of ripe leaves which came drifting down, day after day, in the smoky autumn air.

At last there was a lowering gray sky full of mist, and when rain came in great sweeping gusts through the forest and rushed in a blur across the cleared fields and enveloped the cabin in mist-laden veils, the leaves as they fell soddenly sent up a rich, ripe perfume. The smell of fresh-cut wet wood emanated from the newly-built cabin. When the rain was over, the southward flying geese were calling in the sky, and most of the trees stood bare. Abraham could see a long way now through the aisles of the forest where trees stood as they had stood for centuries, with the younger growth beneath.

Sometimes when Abraham wanted company he mounted Duchess and rode back over the narrow trail to Boonesborough, to the east, for a visit with Daniel Boone, who was more restless than ever and more concerned with the growing ferment of the Indians.

"Mark you my words, Abe," Dan said one November day, his troubled eyes seeing far off where no man could follow his gaze, "mark you my words, there'll be trouble soon, dreadful trouble, and blood everywhere. I can smell it now, I vow I can, and it makes me fair sick!" But men around about laughed at Dan's words. Indians hadn't been bothersome for months on end; they were a-clearing out of Kaintuck, sure as fate. No matter about the English egging them on; hadn't the Delawares and the Shawanese been plaguing the British up around the big lakes all this long while, and hadn't Lord Dunmore sent the Cherokees packing into the wilderness of Carolina and Georgia? Kaintucky was getting to be safe as a baby's cradle now, that was certain. And Boone looked mournfully with his bright blue eyes into the future and knew—because he thought like an Indian and knew what they were thinking even now—that trouble was a-coming.

That time in November when Abraham rode in to Boonesborough, he knew that some of the trouble had already struck. He found Dan just in from an expedition up to the Ohio, trailing Indians. The party had just arrived, loaded with venison for the fort, and while Dan unpacked his gear, he told Abraham what had happened. From the sober face on him, it was plain that Dan had been hit hard.

"They got my brother Edward, Abe," he said simply, pausing to peer with innocent-appearing blue eyes into Abraham's face, and Abraham Lincoln saw a moisture in those eyes he'd never seen there before. "We'd gone to the Upper Blue Licks to boil salt, and on our way back to Boonesborough, they killed him."

"Tell me about it, Dan," said Abraham in sympathy, his hand on

Boone's shoulder. "Sit down over here; you look about done in. Now tell me the whole thing—it'll ease you to let it out."

"Well, 'twas this way, Abe," Dan Boone began. "We was restin' to let the horses eat and drink, and Ed was a-sittin' on a rock, crackin' hickory nuts betwixt two stones. Just then I seen a bear off in the brush, and I fired, but I didn't do so good and the bear, though 'twas hit, wasn't mortally hurt, and off it tore down the stream, with me after it, lickety split. Ed stayed with the horses; he was havin' a good time with them hickory nuts; he was always partial to 'em. As I ran after the bear I could hear him goin' 'crack, crack' with the two stones, breakin' the nutshells. That was the last I ever heard of him, Abraham, the very last.

"Just as I reached the bear, which had keeled over dead, I heard shots back where I'd left Edward. Then I heard no more and I got worried. I was just startin' back on the run when, lo and behold, what should I see but that black-and-tan hound of mine followin' my trail. I knew then that somethin' had happened to Ed; that hound never trailed me 'less I told him to. Listenin' careful, I heard Injun voices, so I slid into a canebrake, thinkin' to hide. But that consarned hound—he never did have any sense, that I vow—kept on followin' me, and when I ducked into the cane, there he stood in the path, waggin' his fool tail, a good enough sign to anyone that his master was hid near by. Every time I threw a rock at him to make him quit, he'd look hurt at me, and run back to where the Injuns was, and when they took after him, back he'd come a-peltin', skeered to death. So the Injuns naturally knew where I was at."

Serious as the situation was, and full of tragedy, Abraham could not keep back a smile at the vividness of Daniel Boone's narrative. Dan might be on the verge of destruction, but he could always make a rousing good tale out of it when he escaped.

"Land, what a time I had," he went on. "I pushed through the cane, but I'd lost my ramrod somewheres so I couldn't reload— hadn't reloaded since I shot that bear, which was a mite careless of me—and my shoes, bein' new, got slick on the soles as I went through the wet cane, and there I was, with that dog comin' and slobberin'

on my heels, almost, and me slippin' and slidin' around in that con-
founded cane, and the Injuns right behind! Eh law, I thought sure
I was a goner, Abe, I really thought I was that time!"

"But what about Ed—where was your brother all this time, Dan?"
asked Abraham.

"I'll come to that part," answered Boone. He always had to tell
a story in his own way, the long way around. "Well, I had to do a
thing I hated, I purely did. I saw a piece of cane about the size of
a ramrod, and with it I quick reloaded my rifle gun and I shot that
black-and-tan hound of mine. He died without a yelp. I had to do
it; it was either him or me, and I didn't hanker to die just then. So
I got out of the cane patch fast and hid behind a tree, and waited.
My, you should have heard them Shawanese yell when they come
upon that poor dead dog of mine! They give up the chase after that,
after they beat about in the cane for a while.

"But Abe, they'd killed Edward, they really had. My poor, poor
brother! I circled back to Boonesborough and came back with a
party of men with guns, and there we found him lyin' dead in the
forest, them cracked nutshells lyin' pitiful all around him, and his
head cut clean off. Them devils! I'll make 'em pay, I vow I will!

"We set off to trail 'em," Dan went on morosely, wiping his sleeve
quickly across his eyes. "We tracked 'em as far as the Ohio, but they'd
got across by that time, so we come back. Just got in, as you see.
We'll have plenty meat for supper, so I'm glad you dropped in.
How's your cabin—'bout finished? I reckon you'll be goin' back to
Virginia for Mrs. Lincoln and the young ones soon."

"Not till next spring, Dan, not till next spring," said Abraham
soberly. "And if the Indians get any worse around here, we'll wait
a spell before comin' back. I'm sorry about Edward, Dan, sorry's
I can be, and all you say worries me some. Yes, the cabin's about
finished, and I'm clearin' a lot of land. Ride over some day and take
a look. It's a right pretty little cabin, if I do say so myself."

There were times when loneliness and foreboding unhappily
closed down over Abraham, and the isolation of his new farm was
suddenly intolerable. It was then that he sometimes rode up to
Harrodstown to talk to Adam Marlow. Adam's steady personality

and his wise, far-seeing counsel always made Abraham feel better. Adam was going back for his family before the snow flew, and wanted Abraham to go with him.

"I can't leave yet, but I'll send a letter you can take to my wife, if you'll be so kind," he said. "I still have a field to clear and I want to build me a barn and more furniture for the house so's it won't look too bare when Basheby comes next spring. I wouldn't want her to see it the way it is now!" And he laughed ruefully as he thought of his bachelor quarters in the cabin—a floor littered with wood shavings right now. It would need considerable cleaning and fixing up before his family came. So he scrawled a letter on a scrap of paper which Adam tore out of his Bible and said his good-bys, and went back to work on the farm.

When he pushed open the door of the new cabin that day, he saw at once that someone had been there. Remains of corn pone were strewn on the planked floor, as if whoever had come there had left hastily. But there was no one in sight, nothing for evidence. Down by the spring, however, when he went to get water, he discovered the deep imprint of a moccasined foot. Not necessarily that of an Indian, he reasoned with himself; lots of frontiersmen wore buckskin moccasins because they were easier on the feet than boots when you were on the trail. But it *could* have been Indians, though they mightn't be hostile ones, like the Shawanese and Wyandot, either, he told himself. Could have been a Piankeshaw, and the Piankeshaw were friendly. There was one up at Harrodstown, fellow named Talking Crow, who had been a big help to the settlers. But Abraham couldn't fool himself very well. The stories Daniel Boone had been telling him of how the Indians were slipping around, all but out of sight, but not quite, planning and plotting and killing here and there, and waiting . . . and an Indian waiting can stick it out longer than a white man can before he begins to get pins in his toes from impatience; he can strike when a white man least expects it. If they could creep up on Dan Boone, the smartest Indian fighter in Kentucky, then it would be easier still for the varmints to slip up on Abraham Lincoln, who was only a farmer. That night he took care to bar the door and the heavy shutters, but no one disturbed him.

CHAPTER EIGHT

The PEACH BLOSSOMS had been drifting away on a breeze blowing up the Valley of Virginia when Abraham Lincoln rode off on his errand into the wilderness. New leaves came out and tiny young green fruits formed on the peach boughs, and it was high summer. Summer, and at last the peaches were ripe, and the slaves with great care picked the ripe golden fruits with their flush of rich red, and laid them carefully in leaf-lined willow baskets. Bathsheba sold the peaches for a fair price in Harrisonburg that year, and put the money away on the top shelf of the big cupboard.

Bathsheba slowly regained her strength and battled with the illness which had kept her so weak and listless after Nancy was born and Abraham went away. But with cold determination, even during the months of convalescence when Bathsheba Lincoln was not able, without help, to walk to the barn and back, she was planning on riding a horse and taking five young children over one of the cruelest and most dangerous wilderness trails in America. And her determination conquered her weakness, and her strength came back.

With Leah's help, Bathsheba, in autumn, began her preparations to leave the farm in Virginia for the unknown house and land in Kentucky.

"We simply can't take much with us, Leah," she explained one day when the autumn rain slanted steadily against the window panes of the brick house. "Mr. Boone says that not even wagons can climb the Gap, though he predicts there'll come a time when they will, and carriages, too."

"Dat Mistah Boone talk mighty big," grumbled Leah, her eyes smoldering. She stood erect above the open trunks where she and Bathsheba had been sorting clothing all that rainy day. "He say plenty, but do he help out when de helpin' time come along? No! Mistah Boone, *he* set in his fort somewhar up dar in dat blessed *Kain*tucky he talk so much about, whilst all dem po' folk work and struggle over dem trails and de Injuns creep up and kill 'em. I hear dem folk talk, dat I have, and I wish to de land dat you ain' goin', Miss 'Sheba!"

"Oh, Leah, don't feel badly!" cried Bathsheba, laying her hand on the woman's strong black fingers. "People get through all the time now, and the Indians aren't so much danger any more; leastwise they don't bother if there are plenty of men and guns in the party, and we'll make sure of that. But I *will* miss you, that I will!"

Her own eyes misted for a moment, as she remembered for the thousandth time how staunch and loyal Leah had been for so many years, nursing Bathsheba and her children when they were ill, cooking superbly in the big, brick-floored kitchen, levelheaded and serene and a source of wisdom in time of trouble. Leah was the one person she most hated to leave, the one strength she clung to. In the silence, the rain beat on the window panes of the pleasant plantation house.

The tall dark woman turned abruptly and busied herself with folded garments. When she spoke it was in a low tone, full of held-back tears.

"Miss 'Sheba, I know I cain't go with you-all into de wilderness, but if ever's you need me, send me word somehow, and I come, ma'am. I come if I got to swim me across dem rivers and fight my way through all dem forests and Injuns and bears and sich. Miss 'Sheba, I come!"

Day after day, week after week, Leah and Bathsheba sorted and stacked and boxed the items which could not be taken into the wilderness and which would be transported by cart to Bathsheba's kin in Charlottesville. By winter the brick house had a bare, clean-swept look. Only the essentials remained, only the things they needed for daily living.

"Really, Leah," commented Bathsheba one day, surveying her cleared-out house, "if we can live comfortably with so few things, why then do we bother with so much? It will be a lesson to me to be content with little and never again lay up for moths to corrupt and rust to decay!

"But I simply can't bear to leave behind my best silver candlesticks!" she cried in a different tone. "We'll take them somehow. I shall persuade Abraham, I know. And my damask tablecloth. Do you think we could possibly find room in a saddle pack, Leah? We must! We can't always live like savages in the wilderness, and if I can set a table with linen and silver and candlesticks, it will at least be a sign that we are not wholly lost." So the candlesticks and silver sugar basin, and Bathsheba's best spoons and forks, and the tablecloth went in a special spot where the things to be taken were kept. There could be so few: clothing, food, a few dishes and utensils, only the items which were most needful and which could be packed in saddle bags and secured to the backs of horses for the long journey.

The peach leaves long since had fallen and the glossy twigs stood bare in the wind sweeping down from the north into the Valley of Virginia, and the pleasant chill of the mild Virginia winter lay in the air. Josiah and Mary and Mordecai were attending school down the road, and Tommy and Nancy stayed at home with Bathsheba while she went about her sorting and mending and packing. She often could have used Mary's help, but she wanted the eager little girl to get some learning while she had a chance, young as she was, for goodness only knew when she would again have a school to go to. Bathsheba doubted whether there were many schools or school masters as yet in Kentucky. Maybe some day, but not for years, and meanwhile her children would grow up ignorant and untaught. Mary should learn, therefore, while she had the opportunity, and maybe the boys could help her later. Bathsheba herself had had no schooling at all; her father did not hold with the education of females. But she felt the lack keenly. She could write her name, but it was hard to do it, to curl her slim fingers correctly around the quill so that it would form the painful pothooks which made her name, and even then Abraham, laughing, said she didn't spell it right. With a gnawing desire that was like an unfilled hunger, she wished desperately that she could read and write as Abraham could.

"Long as you have me around," he had said consolingly when she mourned her ignorance and begged him to teach her, "I'll do all the reading needful and tell you what-all it says!" But somehow it wasn't quite the same and she knew it. Might be that Abraham wouldn't always be handy, as happened now, and it would be a good thing if she had an education.

When Mord came home from school one day, he dashed in with a rush of chilly November air, for a norther had blown down the Valley from somewhere up in the Ohio country, and it was cold in Virginia. He threw his cap on the table and slammed the kitchen door, all in one lithe movement.

"Cousin Hananiah's comin' down the road!" he announced cheerfully, picking up an apple and sinking his strong white teeth into the red skin so that juice dripped down his chin. "Hey, Jo, did you see what a fine horse he's ridin'? Looks like a new one, slick as grease, and see those legs—bet that's a racer, eh, Jo?"

Little Tommy climbed up to a window and looked out. Then he scrambled down and before his brothers knew what he was about, Tom was out in the yard and his stocky little figure was trotting down the graveled drive to the gate where Hananiah Lincoln was just turning in.

"Up! Up!" cried Tommy, holding up his arms, and with a laughing swoop Hananiah bent down and scooped up the child and placed him on the saddle in front of him.

"Hi, Tom, old man, is your mother home?" he asked as the horse walked to the house.

Tommy nodded his black-thatched head. He patted the sleek neck of his mount and held on to the reins. "She's home. Goin' away when Pa comes back. 'Way off."

"Yes, I know," said Cousin Hananiah. He paused at the hitching rail and stepped down on the block, and lifted the reluctant Tommy down.

"Want to stay up!" he protested, starting to cry. Tommy always wanted to be near horses.

Hananiah Lincoln went in without knocking, as if he owned the place, Bathsheba thought angrily. He was as sleek and spruce as his own horse, but Bathsheba, giving him a quick, keen look, noticed frayed edges on his sleeves and a not-quite-new look to his clothes. She wondered quickly if the young, debonair Hananiah had fallen on poorer times, and what he was here for. And she could almost have guessed.

"Well, Cousin Bathsheba, and how are you?" He spoke affably, warming his long hands at the fire, then slowly circulating his handsome body around and about to warm all sides of his tall form. "I've been thinking of you, Cousin, especially lately, with winter closing down. Haven't heard from Abraham, have you?"

"No, I haven't," she said quietly. "Leah," she called, "set another place for dinner."

"Have you ever thought what you would do, Basheby," he said cautiously, not meeting her eyes but bending his gray ones to the flames, "if Abraham did not come home again?"

Bathsheba Lincoln felt a cold hand clutch her heart. It was a possibility she had tried not to think about, had pushed resolutely over and over into the background of her mind, something to be thought about later—if there was any reason for it—something to be shunned as unclean when there was no real reason to think about it—yet. Now Hananiah had brought the ugly thing out into the open, indecently, cruelly, like a vulgar topic of conversation.

"Oh, I know it isn't a pretty thing to say and you must forgive me for being blunt," the tall, lean young man said hastily at the sudden hurt in her face. "Truth generally isn't. But you know as well as I do that the Indians are getting worse instead of better, in spite of talk to the contrary. I've heard things about that bloody Kentucky country, and your precious Dan Boone is a scoundrel for

luring folk into that wilderness and then abandoning them to the
mercies of savages, not fortifying his forts, going off to connive
with old Blackfish himself. Oh, he isn't popular in Virginia, I tell
you that. I don't pretend, though, that I wouldn't go to Kentucky
myself, if the opportunity arose, and I may do it soon, but I don't
fool myself it's exactly safe for women and children. Now you,
Basheby, you're a young, beautiful woman, raised gently, and you
belong in a city like Charlottesville, with a carriage and a nice house,
your children in a good school—not stuck off in a cabin out in
the backwoods forests with Indians on your doorstep and no slaves
to help out with the work. Now listen a minute, Basheby, honey,"
he went on, before she could get in a word. "I'm thinking only of
your welfare. I've got it all thought out and you'll agree it's a pretty
good plan when you hear it."

Bathsheba stood still obediently and held her hands clasped quietly
before her, but, unseen by anyone, her two thumbs bent into the
hollow of her hands dug their nails into her palms as she waited for
what he was going to say.

"I'll listen, Hananiah," she said in a low voice, "but that's *all*
I'll ever agree to do to any of your propositions."

"Wait till you hear it, Cousin," he said jovially, now that he had
her attention. Leah in the kitchen, meanwhile, seemed to be making
an undue amount of noise as she prepared supper. Pot lids dropped
with a clatter on the bricks and she exclaimed loudly in vexation as
she stooped to pick them up. An iron pot tumbled off the table with
a ringing clang and rolled all the way across the kitchen, or so it
sounded. Leah stepped on the cat's tail and the creature with a yowl
sprang into the air, upset a water bucket, and leaped off the doorstep at the end of Leah's broom. Bathsheba, waiting, listened with a
detached, inward mirth to what was going on in the kitchen quarters,
and knew that Leah was expressing her disapproval of Hananiah
Lincoln and his fine plans in the only medium at her command.

"Now then, Cousin," Hananiah was saying briskly, "I've a nice
little house on Albemarle Street in Charlottesville, big enough for all
of you. I'll sell it to you for four thousand pounds, house and garden,

a carriage, and two slaves besides. You can leave this big place—
Michael Shanks is ready to take possession any time—and move into
the smaller, more comfortable house. Then if Abraham does come
home, which I'm beginning more and more to doubt, rest his soul,
you can sell the Charlottesville house easily and be ready to go with
him into that forsaken wilderness of his. And if he doesn't come,
you're all set, with no farm to worry about."

Bathsheba felt herself growing colder and colder. It was as if
there rose in her a dreadful, icy certainty that all Hananiah said with
such conviction was true . . . that Abraham indeed would never
come back . . . many never did . . . that she would have the sole
care of the big farm . . . that she would have to give back to
Michael Shanks the five thousand pounds he had paid for the Lincoln
land, would have to make a living somehow for herself and her five
fatherless children.

The certainty rose in her as if she were slowly freezing to death,
as if she could see Abraham stretched out dead on the forest earth,
his red blood running slowly into the secretive darkness of that earth
and staining the green mosses an ugly brown. It had been so long since
he had gone away from her. What was the use in continuing to
hope and plan . . . and the thing which Hananiah, the always per-
suasive Hananiah, was saying, seemed to make sense.

The kitchen door slammed and Bathsheba, as if from another
world, heard low voices. Red-cheeked Josiah pranced into the room.
In his hands he had some little cloth bags neatly tied up with thread,
and there was pride in his voice when he spoke.

"Look, Mammy, my seeds!" he cried, holding them out to her.
"All my best garden seeds that I've saved from the crops this year,
all ready to take along to Kentucky to plant in Pa's new fields! Do
you think they'll grow as good in Kentucky as in Virginia, Mammy,
do you think so?" And he turned his blue eyes up to hers—so like
her own—for confirmation of what he was so sure was right.

The freezing in her vitals stopped as a warm love rose in her and
she bent to kiss the little boy's forehead.

"Yes, sweet, I'm sure they'll grow. And Pa will be so glad you're bringing them. I doubt he even thought of seeds, and there he's been, likely clearing land for all manner of fine gardens and fields, and *you're* the one who thought of saving seeds to plant in them! I'm proud of you, Joey, and I'm very sure they'll grow!"

She stood taller now, five feet of assurance, and she smiled with a fine peace in her face which disconcerted the handsome young man by the fire.

"Thank you, Hananiah, for being so solicitous of us," she said. "You are truly kind, I know. But we'll stay here so that we'll be ready when Abraham comes in the spring. *And I'm very sure he'll come!* As for that four thousand pounds—I've told you many a time, Hananiah Lincoln, that it's not for you and never will be. Not while it's in my possession at any rate!" she said crisply, biting off her words. "Now," she added, her voice pleasant and low again, "do rest yourself. You look tired. Leah will have supper ready soon, and it smells like fried ham and spoonbread, if I'm not mightily mistaken." And she went out to the kitchen.

Leah gave her a quick, thorough-going look which saw all the way through her. Bathsheba suddenly smiled a roguish, very young, triumphant smile.

"Never fear, he didn't get it!" she whispered.

CHAPTER NINE

"Mammy, when's Christmas?" asked Jo, starting off to school with Mord and Mary one bright, mild, unutterably beautiful December morning. "Ain't it soon now?"

Christmas! Bathsheba, in her preoccupation and her growing uneasiness about Abraham's long, wordless absence, had forgotten all about Christmas. Hastily she figured in her mind. Christmas—why it would be soon, less than two weeks. She consulted with Leah, who always knew about such things.

"Chris'mus—why, yes, Miss 'Sheba, 'tis comin', that it is. Dis de fifteenth day of December, 'cordin' to my reckonin', and you got ten days yet to go."

Well! Bathsheba took hold of herself, mentally shook herself for a mooning simpleton, and sat down to think. They would just have to have a Christmas. It would be too bad that Abraham couldn't be there, but they should have a Christmas anyway. He would want them to. It mightn't be so easy later on in Kentucky. Now was the time.

She held a long conference with Leah, who smiled and nodded her tall-turbaned head and smiled again.

"We do it! Miss 'Sheba, we sho'ly will do it, and have the bestest Chris'mus we ever do have!"

For nine days the household was busy with more-or-less secret doings. Plump Angeline took care of Nancy and Tommy, to keep them out of Bathsheba's way. Suddenly Bathsheba felt gay and happy

72

again, and the children looked knowingly at each other, smiling secret smiles at how Mammy was singing again like she used to do when Pa was home and before she was sick. They loved to hear her sing, and though she couldn't read a note of music or a word of print, she knew all the old songs which she'd learned from her own mother. The children let her sing what she wanted to, and then Mary quietly one day asked for something special:

"Mammy, do you recollect *Barbara Allen?* Won't you sing that for us, Mammy? Do!"

"*Barbara Allen*—why, Mary, guess I do remember it." And Bathsheba's clear voice started off, sweet and true without a tuning fork, on the old English ballad which had come all the way to America and up into the Valley of Virginia, and which, in turn, many a Virginian would carry into the Kentucky country.

> "In Scarlet Town where I was born
> There was a fair maid dwellin'
> Made every youth cry, Well-a-day—
> Her name was Barbara Allen."

The ballad-tale went on for quite a space, and when Bathsheba had ended with the last sad verses—

> "When he was dead and laid in grave
> Her heart was struck with sorrow.
> O Mother, Mother, make my bed,
> For I shall die tomorrow!"

Mary was in tears. "Sweet, you mustn't cry!" exclaimed Bathsheba, aghast, wiping the child's tears away. "I won't sing if it makes you feel so sad."

"Oh, Mammy, do, I love it," protested Mary. "It feels good to cry and be sad when it's only a song. Sing more, Mammy, do."

Bathsheba smiled. "Leah taught me this one—you've heard it a lot, but you always liked it. 'I am a poor wayfaring stranger,'" she began, and Leah began softly to hum the tune in the kitchen, until she carried a gentle accompaniment of the words—"'I'm goin' over

Jordan, I'm just goin' over home . . .' "

Oh, the house fairly rang with singing on the days before Christmas. Bathsheba remembered all the long verses of the *Twelve Days of Christmas*, though she hadn't thought of them for years. And she taught them to the children, so that they could come in at the right places. Mary especially liked to sing the verse about the nine ladies dancing, and the partridge in a pear tree. Mord came in strong on the last verse with the twelve drummers drumming, while he beat time on an upturned kettle Leah handed him with a broad smile on her shining face, and Jo sang the seven swans a-swimming, because Pa had told him about how white the wild swans were when they came down on the sounds of the eastern shore, and he thought seven swans a-swimming, like in the song, would be a pretty thing to see.

So altogether the house quite rang with fun, and it looked like the very best of Christmases, even though Abraham wouldn't be there to have fun with them.

For days Leah was busy with her baking, and wonderful smells filled the house. She made cakes and boiled a pudding, and baked a great spicy-smelling ham which she had lifted down from where it hung in the rafters. Two days before the great day, Demaris came in with a fine wild turkey which he had shot in the woods, and Leah prepared it just right, with corn bread and chestnut stuffing.

One day Bathsheba asked Demaris to drive her in to Harrisonburg where she spent the day in making purchases—bolts of cloth to be cut up in lengths and given to the slaves, tobacco and thread and trinkets for little presents, gifts for the children, too. She was gone until almost dark.

The neighbors were invited in to dinner on Christmas Day. Bathsheba herself rode along the red-earth road to Colonel Colson's plantation, down to Madame Rees' house with its neat acres given over to tobacco, and to the Lees' and to Carter Randolph's plantation, and she invited all the children to come, too. It would be a fine Christmas—which in all likelihood they might never have again, at least not among these good Virginian neighbors who had been so watchful for her welfare while Abraham was gone, and had always been so ready to help in time of need or emergency.

And then it was Christmas Eve.

"Children," began Bathsheba at supper. They all turned from their bowls of porridge to look at her. Mammy had such a bright light in her face, such a starriness in her eyes. She looked as if she could start to sing again, right this minute, thought Mary. It made all of them feel good to see her so.

"Children," she went on, "this is Christmas Eve! Think of it—so long ago it was that the little Jesus was born in a manger in Bethlehem, and now we, far off in Virginia, are celebrating His birth."

"Oh, I know," broke in Jo. "Demaris told me about it and how the animals at midnight bow down in the stable."

"That's what some say," agreed Bathsheba, smiling at him.

"Was it a long time ago?" asked Mary, holding on to Tommy, who was reaching for the honey pot.

"Oh, so long ago, child, you can't even figure it. But it happened, and that's why we go to church and that's why we have Christmas. Pa won't be here, but we'll have a Christmas anyway. The eggnog, Leah!"

And beaming all over her big kind face, Leah appeared at the door with cups of eggnog flavored with a drop of rum and a grating of nutmeg, and handed one with ceremony and a curtsy worthy of a great lady to each wide-eyed child, and one to Bathsheba. She lifted her cup, and the children, watching her guardedly to see what to do next, all lifted their cups, too.

"To Christmas!" Bathsheba cried gaily. "To Christmas, and to Pa off in the wilderness, and may he come home soon." And she took a quick sip of the eggnog to hide the sudden quaver in her voice. The four children tasted gingerly, then drank eagerly. Smiling, Bathsheba held her cup to the baby's pink mouth and gave her a tiny sip, too.

There was a hammering at the door. Bathsheba set down her cup. She put her hand to her heart and felt herself grow a little pale. "Go to the door, Leah, will you please?"

Tensely, Bathsheba and the children waited at the table. It seemed that time stood still, that the sun and stars would not move again until the moment was past. The candle flames flickered suddenly in the gust of air which came from the door when it was opened, then steadied when the door was closed again. Leah came back.

"It was a gennelman come from de wilderness. He brung you dis from Kaintucky. Say he got it fum Mistah Lincoln hisself!" Holding the piece of paper at arm's length, as if it might bite, Leah handed Bathsheba a crumpled, soiled note.

Her heart pounding now, Bathsheba's trembling fingers took the paper and smoothed it out. There were words on it, to be sure, but she could not read them. They might as well have been Chinese or Greek or Cherokee. Almost in tears, suddenly, she handed it back to Leah, wailing,

"Oh, *if I could only read!* Leah, get someone—find out what's on it!"

Mordecai's quiet voice broke in. "Hand it over here, Mammy," he said soothingly. "*I* can read." Mord—of course—she had forgotten he could read so well. Bathsheba Lincoln handed her eldest son the paper.

It was like Abraham speaking to hear the words come off the paper, uttered in Mord's careful tones, which were so like his father's.

"Dear wife and children," he read, smoothing out the thin paper still more with his stubby fingertips. "I think of you often and hope to be home in the spring. I am well and hope you are the same. The land is good and the house is built.

Abraham Lincoln, Esquire."

Bathsheba's pale face beamed with a light which came from joy deep within her, relief to know that her husband was safe, that he had written with his own hand to tell them so.

"Oh, where is the man who brought it, Leah?" she cried, jumping to her feet. "I forgot all about him. Bring him in for refreshment, do!"

But Adam Marlow had not waited, for his family would have its own surprise that Christmas Eve when he walked in upon them. It was a long time before Bathsheba Lincoln knew who had brought the letter to her, or how he happened to be given the message by Abraham to deliver in person to her.

Hananiah Lincoln came riding up late that night. The children were in bed and Bathsheba, sitting alone by the fire, had finished all the Christmas surprises and was thinking of Abraham again for the thousandth time. Leah let Hananiah in and went to stir up a mug of hot buttered rum.

Bathsheba could have thought of many people with whom she would have preferred to spend Christmas than with Hananiah Lincoln, but she made him welcome.

"It is late and I am about to retire, Cousin," she said courteously. "Leah will bring you some refreshment. Will you honor us by spending Christmas with us? The neighbors are coming in tomorrow to dine at three—for the last time in this house—and it would pleasure me if you would join us."

"Gladly, Cousin," he said, flashing his handsome smile. "I had the notion you were angry with me after I tried to help you invest your money, but maybe some day you'll see that dear Cousin 'Niah has some sense and knows best, eh, girl?" He sauntered over to where she stood beside the door and kissed her on the cheek.

Bathsheba turned coldly away from him. Why did this pleasant, personable young man always make her seethe inside; why did everything he said bring to a boil a deep-lying anger?

"I will *never, never* entrust our money to you, Hananiah Lincoln!" she said furiously—courteously still, but without a doubt the chill was on and was on to stay. "You squandered your own and you've squandered the sums Abraham loaned you before this, and you've never repaid a penny, not a single penny. *Why* would I let you have this money—even in return for property—when it is all that stands between us and poverty if Abraham never comes back? I bid you good night, Hananiah. I hope you sleep well!"

Hananiah Lincoln sat for a long time in the warm light of the hearth. He finished his cup of hot buttered rum and the sliced ham and bread which Leah had grudgingly brought to him, and he smoked a long clay pipe of sweet Virginia tobacco. Demaris came in to bank the fire for the night, and Hananiah still sat.

"Go to bed, boy," he said lazily. "I'll put out the candles."

"Yes, suh," said Demaris and left the room. When all was still in the house, Hananiah snuffed the small flames and stood a while in the dark to accustom his eyes to the blackness. A full moon blazing on a light frost over the meadows sent a shine into the room which was soon ample to see about in. Somewhere in the house a clock chimed briskly eleven times.

Methodically, then, Hananiah Lincoln stepped lightly to the wall cupboard and raised his long arm up to the top shelf. He was tall enough to reach into the farthest back corners of the cupboard. His thin, sensitive fingers, which could so deftly misdeal a pack of cards, swept quickly along the shelf until they touched a cool china substance, closed around it, brought it down. It was a sugar bowl and there was money in it.

He went hurriedly on quiet feet to the window and in the moonlight counted the money, and his face contracted in bitter disappointment. Not enough. Not nearly as much as he sought. Just small change, really, probably Bathsheba's peach money or egg money or something. He gently put it back into the sugar bowl, which he placed in its exact spot on the top shelf. The long, questing fingers hunted over the remainder of the shelf and examined the bowls and pots and pitchers on all the other shelves. He explored every shelf and cupboard in the brick house, except in the bedrooms, and he investigated the hearthstones to see if any were loose and concealed a hiding place for money, but he did not find Bathsheba Lincoln's forty-five hundred pounds. In angry frustration, Hananiah was about to take himself off to bed, when a small sound came to his sensitive ears and he froze where he stood.

There were whispers along the passage. Hananiah thought he recognized them. He stepped softly to the doorway to hear better and in the moonlight saw Josiah and Demaris unbolt the big door, open it quietly, and step outside. Hananiah, overcome with curiosity, followed.

The two figures vanished in the darkness of the barn, and pretty soon Hananiah, who stood, shivering a little, just outside the big doors, saw a glow of light from a lantern in the stalls.

"How will we know it's midnight, Demaris?" That was Jo's sweet voice, wondering. "And how do the animals know when it's time to kneel?"

"Oh, they knows it somehow, suh, they sho'ly do know it. My ole mammy done tole me all about it, and many's the time I seen it myself on Chris'mus Eve. Midnight come, and how they knows it is sho' a mystery, but knows it they do, and down they kneels, just like folk before de King Hisself!"

"Do you suppose Jesus knows they do it?" the little boy asked, standing closer to the stout young Negro. "He'd like it, wouldn't He?"

Hananiah could see them silhouetted against the small glow of the light. He could see the dozing cows and the alertly pricked ears of the horses in the stalls beyond, could see the oxen silently champing as they lay in the straw. The warm, fast, thudding sound Hananiah heard—that must be his own pulse hammering in his ears, he thought in amusement. What was he doing out here, nigh on to midnight Christmas Eve, waiting with a superstitious slave and a little boy to see the animals bow their knees to the King! Silently Hananiah laughed. But he did not take his eyes off the two figures in the dusky barn.

Suddenly a shiver prickled down his long back as a cock woke and, like the bird of the Angel Gabriel himself, crowed loudly and with unusal gusto in the darkness. Jo gripped Demaris' arm and stood a little closer.

"Watch now, suh," Demaris said in a jerky tone of awe. "Watch now. De cock he say 'tis midnight, and de King born again.

79

Watch—" And Hananiah, watching, too, saw one of the oxen start to rise, and pause for a long, potent, exciting moment with its hind quarters raised, undeniably resting—kneeling—on its stout, bony forelegs. Then the beast stood up. The other, following the same procedure, stood up, too. The cock crowed again, and off in the distance, at Randolph's plantation, Hananiah heard another, like a dim, insistent echo, and he wondered if the oxen in Randolph's barn were kneeling, also. When he brought his eyes back to the barn, the lantern glow was gone, and he had to step fast to get out of sight before Demaris and Jo came out of the barn doors again and latched them so varmints couldn't get in, and walked quickly to the house.

Hananiah was awakened at an early hour by joyous sounds in the household.

"Chris'mus Gif'! Chris'mus Gif'!" cried the slaves as they went to each bedroom door and knocked, grinning with anticipation. "Chris'mus Gif'!"

"Chris'mus Gif', Miss 'Sheba!" said Leah in her low, throaty, loving voice, opening Bathsheba's door. The tall woman was dressed like an African queen in crimson calico of utmost magnificence, and bore in her hand a parcel wrapped in cloth. Bathsheba sat up in bed, pushed back her braids, and smiled affectionately at Leah. What would she ever do without Leah when they had gone off to the wilderness? Every time she thought of it her heart gave a wrench of positively physical pain.

Leah laid her offering in Bathsheba's hands. She opened it with delight and held up the piece of fine embroidery work which Leah, with infinite care and patience, had created in her few spare moments. "Oh, it's lovely, simply lovely, Leah!" Bathsheba cried. "And *somehow* I shall take it with me to Kentucky. I could never leave it behind. Now for your present—Christmas Gift, Leah!"

Tears stood in the dark woman's calm eyes when she saw the earrings. The gold hoops sparkled in the early light coming through the window. Bathsheba had spent some of the peach money for those earrings; she had to leave something tangible and valuable for

Leah when they went away.

"Wear them always, Leah, to remember us by," Bathsheba said softly.

The house by this time was in a turmoil. The children were shouting the traditional cries of "Christmas Gift!" and the slaves were shouting, too, in great delight, over little presents the children bestowed upon them. It was high time, Bathsheba thought as she lay languorously in bed, putting off the necessity of entering the joyous racket in the house, time for her to dress and to go out and distribute the lengths of cloth, the tobacco, the meal and the side meat, which were given to the slaves each year. And the children themselves must have their Christmas surprises—knives for Mord and Jo, a doll baby for Mary, a toy soldier for Tommy, a soft little ball for Nancy.

Hananiah lay in his bed and smiled wryly at the ruffled canopy. No one came to his door. It was quite right that he was left out; he had brought nothing; after all, they hadn't expected him. And he didn't exactly deserve a Christmas present from aggravating, sweet, firm Cousin Basheby.

Dressed now, neat and trim in a gray-blue gown, a white apron and fichu and cap, she rapped on his door and came in with morning coffee and a roll on a little tray. On the tray was a parcel with a sprig of holly berries upon it.

"Christmas Gift, Cousin!" She smiled, and set the tray on a table beside the big canopied bed, and went out.

Hananiah gingerly reached forth his long fingers to pick up the little parcel, laid aside the holly with care that it didn't prick him, put back the thin paper, and took forth—

A silver snuff-box! Must be Abraham's—she thinks he won't have much use for it in Kentucky. . . . Guess she doesn't know I'm going out there, too. . . .

With a sudden, unaccustomed dew in his sharp gray eyes, Hananiah Lincoln lay back on his white pillow while the coffee cooled, and he wished with a sudden and indefinable wish that he had been a different person all these years.

CHAPTER TEN

CHRISTMAS IN VIRGINIA! A green Christmas, a mild-mannered Christmas, the forest bright with pine and holly and sweet bay, draped with festoons of glossy green smilax where Carolina wrens sang their jovial songs in the bright, gentle Southern sunshine. The air was cool, yet so comfortable that no one needed to wear a cloak after the sun got up, so warm that Bathsheba's daffodils already were thrusting leaves above the ground and the chickens went about cackling and crooning and scratching as if they, too, thought it was spring.

Mary, Jo, and Mord had gone to the woods right after breakfast on that bright Christmas morning and had found enough holly to dress the whole house and some left over.

"We found a great big holly tree, Mammy," Mary cried, bubbling with the gaiety of the day and the whole lovely morning in the woods. "And what do you think—when we started to break off the best boughs full of berries, a whole flock of birds flew out! And they went and sat in the trees all around us and sang and sang!"

"They were robin-redbreasts, Mammy," said Mord authoritatively, "and they'd been eating the holly berries. We saw a buck deer, too, and three does and a big fawn, and there was a possum up in a persimmon tree. I wish I'd had a gun along!"

Bathsheba and Leah laid holly on the mantelpieces and on the window ledges, and upon the long table which was spread now with the great snowy damask cloth. Demaris scrambled up into an elm

FROM THE HOUSE THE EXCITED GUESTS POURED FORTH TO HELP. BATHSHEBA
AND MADAME REES . . . LED THE FRIGHTENED ANIMALS AWAY

THEY HAD TO WAIT FOR HIGH WATER TO SUBSIDE BEFORE CROSSING. . . .
WHEN THEY'D GONE ON, ABRAHAM FOUND THAT HE HAD LOST HIS BEST AX

down the road and cut off a spray of mistletoe full of waxen white berries, and he and Angeline, nudging each other and giggling crazily, contrived to fasten it in a doorway, and managed several kisses under it before they had finished.

"Silly stuff!" muttered Mord, fingering the new knife which was his greatest Christmas treasure. He'd hoped for a rifle gun like Pa's, but Mammy'd said he was still too young. The knife, though, was pretty fine, and he guessed it would do.

Everything was ready when the guests began to arrive on horseback and in carriages down the long red road. The men went out to look at the stock, and stood about talking and drinking glasses of Madeira until three, when promptly on the minute Leah rang her big bell and Christmas dinner was served.

And all those wonderful and tantalizing smells of the past few days and all the concentrated odors and excitement of that one day of the year materialized in Christmas dinner, the last Christmas dinner Abraham Lincoln's family believed they would have in Virginia. The thought of it made Bathsheba want to cry, but she continued to laugh and talk and to keep things moving as a hostess should.

The long table was crowded with food, and the slaves, deftly and quietly as Bathsheba had trained them to do, passed the platters and bowls. Bathsheba carved the big wild turkey and spooned out the rich corn bread and chestnut stuffing with the long-handled pewter spoon which her mother had brought from Massachusetts. Carter Randolph, substituting for Abraham at the head of the table, carved the ham, and under the sharp blade which Demaris that morning had honed to a razor's edge the rosy slices, edged with pearly fat and rimmed with pepper and spice, lay over softly on the blue platter. There was a roast pig to be carved, too, and bowls of peas to be passed, and the cucumbers which Madame Rees' gardener had brought over from her hotbed. There were yams and there were condiments and relishes, and there were Leah's feather-light hot breads and her best golden-sparkling peach preserves. There was Abraham's choice wine, too—better to have it drunk now than to leave it behind for Michael Shanks—Madeira and port laid down in the cool, spidery wine cellar under the brick house.

When the long cloth was taken up before the pudding was served, and there was a break in the conversation as everyone sat back replete with food and talk, Hananiah excused himself for a moment and went out to the barn. He was concerned with the way his mare's left forefoot looked; there was a slight swelling of the fetlock joint which worried him. He was smoking his clay pipe and laid it down on the edge of the manger while he examined the animal's leg.

"Cousin Hananiah!" called Bathsheba's clear voice from the house door. "Will you please come in now so that Leah may serve the pudding?"

Hananiah gave the mare an affectionate pat and departed for the house.

It was Demaris who discovered the smoke. He came pounding at the kitchen door and Leah opened to let him in.

"*Ssshhh!* What in de livin' world de mattah, you Demaris?" she demanded.

"Fiah!" he gasped, panting, his eyes rolling. "De barn—fiah!"

A quick glance from the open door showed Leah the truth. She handed Demaris the bucket of water standing on the kitchen table, grasped up a bucket of waste water from the floor and they flew to the barn. The other slaves were already frantically drawing water from the well.

"Fastah!" cried Leah. "Move, you lazy ones! Pass that watah along to me and Demaris—you chillen haste with dem buckets back to de well!"

Rapidly the flames spread. "Get out de horses! Ain't you got de horses out yit?" Demaris and two helpers dashed to open the doors and lead the horses out.

From the house the excited guests poured forth to help. Bathsheba and Madame Rees, who had a way with horses, led the frightened animals away when they were brought out. Carter Randolph and Hananiah were everywhere at once, working desperately to stem the flames. Mord and Jo carried buckets. Colonel Colson and his boys and the Lee men rushed the buckets of water to the flames. Mary looked after Nancy and Tommy. But Tommy slipped out of her reach and was lost in the confusion.

"Tommy, Tommy," Mary wailed. "Oh, I can't find Tommy!" she cried as Leah flew past.

"Tommy!" Leah stopped in her stride. "Where at he go, baby?"

"In there," wept Mary, her face smudged with soot and tears, pointing to the open door where the men were bringing out the last of the snorting, rearing horses. "He said, 'Go get 'Niah's horse!' and ran in there. Oh, Leah, get him, won't you? Mammy told me to take care of him and I can't leave Nancy!"

Leah gave a swiftly calculating look at the blazing barn. Rafters were beginning to burn through and fall. If Tommy had gone in there—the tall Negro woman took a deep breath, held her hand over her nose and mouth, and raced for the doorway where smoke was billowing thick and choking. The gold hoops of earrings caught the red glare of flame, flashed in the blur of smoke.

Bathsheba saw her. "Leah! No!" she shrieked.

In a moment Tommy was tossed bodily out of the smoke and landed on the ground just as a blazing beam crashed in a great shower of red fire and the roof went down.

Hananiah leaped to get the child out of the way of flames and falling beams. But Leah did not come out.

Leah. Leah. That night Bathsheba lay with wide, burning eyes staring into the darkness of Christmas night, the Christmas which had begun so beautifully and so happily, which had ended so unbelievably, so hideously. Leah. In losing Leah, Bathsheba felt that she had lost a vital part of her life; part of Bathsheba, too, had died in the flaming barn. Now indeed was she ready and willing to go to Kentucky—as soon as possible—if only to get away from the memory of this Christmas night, away from the smouldering black shell which was the barn, and the remembering of Leah. But that remembering would go with her always wherever she might be.

In fortified Boonesborough Christmas lay as brightly as it lay in the Valley of Virginia—but with a difference. That gay December sunshine might hold lurking Indians waiting to attack the forts of white men audacious enough to have tried to settle the wilderness. All about there were growing signs of Indian unrest. When? When? Vainly Dan Boone had sent back desperate requests for ammunition and men but none had come. He had gone to Richmond himself to beg for help, but the Virginians were too far away from the terrors of Kentucky, and he found neither sympathy nor supplies. He wondered now what would be best to do, send folk out of Kentucky until the Indians had calmed down and got their quittance, or go back in person again and by main force get the men and guns he needed to take care of any uprising? When? How?

Abraham spent Christmas with the Boones. The cabin was not decorated with holly nor was it bright with candles and silver and smoking platters of fine food. Rebecca had roasted a haunch of venison. Turkeys were scarce thereabouts and Dan didn't want to waste shot on them and didn't want to roam far afield in search of some. Venison would have to do for Christmas dinner, though there was nothing different or special about venison; they had it most of the time, when they weren't eating buffalo meat. That and corn pone baked hard in the ashes, and a sort of pudding made with dried huckleberries instead of raisins and currants. Persimmon beer, not wine, topped off the meal.

Abraham ate heartily enough, but he wondered lonesomely about Christmas on the other side of the mountains. What were they doing on his plantation that Christmas Day? So close, as an eagle would fly, so far as a man must walk.

He spent that night with the Boones, and rode back to his own cabin the next morning when frost was white on the buffalo road. He found everything in his cabin safe and untouched, just as he had left it.

CHAPTER ELEVEN

THE MAN who came up the road was bearded and rough, but Bathsheba would have known him anywhere—that tall, broad-shouldered form, the way he held his head proudly on his neck, even when he was wearied to death—would have known it was Duchess by the way she put her feet down and picked them up, lightly, like a dancer, even when she, too, was bone-tired from the long journey from Kentucky. The peach buds were pinkening and Abraham Lincoln had come home again to the Valley of Virginia.

She flew from the house, the children streaming after her like the tail of a comet, and the slaves following, and all the dogs, and she was in his arms as he leaped down from Duchess.

"Abraham! Abraham!" she murmured into his dirty leather shirt. "You did come back. Oh, I knew you would, I knew it!"

"Of course I was coming back, sweet," he said, smoothing the bright hair he hadn't seen for so long a time. "What ever made you think I wouldn't?"

"Hananiah," she said in a weary tone. "He was so sure you wouldn't—couldn't—he wanted me to buy a house in Charlottesville. . . ."

Abraham, who hadn't given much thought to Hananiah for some time, immediately said some highly uncomplimentary things under his breath about his dashing young cousin as, with Bathsheba on his arm and the children hanging on to him wherever they could catch hold, he walked to the brick house. It surprised him somewhat to find it so large and spacious, the grounds so well kept, the trees so far in the background as a forest should be. For so many months he had lived in a smaller house, in grounds he was battling to open up, with the forest always ready to encroach on his cleared fields, always standing too close to him for comfort.

But although Bathsheba was anxious and ready to go to Kentucky, they waited. Abraham was in no hurry, he told himself. With Indian troubles growing worse instead of better, he hesitated to take his family immediately into that hornet's nest of danger. Had he known what he knew now, he told himself over and over, he'd never have sold the farm and gone to Kentucky when he did. He'd have waited till things were quieter. But then land would have gone up in price, he argued; you had to brave certain amounts of danger if you wanted to get in on the opening of new land at the low prices the government was asking. With the land agents coming in even now, before the Indians were settled once and for all, prices were shooting up.

It was not until 1782 that the time seemed right. By then, Abraham was homesick for the new cabin, homesick for Kentucky, for his bright, green, dangerous wilderness. But when the Lincolns started for Kentucky, the time perhaps could not have been worse, for 1782 was called the Year of Blood.

There was the final wrenching away from the old home and the old friends, the final discarding of things which simply could not be taken along, the final packing of only necessities in the saddle bags, and they were crammed until they would hold nothing more. The house doors were locked, and the slaves, who now belonged to Michael Shanks, weeping and crying out their grief, stood by the gate to see them off down the red Virginia road. The Lincolns made an imposing procession. There were five horses, the best cow, Abraham's two favorite hounds, and two hens and a cock in a big willow basket.

Bathsheba mounted. Angeline set Nancy in her arms and settled her skirts with a lingering affection, as if she could not let her go. Four-year-old Tommy was tied to the back of Bathsheba's saddle so that he could not slip off. Abraham rode alone, and so did Mord but they took turns sharing the lively Tommy. Jo and Mary rode together and sometimes walked when one was tired of the hard saddle. The fifth horse was loaded with the bulkiest of the baggage.

In the saddlebags and packs were clothing and food and dishes and cooking pots. There were Bathsheba's candlesticks and the silver sugar basin, and the best damask tablecloth, though it was heavy and bulky, and Abraham for a time thought they would have to leave it behind in favor of oats for the horses. But Bathsheba looked so desperate when he suggested the substitution that he relented and let the tablecloth be packed.

The party had gone a mile or so down the road, had waved to Madame Rees, who came down to her gateway to bid them a last farewell, when they heard the sound of racing hoofs behind them. Bathsheba turned quickly and almost lost her grip on Nancy when she saw that it was Hananiah galloping to catch up with them. Not Hananiah!

"Greetings, greetings!" he panted, as if he himself had been doing the hurrying, not his lathered horse. "Almost missed you, didn't I! Thought I'd get here sooner, Abraham, but all's well now, and let's be on our way."

Bathsheba was genuinely startled. It had never occurred to her that Hananiah Lincoln would accompany them. Apparently Abraham, though, knew that his cousin was going along, but no one had said a word of it to her. Seething again as she let her thoughts dwell bitterly on Cousin 'Niah, and filled with an unsettled feeling of impending disaster, she rode in heavy silence along the red earth road, down the long trough called the Valley of Virginia.

The dreadful journey remained in Bathsheba's mind merely as spots of memory punctuated by a blur of endless uncomfortable days of hard riding, incredibly hard riding, over rocky trails and fording endless streams. She remembered the night the party spent at Captain Bledsoe's after they got on the Wilderness Road itself, how they stayed with fat, kindly Mrs. Callaway, who told stories to the tired children and gave them some molasses candy she had made. How the family waited for more travelers with plenty of firearms at Captain Martin's place in Powell Valley—she remembered that

89

rain kept them there three days, and how irked she was at the delay. Now that she was on her way to Kentucky, Bathsheba wanted no more waiting. And ahead of her always reared up the higher blue mountains, with rain clouds resting damply on their summits.

When the party of thirty people set out from Captain Martin's fort, she hardly recognized dapper Hananiah in the deerskin wilderness outfit he had bought from the Captain, who was as tall as Hananiah. But no matter what he wore, Bathsheba grudgingly admitted to herself, Hananiah always was a handsome, well set-up figure.

Bathsheba would always recall how steep was that hideous trail over Cumberland Gap, and how she climbed up painfully on foot with Nancy in her arms and little Tommy pulling at her skirts or scrambling among the rocks like a squirrel, until he fell and skinned his nose and knees and howled as if he was half killed. Hananiah picked him up like a meal bag and carried him, kicking and squawling, under his arm to the top of the Gap. She remembered how the poor cow had bellowed going up that steep incline and sometimes had to be urged from the rear by Mord and Jo when she decided she'd had enough of pioneering and wanted to go back to her comfortable green meadow on Linville Creek. Bathsheba wondered what all the distress and straining would do to the unfortunate creature's future.

Bathsheba climbed. The sharp rocks were felt through her thin soles; her feet ached intolerably. Nancy grew heavier and heavier; Bathsheba's skirts dragged around her ankles and she stumbled now and again and almost fell. Abraham took Nancy, then, and it went easier.

She reached the top. Everyone reached the top. They mounted and set off down the other side, down into Kentucky, which to Bathsheba didn't look so much different from Virginia. From what Daniel Boone had said, she had expected to find a different sort of place, unlike anything she'd ever beheld before. Here was only a great sea of trees and endless lines of hills growing blue in the distance, and wild rivers and wilder trails. They were like that in Virginia, right enough, in some places.

She remembered how they felt lucky if they covered fifteen to twenty miles in a day, and how, one morning when she woke, she saw the men of the group talking soberly among themselves, and discovered that Indians had walked around the camp in the night and had lain on their bellies like snakes or catamounts, watching. Bathsheba still turned cold, thinking of what had been so near them.

Bathsheba went on day after day, riding her horse or walking with Nancy when the trail was bad or the saddle unbearable. Bathsheba thought she would never, never be rested again. She woke as weary as when she lay down on a blanket on the hard earth, and she ached all over when it was time to go on each morning. On, on. Oh, will we *ever* get there—*ever*—how can I bear another day of this . . .

She remembered the rain, the beating rain, and how they had to wait for high water to subside before crossing Richland Creek. When at last they'd crossed, and had gone on a way, Abraham found that he had lost his best ax. He rode back hurriedly to see if he could find it, but it was gone, likely dropped into the rushing waters of the creek.

She remembered how peevish the tired children grew and how Tommy squirmed and kicked the horse's rump, reached around to pinch Nancy and make her scream. Sometimes to ease the situation, Hananiah took Tommy with him on his own horse, and Bathsheba, in her relief at being rid of her unmanageable son, could almost feel affection in her heart for Hananiah, could almost forgive him for irritating her these many years.

When the party crossed the terribly difficult ford on Dick's River, one of Abraham's saddle packs fell off the pack horse and was swept away before it could be recovered. And Bathsheba, with an empty feeling and blank eyes, had known that in that saddle pack had gone her best damask tablecloth. And she would never forget how hard it was for her to eat the coarse food provided by the cooks of the party, and how it went against her stomach to try to eat half-cooked, tough buffalo meat and gritty corn bread made by Mr. Drake, who never, never washed his hands.

The journey took a month. In spite of the discomfort, in spite of the hardships, the party had been in no immediate danger. Although they saw Indian signs as they traversed the Warriors' Path and the Buffalo Trace and took the fork in the road which led to Boonesborough, no Indians attacked. And at last the party reached Boonesborough. Bathsheba, numb from the long day's ride, collapsed weak-kneed on the ground when she got off her horse. Rebecca Boone and her daughter, Jemima, helped her into the fort.

CHAPTER TWELVE

Dan boone was sober as he greeted Abraham and Bathsheba and the children. Somberly his blue eyes surveyed the people who had come hopefully up from Virginia to make their homes in Kentucky.

"What's the trouble, Dan?" Abraham asked in a low tone so that Bathsheba would not hear. But Bathsheba already had been taken in tow by Rebecca and Jemima, while the children made friends with the other young ones of the fort. Hananiah strolled about, saying nothing but seeing everything.

"Trouble enough," muttered Dan Boone out of the corner of his mouth. "The Injuns are gettin' worse 'stead of better. That Simon Girty—blasted renegade white, I'd like to cut his throat, that I would—he's incitin' the Injuns to take our hair whenever they can get a cut at it. And the Shawanese and Wyandot are strikin' everywhere, off in the wilderness at lone cabins and massacreein' everyone they find. They been hammerin' at Harrods fort and they been hammerin' at mine. George Rogers Clark been here and he's doin' all he kin, and I trust him to convince any redskin of his misdeeds—they're scared to death of that Clark—but he cain't be everywhere, and meanwhile the trouble's growin'."

"Maybe I should have waited a little longer," mused Abraham with an inner quaking when he thought of Bathsheba and the children at the mercy of Shawanese and Wyandot and Simon Girty. Abraham had heard plenty of tales of what the redskins did to defenseless white women and children. With a momentary revulsion, he won-

93

dered what in the world he and his family were doing in Kentucky.

Mord and Jo came up behind Abraham, and Dan saw them and stopped talking.

"Tell us about the Injuns, will you, Mr. Boone?" piped up little Jo, with big eyes taking in every detail of the hero, the great Mr. Daniel Boone who had laid out the Wilderness Road and fought the Indians.

"Injuns is it?" Dan smiled. "Well, did I ever tell you about how I shot two Injuns with one bullet? No? 'Course not, you only just got here. Well, listen, this is how it happened—good way to save your bullets, if you can do it!" Dan sat himself down on a puncheon bench and the boys plunked themselves on the ground at his feet. Abraham joined Dan on the bench and listened to the tale, though his mind was still roiling over what Dan had said about that Girty and the Indians.

"It was soon after I got back from Carolina with Mrs. Boone and the young'uns, who'd gone back to the Yadkin when I was captured by the Shawanese and they feared me long since dead. And no wonder, I was captive nigh on to three months. But I escaped from old Blackfish and his people, and went to bring my family back to Boonesborough, where they rightly belonged. Well, boys, soon after I got here, I went out to hunt along the Upper Blue Lick, when a rifle ball whistled that fast past my head I vowed it must be a white-faced hornet aimin' for my eyes. But, no, it were a rifle ball and it scaled a piece of bark from the hickory I'd been leanin' casual against."

"What did you do?" chorused Mord and Jo together. Tommy, escaping Mary's watchful eye, toddled over and sat down with his brothers.

"Well, I ran down the slope, leaped into the creek, and waded across—it was low water and rocky-bottomed—and dived me into a cane brake. Well, once there, I got me down on my hunkers and crep' like a catamount through the cane, 'bout a hundred yard downstream. Then I riz up ever so little—j-u-u-st enough—and parted the cane, and peered out, and lo and *be*hold, there was two Shawanese comin' along the other bank!" Dan paused and calmly and with maddening deliberation looked at the sky. The boys waited with poorly concealed impatience for the great man to go on.

"I knew if I shot one, t' other would get *me* afore I could reload. It were a ticklish spot, I tell you! So I riz up enough to get a bead on the first varmint and waited till the other got into line behind him. Ha, I thought, now this is just what I want. And I fired at the first one's head and the bullet, I vow, went clean through it like it was a punkin, and hit the second varmint in the shoulder. What a howl he did let out! The first one dropped dead in his tracks, and the second flung down his gun and lit out through the forest. *He* warn't interested in botherin' me after that, you may be sure!"

"Golly!" exclaimed Mord, his eyes like stars. "Tell us more. Tell us about when old Blackfish captured you, Mr. Boone!" Abraham was glad Bathsheba wasn't listening.

"Haven't you ever heard me tell of that, boy?" said Dan, mightily flattered at all the attention he was getting. Dan Boone had become so unpopular in certain high places that he wasn't always considered the hero he once had been, and that hurt him. He loved to tell tales of his adventures, and Abraham's young ones were a willing and gratifying audience.

"Well, now," he began. "I been captured twice by the redskins and I ain't sayin' I won't be again. But I reckon if it happens, I'll get me back home, like always. When the Injuns catch me in a tight spot and I see there's naught to be done but give in to 'em for the moment, I just smile real pleasant-like, give handshakes all 'round, pass the time of day, make comment on the weather, and go along peaceable. But that ain't sayin' I'm goin' to *stay* peaceable, and when I find my chance to escape, I take it, I'll tell you that. Remember that, boys, if ever's you find yourselves caught by the Injuns. They'll have more respect for you and give you better treatment, and won't watch you so all-fired careful if you give 'em politeness and pleasantness and act unconsarned, even if you're scared half to death.

"Old Blackfish had his eye on Boonesborough and he done his best to take it. It was in '75, and Blackfish, that old codger—you

95

know, Abe, I always did like that fellow, even if he *is* an Injun and after my hair; now that Moluntha, he's different—well, Blackfish had been layin' siege to Harrodstown, and finally got tired of it. So he changed off for a while and for variation decided to attack my town. But even Simon Kenton and Tom Brooks, who were scoutin' for me, didn't notice them Shawanese comin'. 'Twas a wonder them two didn't sense somethin'. Even the cows acted queer—cow-critters always has been first to smell out an Injun; cain't stand the scent of the varmints. Well, that day the cows inside the fort wouldn't go out to pasture. They just stood there snuffin' and mooin' under their breaths, like they was tryin' to tell us somethin'. But nobody—and I'm ashamed to say I never did either—nobody paid any attention and when two of my men went out of the stockade at sunrise, the Injuns fired. They got one feller, too—tomahawked him and scalped him right in sight of the fort. Sime Kenton was there handy, though, and he shot that Injun. I heard the shot, and I'm tellin' you I come on a run, and them devils mighty nigh got me that time. Simon shot one just at the moment he was drawin' a bead on me. Made the cold sweat stand out on me, that it did.

"Well, it was quite a fight, quite a fight. For a while there I had my doubts of ever gettin' out alive, I or any man or woman inside the stockade. And then if I didn't up and stumble over a log and break my ankle! Craziest thing I *ever* did, that it was. There I lay, helpless, and them Injuns swarmin' all around and bound to get my hair *that* day. In fact, one was just about to scalp me when Kenton whacked him down with his rifle, and then, what did Sime do, but carry me— and I ain't a lightweight—all the way through them Injuns and to the fort. Before he got there, who should run out to help but my Jemima! No fear of Injuns for her; she was bound to help her pappy if it was the last thing she did. I always wished she'd married Sime Kenton; they'd have made a good pair.

"I wasn't much good for a while after that, and Blackfish after a time gave up tryin' to break in, and contented himself and his braves with carryin' off everything that wasn't nailed down. He tried several other attacks, but he never got in. Yes, I always have liked that feller. He's got persistence!"

"But when did he *capture* you, Mr. Boone?" insisted Mord. "You said he did."

"To be sure, to be sure, I'm comin' to that," went on Boone, smiling at their eagerness. "That was back in '78. Our salt supply was low, and I do like salt on my vittles, not to mention how we got to have it to cure meat and salt down hides. So I and some of the men, thirty of us, went with the big salt kettles and set out for the Blue Licks. That's where the buffalo been goin' for years, lickin' salt, and that's where we found it. Not so simple as that, though, we had to boil the briny water in the kettles to cook out the salt. We worked for weeks and sent sacks of salt by pack horse back to the fort whenever we had some ready. It was cold weather, mighty cold weather, and the Injuns weren't out on the prowl so much then; they liked to stay to home and keep warm, or so we figured. Well, but that's where we were wrong. I was out on scout duty, bound to get some meat while I was at it, when lo and *be*hold, I ran onto a bunch of Shawanese. I guess they was as startled as I was. I tried to run—my horse was plumb loaded with buffalo meat and the green, slippery hide, and I couldn't get on—but they tracked me easy in the snow and it was slick underfoot beside. They started firin', and then I knew I hadn't a chance. So I just stopped, leaned my rifle beside a tree, and when the Shawanese come up, I just held out my hand, said howdy, and shook hands all around, commented on the weather, and off I went with them. They was proud as anything to have captured Dan Boone; they'd heard of me, plenty, and they knew old Blackfish would given them a reward.

"Hah! And there was old Blackfish himself in camp—but what else I seen made my blood run cold, I tell you it did. For it was a war party, more'n a hundred Shawanese, painted like devils for certain, sittin' around a big blazin' fire—and they wasn't *all* Injuns, either. I saw right away there was white men amongst 'em, and white men who go off to fight with the Injuns are worse nor any Injun alive. And what made me really curl up, boys, was the sight of the Girtys —you've heard tell of the Girtys, ain't you? Womenfolk tell their

young'uns when they're noisy, 'Be quiet, Simon Girty'll git ye!'
Well, Simon wasn't there, but his brothers George and James were,
and they're nigh as bad. How they did grin when they caught sight
of me!

"Well, it's a long story," said Boone, sighing, "and I won't tell
you all of it. 'Tain't fit for young ears. The upshot of it was I was
taken to Detroit as a prisoner, but when General Hamilton, the old
Hair Buyer, offered to buy me from Blackfish for a hundred pounds,
Blackfish decided I wasn't for sale! Hah, first time I ever had a price
put on *my* head! Then back we went, Blackfish keepin' a close eye
on me, back to Little Chillicothe, and when we'd got to Blackfish's
home town, they had a ceremony to adopt me into the tribe. They
named me Sheltowee, Big Turtle, though why, I don't know. They
plucked out my hair, one by one, just leavin' a scalplock—and I
tell you, the rest of the ceremony was no more pleasant!

"Well, there I was a Shawanee for certain, whether I liked it or
not. Blackfish was kind to me, though; he never made me work when
I didn't feel like it, and he was so agreeable I felt mean to be plannin'
to escape. He knew I could repair rifles, and let me do it; I was a
big help to him. How they did gather around to watch and admire
me, all them braves and little boys. I managed to keep out a rifle for
my own, though, and some bullets they gave me just to be polite.
To throw 'em off the scent, I made jokes about how I'd escape some
day, and had 'em convinced I was a mighty powerful magician and
could spirit myself out of that Indian town any time I so wished.
Well, one day when the men was sittin' around doin' nothin' but
act lazy and important while their womenfolk worked, I managed
to slip all the bullets out of their rifles. Then I up and said:

" 'Blackfish,' I said, calm as calm, 'I'm a-goin' home.'

" 'You try it and I'll shoot you dead!' says he, right pert and not a
little startled.

"So off I trotted and yelled back over my shoulder to shoot me if
they could! They all fired, and of course not a bullet came out, but
I made a great show of pretendin' to catch bullets in the leather apron
I wore. My, my, you should have seen them Injuns stare, with their

98

mouths hangin' open, and, I swear, their eyes was all but poppin' out.

"I walked back then, peaceable as you please, and shook out of my clothes all them bullets I'd taken from their rifles."

"What did you say to them?" cried Mord and Jo together, rolling on the ground with laughter. "Oh, my, what a thing to do!"

"Say? Why I said, says I, 'Here, Blackfish, take your bullets back. *I* ain't goin' no place!' You should have heard them Injuns whoop. They thought it was a great joke." Boone's big mouth curved in a great smile and his bright blue eyes in his pink-skinned face beamed.

"But how did you really get away, Mr. Boone?"

"Oh, I managed it, I did. Cain't keep Dan Boone prisoner very long and I was gettin' anxious for my family, that I was. So one day in June I just up and walked off. We'd been on a hunt and then I knew they was gettin' ready for an attack on my town. The men was off gettin' wild turkeys, and I was left with the squaws. I jest walked over to my horse, the one Blackfish had given me, said good-by to Blackfish's big fat wife, who was scandalized, and off I rode. And by gracious, you ought to have heard them squaws squeal! You'd have thought a catamount was loose amongst 'em. I vow, what a caterwaulin' and a screechin'! But I got away all right. I had a tough way to go, too; it were 160 miles to Boonesborough and I only ate one meal in four days. I crossed the Ohio, which was floodin', by pluggin' up the holes in an old leaky Wyandot canoe I found along shore, and finally got me to Boonesborough.

"But what do you think? All I found of my family was Jemima, who wouldn't give up hope, though everyone else believed me long dead and et by buzzards. Jemmie was there, but Rebecca with the other young'uns had gone off to the Yadkin to be with her kin. I went later, though, and brought 'em back, as I told you in the beginning."

The boys were grinning and Abraham had relaxed on the puncheon bench.

"Did I ever tell you about the way the Injuns captured my girl, Jemima? Now that was a worrisome time, I do declare. It was back in the summer of '76. Things had been mighty quiet for a long spell

99

and we'd got the idee it always *would* be peaceful and the Injuns
would forget we were there. But one hot afternoon, Jemima, along
with Lizzie and Fanny Callaway, who lived at the fort, too, decided
to take a boat ride on the river. It was of them hot, sultry days and
the gals they had themselves a nice cool time lettin' the canoe drift
on the current and dabblin' their hands in the water. And they didn't
have the wit to see how the canoe was bein' carried by that self-same
current toward the far shore. But they weren't afeerd none. No
Injuns had been seen nigh to Boonesborough since the winter before,
I guess. But there was some Injuns that wouldn't abide by the treaty
makin' and they got to itchin' for devilment until they couldn't
stand it no longer. So there was a party of young bucks that left the
Shawanese towns and crossed the Ohio into Kentucky, with the idee
of scatterin' amongst the settlements and doin' what damage they
could, all by their lone. Five of these redskins decked out in war
plumes and painted up like devils come up near Boonesborough and
I guess they was hidin' in the cane when the gals in their canoe
drifted near.

"My, my, what a chance it gave them! One of the critters waded
out and pulled the canoe toward shore while the pore gals was nigh
crazy with fright. Lizzie, she hefted up her paddle and bashed it
down over the Injun's head, givin' him a cut to the bone, but that
didn't help her none. All three shrieked like bobcats but no one
heard 'em to come to their aid. And them blamed redskins made them
pore gals walk, barefoot, off through a clover field and across a
meadow, through the cane brakes that slashed their gowns and cut
their feet, and into a maple grove. But Jemima's a smart one, if I do
say so myself. She's a true daughter of a wilderness man. Some
gals might have swooned then and there, but not my Jemmie. She
quietly begun to rip bits and tatters from her apron and dropped them
on the ground to make a trail—fastened some of the tatters to the
thorns of bushes as they passed, too, and the other gals, seein' what
she was up to, did likewise. Whenever the ground was soft and
marshy, the gals trod heavy with their pore cut feet so's to make a
trail for us to foller."

"How did you ever get them back, poor things?" cried Mary, who had come up in search of Tom, and stayed to listen, wide-eyed at this frightful tale. She doubted if she'd have had the presence of mind to do as those brave girls did if *she* was captured by Indians. The very thought made her shiver.

"Oh, we got them back, but it was a piece of luck we did, I assure you," said old Dan. "Two parties set out soon as we discovered what'd happened. Dick Callaway, the pappy of the other two, headed to the Licking River, thinkin' to cut off the Shawanese at the ford of the Lower Blue Lick. But John Floyd and I led another five men— and I tell you, *I* had the eager party! For what do you think, Sam Henderson, Flanders Callaway, and John Holder were one and all in *love* with them three purty gals, and nothing would hold 'em from goin' to the rescue. My, my, it was all I could do to hold them back from doin' somethin' real rash, they was that worried!

"It was dark before we'd gone five mile, so we camped in the brush till daylight. We covered thirty mile that next day, led on by them pitiful tatters of calico we found on the bushes. By next mornin' we'd traveled only two mile or so when we come to the Upper Blue Lick, and saw a wisp of smoke risin' in the mornin' air. Hah, we thought, there they be! So we crep' up cautious-like—we didn't want to alarm them savages lest they tomahawk the gals in pure spite at bein' discovered—and we seen the redskins was cookin' buffalo meat for breakfast. The gals sat a little way off, lookin' sad and tired, as well they might be.

"Just as we rushed in, firin' off our guns, the gals looked up. My, they was glad to see us! Four of us fired, and the Injuns was so alarmed they didn't so much as fire a shot. Fact is, they hadn't even their moccasins on, nor their guns in hand, when we chased 'em off into the brush. But we didn't chase 'em far. We was too glad to rescue them three brave little gals. And what do you think?"

"What?" cried Mord and Jo together, thinking of other horrors.

"Well, three weeks later, Sam Henderson up and married Lizzie Callaway, and it was the first weddin' in Kaintucky! Squire Boone, my brother, was a magistrate and he said the words. There was a high time in my fort that night, I tell you! Jamie McPherson played his fiddle so hard he broke two strings but kept right on sawin' away, and for refreshment we had the first watermelons grown in Boonesborough."

"Oh," said the boys in disappointment, though Mary beamed at this romantic ending. To the boys it was poor stuff to climax an Indian attack with a mere marrying and watermelon feast.

"Yes, and Flanders Callaway married my Jemima, though I didn't much approve, and John Holder married Fanny, so you see that all turned out right, after all. Howdy, ma'am," he said to Bathsheba, who had come out to gather her brood in for the night. "I was just tellin' tales to keep 'em amused." And Abraham wondered how much she had really heard.

The Lincolns spent two days at Boonesborough. Still accompanied by Hananiah, who was growing more enthusiastic about the quality of the country, they set out over the buffalo road toward Harrodstown and turned southwest to the farm near Green River, where Abraham's new cabin waited. Abraham had been wondering for some time if it would still be there. He had had no more unseen visitors, but the cabin was remotely situated and, although men of Harrodstown promised to look after it when they could, they were too far away for constant watching.

When the Lincolns rode over the last hill, Abraham discovered in immense relief that their new home was indeed still there.

He threw open the smoothly planed front door and bowed low to Bathsheba, whose knees were trembling again with fatigue, though her back was straight and there was a smile on her lips.

"Here, my lady," he said with a flourish of his old hat, "is your Kentucky mansion!" And Bathsheba Lincoln walked in.

The cabin smelled damp and it was dark in there, and furnished only with the rough pieces which Abraham had contrived to make all during the long lonely autumn and winter. But the fireplace was big and beautiful, and ashes of old fires gave a feeling of warmth-to-be. On the broad mantel she would put the silver candlesticks, and on the table her silver spoons and sugar basin. This was not a vacant house, but a home in which a man had lived and which he had built for his children and the wife he loved. And because she loved her husband, Bathsheba Lincoln accepted the crude log house, and seldom again, except in her deepest inner memories, did she think regretfully of the house in Virginia where life had been so different.

CHAPTER THIRTEEN

AND STILL the terrible tales continued to be told. Still news was heard of Indian troubles, and Abraham could feel them coming closer and closer to the unprotected cabin which he had built so trustingly and so foolishly in the clearing above the river. Simon Girty, the renegade white man who long ago went over to the Indians and connived with the British to thwart the struggle of the colonists for independence, was carrying on his private battles into the remote frontier. Here warfare meant massacre. Women, children, and men trying only to cleave a living from the wilderness were betrayed by one of their own kind. Simon Girty had been hand-in-fist with Hamilton-the-Hair-Buyer at Vincennes, and even after the General was ignominiously hustled off to justice after George Rogers Clark captured Vincennes, Girty and his men continued to incite the Indians against the Kentuckians. For if the people of Kentucky, then a county of Virginia and an outpost of that state, could be destroyed or so discouraged as to return to Virginia, he reasoned, thus leaving Kentucky wide open to the Indians, then all of Virginia would be exposed to ruthless attack from the rear. In defeating Virginia, the British and Indians could then attack the seat of government of the struggling colonies.

But the people of Kentucky were not Kentuckians for nothing. They had traveled the Wilderness Road. The weak never got there at all; they had turned back all along the way. It was only the strong, the tough, the bullheaded, the no-quitting, defiant kind like Simon

Kenton and Daniel Boone, and Richard Callaway and John Floyd
who finally settled in Kentucky, the Dark and Bloody Ground, and
it was they who defended it. They had little support from Virginia
itself. They were on their own and they knew it.

But John Floyd of Harrodstown expressed what so many thought:

"I want to return as much as any man can do, but if I leave the
country now, there is scarcely one single man who will not follow
the example. When I think of the deplorable condition a few helpless families are likely to be in, I conclude to sell my life as dearly
as I can in their defense rather than make an ignominious escape."

And so the grim tales of depredation, death, and attack continued
to mount.

There arrived one day on the buffalo road a dusty, weary traveler
who came to the Lincoln door, and while he ate and drank and rested,
he told of what he had heard at the settlements.

"They call her the 'Long-Knife Squaw,'" he said, reaching with
his knife-blade for another chunk of roasted venison. He gnawed
bites from the meat held upright on the knife, and talked greasily as
he chewed. "That Mis Merril, she sure set an example to other females
in this beset land! It was a summer night, they say, when her house
was attacked by Injuns—the dogs barked, and warned John Merril
—'twas up in Nelson county, not so far from here, ma'am—and when
he opened the door, thinkin' it was a traveler seekin' shelter, six or
seven Injuns fired point-blank through the door and broke his arm
and his thigh. He fell to the floor and called to his good wife to come
quick and close the door.

"But no sooner had she done so, than the Injuns beat on it with
their tommyhawks and broke a plank in. But that Mis Merril, I tell
you, ma'am, *there's* a woman could rastle a wild buffalo! There she
stood—six feet in her stockin's, I lay, and broad as an ox—with the
shake-ax in her two hands, and every time an Injun poked his head
through the hole in that door, thinkin' to crawl through to finish
off those inside, she whacked down with the ax on his head neat as
slicin' a watermelon!" Bathsheba, pausing at the fireplace where she
was baking more corn bread, felt her stomach turn over and wished

the man would hush.

"Well, them Injuns didn't know when they was well off. They saw they couldn't git into the door, so up they went on the roof and Mis Merril could hear 'em paddlin' around up there on the clap-boards, and knew they was plannin' on comin' down the chimney. 'Twas summer, and the fire was nigh out for the night. But she thought of what to do. She grabbed up her one and only feather-bed—and sad she was to part with it, you may be sure, goose feathers not bein' easy to come by in the wilderness—and she ripped it open with the ax and poured them feathers on the hot ashes, stirred up the fire so the feathers begun to blaze, and them redskins nigh choked to death on the thick smoke and fumes of the burnin' feathers comin' up the chimney piece! Hah! Two of the varmints was already half-way down the chimney, though, and down they come, *ker-thump*, and lay there, half dead on the hearth, kickin' and gaspin' and chokin' till she stopped 'em for good with a couple good blows of that there trusty ax. She was a great hand with an ax, I vow!

"And what did she hear while she was dispatchin' 'em, but a sound at the broken door, and there was the last of them fool Shawa-nese, undaunted by what had happened to his companions, tryin' to get in! So she whacked *him* with the ax, but missed just enough so's she slashed his cheek to the jawbone, and he yelled bloody murder and went kitin' off all the way to Chillicothe. I heard he gave out with tales of a giant squaw who'd killed more'n *sixty* Injuns with a great long knife!"

The boys doted on tales like these, but Mary had bad dreams which made her cry out in her sleep and kept Bathsheba up half the night soothing her. The little girl had nightmares of Indians coming down the chimney and in the windows and through the heavy door, and Bathsheba herself, though she had better control, had her dark and desperate moments of fear.

Abraham was too busy in his fields to worry very much. He and the boys quickly got the corn planted and put in a field of clover. Jo planted his vegetable seeds and a row of immortelles to surprise Bath-sheba. The cow recovered from her frightful journey up the Wilder-

ness Road and gave birth to a lusty bull calf; and one of the mares pro-
duced a colt with the slender legs and fine head of a blooded racer.
The two hens and cock which somehow had survived the journey,
too, cackled contentedly at the woods edge and laid eggs in the barn,
and Bathsheba managed to bring off a setting of eggs. But the varmints
were bad. The forest was so close that the foxes came out sniffing
about the pen of young chickens, and one morning she found them
all gone. Then one night a large-footed varmint left prints in the
soft earth of the barnyard, and Abraham knew that a wolf had come
looking for the calf or the colt, and he tightened the latches on the
doors of the barn.

That summer the sly raccoons, the lithe-heeled deer, and the scampering wood mice got into the corn and destroyed so many ears in
the milk that Abraham wondered if he'd have any left to dry for
winter. But as the stalks browned and autumn came on, and the
sassafras blazed in an orange and pink glow at the edge of the forest,
he saw that there would likely be enough . . . if nothing else happened to the precious crop.

CHAPTER FOURTEEN

Aₙd still the American Revolution continued. Back in the wilderness it was worse than ever and no one could see how the end would be.

All about there were signs of trouble. And at Boonesborough one day in the spring of 1782, a silent warning floated quietly down the Kentucky River, past the fort. Three logs fastened together . . . fastened by Indians who were crossing somewhere upstream, and their raft-bridge had floated away. But no one knew where the Indian trouble would strike and all over Kentucky folk could not sleep for thinking and wondering and fearing.

Simon Girty inspired most of the trouble. Over in Ohio he had hatched a plan by which he could bring discomfort to the Kentuckians and at the same time give comfort to Captain William Caldwell. The Captain had planned an attack on Wheeling and was thwarted in it, but he didn't want to report back to his superiors at Detroit and admit he'd muffed his campaign. So Simon Girty, who always knew what to do in a situation like that, worked out something that would do as well. There were plenty of unprotected forts in Kentucky which would be interesting and fairly easy to attack. Not Boonesborough, though Girty had a bone to pick with Dan Boone; but Boonesborough by now was too well fortified for an easy and successful attack. And this had to be successful. Girty thought for a bit and let his mind run over the crude map of Kentucky he kept, with the little forts and settlements and isolated cabins set in their lonely bravery upon it. His mind came to rest on the very one: Bryan's Station.

Bryan's Station lay not far east of Boonesborough, and it was, indeed, small, innocent, and unprotected. The stockade enclosed a dozen cabins, each occupied by a family, besides two dozen scouts, surveyors, hunters, and such like who made Bryan's their headquarters.

It was easy for the six hundred men of Captain Caldwell's force —three hundred of which were fierce and bloodthirsty Wyandots and a good many more of which were Shawanese—guided by Simon Girty, to surround Bryan's Station. The plan was to decoy a group of defenders outside the gates, then attack from the rear, in the method which had always been so successful in similar assaults.

On the night of August fifteenth, when the loud zinging and buzzing of night insects filled the warm and humid dusk, Simon Girty and his Indians and British soldiers were slipping in quietly like shadows around Bryan's Station. At sunset, however, a rider dashed up to the gate with his horse in a lather, to tell the men of the fort that Holder's Station, a few miles away, had been attacked by Indians, and men from Bryan's should come early the next morning to help track down the marauders. And so it happened that while the Indians were gathering around Bryan's Station and were slapping quietly at mosquitoes in the darkness, and lying on their bellies in the dewy grass, the men of the fort were getting their rifles in order and their powder horns filled.

When the sun came up over the meadowlands of Kentucky, the Station was completely surrounded by Indians, who were invisible from the fort. Girty had no idea that the men of the fort intended leaving it; if he had, he would have used a simpler method of attack —merely to wait until all the men had cleared out on their rescue mission, then strike. But he didn't know it, and at his signal, a small group of Indians, yelling and brandishing tomahawks, were to race toward the front gates of the fort.

You can fool a Kentuckian a couple of times, but he learns pretty fast, Simon Kenton had found out. When the Indians had only one idea of attack in mind, only one plan to follow, the Kentuckians, from bitter experience, soon discovered what that idea was and worked out what to do. Consequently, when the decoy force appeared at the gates, no one rushed out to defend the fort. Instead, the great gates were double barred inside and every man was ordered to arm himself and guard all four sides of the hollow square with the cabins inside. And the attack began. Simon Girty and the Indians were at it again.

Several days later, Bathsheba Lincoln was sweeping the puncheon floor with a twig broom when she heard the sounds of horse's hoofs pounding the dust of the trail. She hurried to the door and Abraham, seeing the dust, came up from the field. The rider was wild-eyed and his black hair was tousled in the wind. His left arm was in a rude sling and there was a raw, red cut on his cheek, down which was a mark of caked dried blood.

"Adam! What's happened?" cried Abraham, aghast, reaching up his hands to help his friend down. Adam was about to fall, Abraham saw, worn and weary to the bone, and hurt badly, too. They got him into the cabin, and Bathsheba bathed the cut on his cheek. Abraham put a splint on the broken arm, and they made Adam Marlow comfortable before they allowed him to talk. Hananiah came in, saying nothing, and listened intently to Adam's story.

He was eager to talk. Abraham thought for a bit that his friend was delirious in his ranting, but it all made sense, finally, and he knew it had all happened and that Adam had been in the thick of it, because he'd gone to the defense of Bryan's Station when word came of the force of Indians deployed somewhere near by. They had attacked the Station, but unsuccessfully. They had scattered, but the scattering was only a ruse of Simon Girty's.

Adam told the whole story, about how the men in the fort, early in the morning, became aware of the Indians hiding around the fort, waiting for the right moment to attack, and how the women saved the day when there was no water to be had inside the fort. With a probable siege coming up, no one knew how lengthy, a lack of water would be disastrous.

The water supply of most forts in the wilderness was usually at a distance from the walls, so that in time of siege there was no easy access to the vital source. The spring supplying Bryan's Station lay bubbling peacefully at the foot of the slope leading to the river . . . and along the well-trodden path where the women and girls each morning walked to get the water, lay several hundred Indians, hidden in grass and behind trees, waiting.

"The women!" cried Adam. "Bless those pioneer women who are making Kentucky what she is! Listen to this, Abraham. It was Mrs. Johnson—you know, Colonel Robert Johnson's wife, it was—who stepped up and offered to lead a party of the women and girls down to the spring. And that spring was surrounded, I tell you; it was fairly bristling with redskins just waiting for a chance at their scalps. You never know what a woman will do till she does it, I vow!" He bowed his head to Bathsheba, who was listening. Bathsheba's small figure looked a little stooped, a little weary; her hands had grown rough from the work she did, but they were tender when she bathed Adam's wounds, and her blue eyes were bright as she listened to his tale.

"And Mrs. Johnson said, 'Every morning we go to the spring for water, and I allow that the Indians know it; there's precious little they *don't* know about our comings and goings. If we fail to go out this morning, they'll be sure we suspect they are there. But if we all go out as we always do, and pretend to be unafraid, then they may spare us on the chance of bigger game. I'm ready to try it, and I know Betsy will go with me, won't you, daughter?' And the little girl nodded that she would. I hear they hesitated a mite, those women in the fort, and I'm sure their hearts were beating high with fear. Not a one among them but didn't know what Indians did to white women, and then—and then—listen to this, Abraham. *Every one of them spoke up that she would go!* Every one of them. And their men were horrified and tried to dissuade them, but they held to their resolve. They picked up their buckets and their gourds and the little piggins for the small girls to carry, and when the rear gate of the stockade was thrown open, out they marched. Twenty-eight women and girls, and they all set out to that spring. It was like walking into a den of rattlesnakes, that I swear, and I doubt if I'd have had the courage!

"And would you believe it, they laughed and talked and sang a little, pretending they were just after water as always, suspecting naught. And yet they could see, as they came closer, how the morning sunlight struck sparks from the rifle barrels hid in the weeds, saw Indian feathers and doubtless the whites of Indian eyes glaring at them from down in the cane. Those women were surrounded by savages and yet not one faltered, but came to the spring, dipped up the water she needed, and came back in the same leisurely manner. It was a wonderful piece of self-control, and I shall always revere women the more for knowing that they did it so. And the savages, even Simon Girty, they say, were completely taken in. They were only intent on their original plan and the plan didn't include attacking a group of women getting water."

Abraham took a deep breath. Bathsheba, leaning against the door jamb, listened, and there was a rich, deep pride in her breast for the bravery of the women of Bryan's Station. She doubted if she could have been so brave, but you never knew till the time came for your testing.

"Don't stop," whispered Mord, who had come in and was listening with wide eyes. "What happened next, Mr. Marlow?"

"Well, once the females were inside, the garrison went into action. The men sent a decoy force of their own out the gates, and they made a great noise, as if the whole fort had rushed out, and that vile Girty charged with his even viler followers.

"They came leaping out of the grass and the bushes and the corn-field, screeching and whooping like monsters. They say it was that black-hearted Moluntha who led the Shawanese, and he carried a torch to set fire to the fort. And Girty was in the forefront, of course. Trust him to be where dark doings are happening. George Bohannon told me about it, how everyone in the fort was deathly silent and waited as the savages raced up the slope. And our people poured a deadly volley out of every loophole in the fort, while the wives and girls kept the men supplied with freshly loaded arms as fast as they were spent. Again and again they fired, and the savages fell with dreadful howls to be so deceived.

"But even though the Indians fled—all but those laid low by the gunfire—they tossed flaming torches into the stockade and half a dozen cabins were fired. And now the women came to the front again," went on Adam with a light of introspection in his harassed eyes, "and they and the boys put out the fires while the men reloaded and waited for what would come next. I tell you, Abraham, there were brave doings inside that little stockade—but no braver, I suppose, than what has taken place inside other forts under attack." Adam leaned back his head for a moment and closed his eyes. Then he opened them and resumed his tale.

"They all held their breaths, likely, for the second charge, and there was none, which was queer, mighty queer. The Indians had learned enough from the first attack, the garrison concluded. Instead, the Indians contented themselves with lying in the brush and shooting flaming arrows into the fort, and busy the people were inside to keep the flames down and the roofs intact. But a party of horsemen from Lexington arrived, summoned by a messenger who had left the fort early, and now the garrison was so wonderfully strengthened that the siege ended then and there.

"They sent word to Harrodstown for volunteers—that's how I happen to know about all this, Abraham. They sent to Boonesborough and to Lexington, and fifty of us from each town went off to track down the savages. Dan Boone was there; he's been itching for the chance to avenge the death of his brother Edward but didn't want to start anything on his own. Now was his chance, and his eyes were fairly snapping blue sparks, he was so eager. You know how Dan is. His boy, Israel, was with him; a fine lad, a man grown now. It was Stephen Trigg who led us from Harrodstown, and Bill McBride was with him, who hasn't the equal in fighting redskins.

"It was easy to see which way the Indians went, and we followed quickly before the trail got cold. By day before yesterday, we got to the Lower Blue Lick. But Boone was getting more and more disturbed by the whole business. He didn't like what he was seeing. The Indians had left *too* plain a trail.

" 'I tell you,' he kept saying, 'them savages *know* we're followin' on their track. They're leadin' us on. We're not foolin' them one bit, and if we don't watch sharp, we're goin' to be sorry!' But you couldn't tell us anything, we were so anxious to get a shot at those Shawanese. Boone wanted to wait for Ben Logan's force, which hadn't come up yet; he was sure that Girty's Indians were setting a trap, and you can't fool Boone when it comes to Indians. But it was that Hugh McGary, who never knows when to keep his mouth shut, who set us off. He spurred his horse into the water, swung his rifle over his head and yelled:

" *'Delay is dastardly! Let all who are not cowards follow me!'*

"Well, of course," went on Adam, "there wasn't anything else we could do, after that. You know what it does to a Kentuckian— or a Virginian—to call him a coward, and none of us wanted to have *that* label. The commanders had a hard time getting order in the ranks. Every man was plunging madly into the river and trying to get across. You remember how the Blue Lick runs, Abraham— alongside there's that trail up a rocky, barren ridge, but with tim-bered hollows coming down from both sides of the ridge. And it was down in the ravines there, nicely out of sight, that the Indians were hidden, and likely gloating blackly at how we were falling into their trap. *And then they fired!*"

Adam went a little whiter, remembering. He pushed back his tangled hair and his hand shook.

"Abraham, it was horrible," he said in a low voice shaken with emotion. "I never saw anything like it. The Wyandots are worse than the Shawanese any day, and now here they came tearing out, charging with tomahawks in their hands, and slashing and cutting and beating down every Kentuckian who was in the way. And we were *all* in the way. We fought them hand to hand for a while, but the Shawanese poured fire into our ranks, and then—Abraham, I hate to say it—we just cut and ran. It was sheer panic that did it. No

THE INDIANS TOSSED FLAMING TORCHES INTO THE STOCKADE AND HALF A
DOZEN CABINS WERE FIRED

SHE SCREAMED WHEN SHE SAW AN INDIAN STANDING TALL IN THE DOOR-
WAY.... IN HIS ARMS HE HELD TOMMY LINCOLN, FAST ASLEEP

man could stand up to murder like that, and that's all it was, just plain butchery. Some jumped into the river to escape the tomahawks, and I saw them cut down by bullets fired at their defenseless heads. And Dan Boone's boy was killed. Poor Dan, poor Dan. He was close to Israel when it happened, and I heard him give a mighty groan and saw him throw down his rifle. He lifted his boy up from the bloody ground and half fell with him down the stony slope and into the river, just as an Indian bullet clipped him on the shoulder. He kept on, though, but before he got to shore, the boy was dead and Dan knew it. It was all Dan could do to get away with his own life when the Indians began scouting around to clean up any of us who survived."

"How did you get away?" cried Abraham, aghast at the dreadful story.

"I don't know, I really don't know," said Adam dully. "They killed seventy of us, and I feel as if I'd died with every one of them. They captured four and I hear they're to be tortured to death in the Indian towns. Abraham, they killed John Todd, and Stephen Trigg, and even Bill McBride himself, and no Indian had ever before harmed a hair of his head. And listen, Abraham, Dan was right. If we had only waited till Logan's force came, we'd have beaten them. As we were struggling back to Bryan's with our wounded, we met Logan and five hundred men coming to our aid—*five hundred*, think of it! We could have beaten them easily if we'd only waited. Dan Boone always knows best. If we'd only heeded him. Poor Dan! He's all broken up about losing his boy, the second one he's seen killed by savages."

The Battle of the Blue Licks was over, and now from all over Kentucky's settlements came the cry for vengeance. George Rogers Clark rose to the situation. In October, he marched with a thousand men through the dark forests of Ohio, along the old buffalo traces and Indian trails to attack the Indian villages on the Little Miami. His forces burned and killed and destroyed, and that winter the Shawnees and Wyandots were weakened even more by loss of food stores and shelter. And the British were withdrawing their support so that even Simon Girty was not the power he had been.

But Abraham Lincoln, in his lone cabin in the little clearing, surrounded by the vast, hostile forest, could not forget the disaster at Bryan's Station and the Blue Licks, so few miles to the east, nor all the other terrible things which the Indians still were perpetrating in Kentucky. He was restless and uneasy, but because he could never make quick decisions and had to mull ideas over in his mind for a long time before he acted, he did nothing about his uneasiness. But he could not go forward with the plans he had for further clearing and building and improving. The cabin simply had been built too far from other people and the protection of the towns and forts, and he knew he was going to have to move.

CHAPTER FIFTEEN

ABRAHAM COULD NOT decide what was best to do, so he let months go by while he studied the matter, and while he studied he neglected his work. The Battle of the Blue Licks happened in 1782. Abraham felt he should move his family at once to a safer place. But time passed, and when Clark went after the Indians and events were more peaceful, the Lincolns still remained at the Green River farm. The year 1783 went by, with its growing season and its harvest, and the year 1784 blossomed with springtime and burgeoned with summer, and it was autumn again in Kentucky. And still the Lincolns stayed.

The boys spent the pleasant autumn days in the woods, gathering hickory nuts and walnuts. Mord discovered a big old persimmon tree, but the fruit wouldn't be ready for a time yet. Just now, as he'd found out to his sorrow, it was bitterly astringent and dreadfully puckering to his mouth. But he remembered where the tree was, standing tall above a little run in the forest, and before the possums and the paroquets got all the soft, sweet, pulpy fruit, he and Jo gathered basketfuls of them. Bathsheba made a pudding and dried some of the fruit—almost as good as Carolina figs, she concluded in pride—and Abraham put down a keg of persimmon beer. There were papaw trees, too, whose great leaves, thin as paper in the deep woods shade, turned pale yellow and dropped soft banana-like fruits. Bathsheba did not fancy them; too rich, she complained, but Abraham and the children devoured all they could find, and Hananiah sometimes delicately picked at one.

Jo had had a dreadful time with his garden. The fence he put up around it the first summer did nothing more than to invite the deer to high-tail it over the poles and eat up all his cabbage and beans. So he cut longer poles, and with Mord and Abraham to help him, he put up a fence nine feet high—too tall for any deer, no matter how ambitious, to leap over and dine on his tender garden stuff. But Jo mourned all the precious vegetables he had lavished on the ever hungry deer.

Autumn went, and the leaves came down, and the Kentucky countryside lay purple-gray and open, accented by dark green where the cedars topped the ridges, a far, rolling, hilly landscape over which a chill wind from the north swept in gusts as winter came on. And every night the wolves barked and howled, barked and howled, out on the hills, and trotted lightfooted and watchful around the barn.

That was what worried Bathsheba so dreadfully on that day when Tommy got lost. He had been playing with Mary and Nancy in the heaps of dry leaves within sight of the cabin, and next thing she knew the little girls were indoors for their supper of corn bread and milk, and they didn't know where Tommy was.

"He was with us, Mammy, most all the time," Mary explained, in tears and unable to eat. "Only when I finished building a cave in the leaves for Nancy and looked around, he just wasn't there. I *called* and *called*, and he didn't come."

Bathsheba went out with a blazing stick of kindling wood for a torch, went out, a little, lone figure in the gathering dusk, and walked to the fence line. Her voice seemed small and thin against the blackness of the sky and the immensity of the forest. If only Abraham were here—but he and the older boys had gone over to Harrodstown and they might not be back until late. He had told her to be sure to bar the shutters and put the big bar across the door. The horses had to be shod and since he didn't have a forge as yet, they must be taken over to the smithy at Harrodstown. It wasn't a long journey, but they might not be able to get back before nightfall, it came so early in autumn. . . . Hananiah had gone up to Louisville for a week.

Bathsheba wasn't nervous about staying alone, but now that

Tommy was missing, she was in a panic. Never had she felt so lone and small and helpless as when she stood there and faced the vast, mysterious, dusky forest of Kentucky and called in vain for her youngest son.

"Tommy—Tommy—Tommeeee!" Her voice was impotent against the great silence of the autumn night. There was no reply but the sardonic hoot of a big owl somewhere off in the big trees of the river bottoms, no answering pipe of a small boy's voice saying, "Here I am, Mammy!" as Tommy always did when she called him —or almost always. Sometimes he liked to hide and not answer so as to make her look for him until she and Mary were frantic, and then out he would pop with a mischievous sparkle in his big gray eyes—"Here I am, Mammy!"

But never, never had he stayed out so long. He was always ready to run in to the warm, lighted safety of the cabin when dusk closed down.

"Tom—meee!" Bathsheba called once again, sobbing under her breath, and walked heavily in despair to the cabin. As she turned, the back of her neck prickled with the fear of the unknown lying there behind her in the forest. The little girls stood in the doorway, silhouetted against the light inside. Her torch smoked and went out.

"Did you find him, Mammy?" cried Mary anxiously.

"Did 'oo find 'im, Mammy?" echoed Nancy, holding out her hands to be picked up. But Bathsheba was too perturbed to take her.

"I don't know where to look . . . what to do . . . if only Pa were here . . . or Mord . . . oh dear, poor Tommy . . ." Out there in that dreadful black wilderness with all those wolves and catamounts and bears . . . a little helpless child like Tommy . . .

Bathsheba put a candle in a window, left unbarred to let the light shine out so that he could see where the cabin was if he was wandering about lost. A little light would lead him in, her small stray lamb. By and by she put the girls to bed, but she heard Mary softly crying, and went to comfort her.

"We'll find him, sweet, never fear. Pray a little prayer and God will surely hear you."

She was praying, too, over and over, a petition for her youngest son lost in the woods. And *where* was Abraham?

It was very late when the dogs began to bay and bark in a dreadful clamor. There came a sharp rap on the door, and Bathsheba, without remembering what Abraham had always told her—to find out who was there before she pulled back the bar—flung open the door.

She screamed when she saw an Indian standing tall in the doorway. The firelight sparkled on his white eyeballs. In his arms he held Tommy Lincoln, fast asleep.

"He . . . yours?" the Indian grunted low in his throat, as if he had a hard time forming the English words.

"*Yes!*" gasped Bathsheba, holding on to the door to steady herself. "Yes! Oh, where did you find him? He's been gone so long!"

The Indian handed Tommy over to her and jerked his thumb in the general direction of the north forest, nodded his head, and came into the room. Bathsheba stood still, watching. An Indian in her house . . . and she was alone with three helpless children. She staggered under Tommy's weight and laid him, still sleeping heavily, on the bed.

The Indian went to the fire and sat himself down on the floor in front of the flames. And there he remained without a word or with a by-your-leave.

Through Bathsheba's mind raced all the hideous stories which had been told to her—about how vile the Shawanese and Wyandots were. how they abused women and children. Yet this one had brought Tommy home: *Tommy was safe.* The Indian needn't have done it. He could have tomahawked the child then and there, and that would have been the end of it, could have attacked the cabin in the night and killed them all. But he hadn't. Instead, he was sitting before her fire as if he were at his own fireside.

She covered Tommy with a quilt. He was dirty and tattered, as though he had wandered through miles of brush, and his face was streaked and grimy where his fists had gouged at the tears. Poor baby . . . but miraculously he was home, he was safe. And that Indian . . . Bathsheba wasn't sure what she should do, but the eternal hostess in her came forward.

She took the big knife and with shaking hands cut off a chunk of venison from the haunch she had roasted yesterday. She put it neatly on a plate and handed it to the Indian. His black eyes swiveled around to the venison and then up at her. His dirty hand reached out and grabbed the meat and his strong teeth gnawed at it and the grease ran down his chin and over his chest. It made Bathsheba a little sick, suddenly, to see how he ate and how he gave small animal-like grunts and smacking sounds as he devoured the meat. She offered him cold corn bread, but he shook his head and pointed at the meat on the table. She hacked off a great rough hunk and held it out to him on the point of the knife, and he grinned a little and snatched it off.

Somehow he didn't look as ferocious as she'd been led to believe redskins were. Surely this was no bloodthirsty Shawanee or Wyandot or Delaware, nor yet a Cherokee—she'd seen Cherokees in Virginia. But whatever he was, he was an Indian, and he was in her house and she had nothing whatever to defend herself with except the carving knife . . . and the ax, maybe, but she was not a Mrs. Merril to defend her home with an ax.

When he had eaten, the Indian curled himself up with his blanket around him and went to sleep on the hearth. Her knees trembling in the absurd way they did when she was frightened or tired, Bathsheba stepped lightly around him and put on more logs. Then she went over to the bed and lay there, fully dressed, with the knife in her hand. She watched the flames flickering with a ruddy light between the black shadows on the rafters and on the log walls, saw the form of the Indian silhouetted against the licking flames. She would watch all night if need be. There was naught else to do. If only Abraham would come!

But Bathsheba never could stay awake when she went to bed. She woke with a start, saw that the flames had died down and that the Indian was sitting up. She had slept—she had been so sure she wouldn't—and the creature was still there and evidently he wasn't going to do anything to them. Then she heard the dogs clamoring, heard horses and voices outside. With a vast warm relief, she knew it was Abraham and the boys.

She threw open the door and ran out into the darkness.

"Abraham!" she cried breathlessly in a frantic whisper, lest the Indian hear. "There's an Indian in our house! He's been there for hours, and he won't go! An Indian—he brought Tommy home—"

"What on earth, Basheby, are you daft?" cried Abraham, jumping down, a peculiar look on his tired face, while the sleepy boys were thoroughly awake.

"What do you mean, an Indian in our house—and where was Tom—" Abraham's long legs sprinted to the house and there he found the Indian still sitting on the hearth, placidly, where Bathsheba had left him. Tommy was still asleep and the girls had not been awakened by the racket.

"You!" cried Abraham, and a relieved grin spread over his lean face. "It's Talking Crow, Basheby, he's all right. Talking Crow is a Piankeshaw. His people are friendly; he's a friend of Jim Harrod's and I've seen him often up at Harrodstown. And you say he brought Tom home? Where *was* that rascal?"

"Tommy got lost and we didn't know where he was. Night came on—I was desperate, Abraham, alone like this, not knowing where he was. The Indian came late to the door with Tommy. I guess he'd found him in the forest; I can't get the man to talk. And he just stayed there on the hearth. I was terribly frightened—I thought something had happened to you and the boys, you were so late—and I didn't know if the Indian would murder us all! How was I to know he was only a Piankeshaw? Indians look alike to me."

CHAPTER SIXTEEN

"ABRAHAM," BEGAN Hananiah, fingering the bristle of beard on his cheeks and chin and mentally reminding himself to shave more often, lest he get to looking like some hopelessly shaggy woodsy out in this wilderness. "Abraham, it's time I got myself some land here in Kentucky and settled down."

The idea of the lightfooted and flighty Hananiah Lincoln ever settling down like other folk his age amused Abraham. He leaned on his shovel and grinned at his cousin.

"Any place in mind?" he commented smoothly without committing himself one way or another.

"Not yet, Abe, not yet, but seems to me as if Washington County is likely country. Getting pretty well populated and that cuts down danger from the Indians. I don't fancy to get myself a place off in the brush like this and then spend my days and nights wondering when the redskins are going to lift my hair. No, I'll buy some land nigh to the settlements and build a house. Might even get me a wife some day!"

Hananiah had dallied with the affections of many women in Virginia, Abraham knew, but he never went so far as to commit himself to marriage. A man with a wife and a house and likely some young ones couldn't traipse off to Charlottesville or Richmond whenever he pleased, and Hananiah had no mind to let himself in for anything like that. But now, somehow, he had lived so long out in the wilderness that he was getting to think in wilderness ways. Folk

didn't live the same as they did back in the Virginia settlements.
The women were different. Any woman strong enough and brave
enough to have come out here by way of the Wilderness Road and
able to make a home for her man and her young ones would have to
be made of different stuff than the pretty, painted creatures in the
towns. But poor Bathsheba; these women paid a fearful price,
Hananiah thought with regret. A right beautiful woman was
Bathsheba, well cared for and delicate, used to plenty of servants,
and now look—hidden away out here in the forest. Her clothes had
become the utilitarian kind, and she had but few of them. Her skin
was tanned and there were fine wrinkles spraying out from around
her eyes and mouth; her hair had white threads in it already, and it
never knew the care which Leah had given it at home. And her
hands. Hananiah shook his head over the way they looked. He'd
always been one to admire a woman's hands. Now *his* wife would
be different; she wouldn't have the hardships Abraham's wife had
to endure. Hananiah's wife would prove that a woman could live
in Kentucky and still be pretty.

"Well, when do you propose to buy this land?" Abraham inter-
rupted his reverie, for he well knew what was coming.

"I don't rightly know, Abe," Hananiah said, his own tone guarded,
watching his cousin's seamed, thin face with the firm, sensitive,
inscrutable mouth. "Seems as if I've about outstayed my welcome
in your house, crowded as it is with so many young ones and dogs.
I know Basheby would be glad of my room."

"She never said so, did she?" defended Abraham, straightening. He
had been digging sweet potatoes and his back was tired. "She's always
been hospitable to you, hasn't she?"

"Oh, of course, of course," Hananiah soothed. "Basheby is never
anything but kind and hospitable. But I know as well as I know my
name that your house was never intended for me and it's overfull,
and a woman never likes to live crowded in her own house. Now if
I was to get me some land and build . . ." Craftily he watched Abraham, because Hananiah knew well enough how Bathsheba had complained—late at night when she thought Hananiah was asleep—about

how cramped they were for room and how much Hananiah eternally ate and that he didn't work worth a lick of use to help earn his keep. Oh, he knew what they were thinking, and that was good, that was very good indeed. Make them so sick and tired of him, he would, they'd be ready to do anything to get rid of him.

"Now if you'd loan me the money, Abraham," he went on smoothly, "I could negotiate for that land up on Beech Fork I've an eye on, and could begin clearing this winter, maybe, and could get myself moved over there by next spring. What do you say, Abe? You know I've no money and yours isn't doing you any good just lying around somewhere (Hananiah couldn't for the life of him imagine where Abraham had hidden it). Loan it to me on three per cent interest and you'll profit by the investment; you'll get more back than you let out!"

Abraham looked thoughtfully at the field where he and Mord had been digging. The boy was down at the far end of the row.

"Well, 'Niah, what you say seems to make sense. We'll think about it, and meanwhile you go see about that land on Beech Fork and find out what price you'll have to give. And I reckon the money'll be there when you need it."

Abraham went on with his digging, thinking it would be worth the money to get Hananiah out of his house so Bathsheba would rest easy again. He didn't see why she was so set against the man; he was innocent enough, only a little reckless with women sometimes and never could keep any money of his own. Come to think of it, though, when did 'Niah ever work to earn any of the money he had? And if he didn't work, then how did he get money? Abraham shook his head, then dug away and turned over the loose earth where the damp brown potatoes lay open to the sunshine. He was so preoccupied with his thoughts that he almost collided with Mord when their shovels suddenly clashed.

A good many days went by and then pretty soon Hananiah had his piece of land. Abraham didn't know how he was going to tell Bathsheba about the money, but he found that he needn't have been concerned. As usual, Hananiah had beaten him to it.

Bathsheba, her eyes blazing, met him at the door when he came in from pulling corn and stacking the shocks. The boys were still out there in the fragrant November twilight, playing Indians around the tepee-like shocks and whooping like Wyandots, the dogs barking in joy at the game.

"Abraham Lincoln—so—you did it at last! *You—you've given Hananiah our money!* You—oh, why did you *do* it? You know that's all we had in the world!"

Abraham's thin face froze in the stubborn gray lines it took on when he was deeply angry and on the defensive.

"Yes, I did it, and you've no call to blaze up like that and ask me *why* I did it. I take care of the business affairs of this family and you've got to remember it, Basheby Lincoln! If I loaned Hananiah that money, then it was in a good cause. I should think you'd be glad of the chance to get him out of this house; you been complaining about it long enough, how he never knew when to leave, once he got his foot in the door! Well, now he's going and you won't have to feed him and wash his clothes or wait on him. Isn't that what you've been scolding about all this time?"

"Yes, that may well be," she said acidly, her mouth set in bitter lines, her hands defiantly on her hips. "But for years I've been out-thinking that man so as to keep that money in our own strong-box —*not in his pockets!* Time after time I've outwitted his arguments and never let him have a cent. And now you up and give it *all* to him, Abraham Lincoln, like any simpleton. And I suppose he didn't even sign a note, did he?"

"Yes, he did," said Abraham sullenly, defensively. "It's in my strong box and there it'll stay till he pays it back with interest. He'll pay three per cent interest and that isn't a small sum, I'm telling you. You'll be glad enough for it when it comes in and we have plenty of money. Now I don't want to hear any more about it; hush your talk and leave me in peace, woman!"

"Yes, Abraham," she murmured tightly. She knew when to quit, but she was seething inside, boiling and blazing and ready to scream at how Hananiah had so neatly circumvented them. It would be like the other debts he had; all nice promises and handsomely signed notes, and never any payment. Three per cent! Hah—where would he even get the principal to repay, let alone the interest? But she'd hold him to it this time if it killed her. And then, in a sudden, deep-seated panic which kept rising like yeast in her breast until she could not but acknowledge it—what if, as always, he *didn't* pay? How, then, would they improve the farm, how, then, would they educate their children? If the Lincolns of Kentucky became poor and shiftless frontier people like so many she had seen, then it would be Hananiah Lincoln who had made them so.

What if he didn't pay . . . what if he didn't pay . . . what if . . .

CHAPTER SEVENTEEN

WHEN THE CROPS were in that winter, Abraham told Bathsheba what he proposed to do. She had not entirely forgiven him for loaning the money to Hananiah, but the new plan eased some of the tension which had lain tautly between them for so long.

"I'll never rest easy out here in the middle of the forest," Abraham began with a sigh, "long's those red varmints are still around. We'll move up to the other farm in the spring, early enough to get the seeds in. The boys and I'll go up maybe during the winter to get a headstart on the clearing. And we can all live at Hughes Station half a mile away till the house is built and the land all cleared. What say you, Basheby?"

She smoothed down her homespun gown with her work-worn hands and stared from the open door to the ever-menacing dark forest, empty now of leaves, and remembered how Tommy had been lost in it. She wondered, as always, how many Indians were lurking there; looked to the barn where the horses and cows stood in the barnyard waiting to be fed, but where the young never were safe from wolves; saw how wild the children looked, unkempt and like woods folk who didn't know manners nor a proper way for gentlemen and ladies to act. It would be good indeed to live nearer to other folk, nearer to where there might be a school, where the children needn't grow up ignorant and wild.

She smiled suddenly, and in the light of her face he saw the old Bathsheba again.

128

"Yes," she said happily. "That will be good! This is a nice place you've made for us, Abraham, it really is, but likely we can let it out to someone who might *want* to live so far from the settlements. I'll be glad to move to the other farm as soon as you think it's time to go."

But the winter was unusually cold and wet, and there came more snow than the boys had ever seen. It lay, sodden yet stubbornly unmelting, until April, so that Abraham, in vast impatience, wondered how he would get his crops in if the earth didn't mellow up soon. The winter of 1784–85 was so disagreeable that he and the boys didn't go up to the other farm at Floyd's Fork to start the clearing, so that in the spring of '85, when the Lincolns moved with their livestock and belongings to Hughes Station—with bundles and bedticks and kettles and fowls and cows and horses and dogs—no start had been made on the new farm. It was difficult for Abraham to get up enough inner push to start the job of building a house and barn all over again. It seemed to him, sitting quietly before the fire in the evening and staring thoughtfully into the flames, that all his courage and ambition had melted away under the constant threat of danger from Indians. How could a man plan and work toward the future when he could not see into the future at all, except with fear and misgivings? And so, with the excuse of a bad winter to abet him, Abraham did not go to the new farm until spring was upon them and he knew he would have to get a field cleared in order to plant for the coming season's food supply.

Bathsheba had not been sorry to leave the house on Green River. There was nothing in it of much value; none of Abraham's furniture had been lived with long enough for it to have that mellow attachment which she had felt for the furniture left behind in Virginia. The contents of the cabin were to be left as they were for the next folk who would live there. Abraham felt that it would be simpler to build new furniture for the next house than to haul the other pieces over the rough country to the new cabin. The cabins at Hughes Station were meagerly furnished; there was nothing good or comfortable in them, but when Bathsheba had set her silver candlesticks upon the rough mantel and lit her candles in the evening, their gentle glow cast an aura of unreality and comfort over the unkind surroundings. In the light of candle flames, Bathsheba could be transported back to the big brick house in Virginia—not unhappily or longingly, for Bathsheba Lincoln long since had accustomed herself to believing that home was where she and Abraham and the children were, and she did not pine for Virginia. But she could think gently of hardships when she could see her silver candlesticks, symbol of what used to be and what, with the help of God, she would make in the wilderness of Kentucky when it was tamed.

Hananiah Lincoln came along, but Bathsheba had ceased minding his once unending company. He had acquired a piece of land and soon would build his own house upon it. Because Hananiah needed assistance with his cabin, Abraham went over to Beech Fork to lend a hand. His own clearing and building waited while he helped Hananiah clear land and build a fine cabin—a well-made house with a porch and three rooms, and windows all around. Abraham didn't much begrudge the time it took from his own place; the earth was so wet and cold, even in May, that the seeds he had planted rotted in the ground and he would have to replant as soon as the weather warmed.

"Soon's I get settled," Hananiah declared, standing back admiringly to watch Abraham laying the planked floor, "I'll have a regular frame house, or maybe brick. This isn't going to be backwoods much longer. This is settlement country, sure and certain. The backwoods is off yonder where your old cabin stands, and I'm expecting towns to grow up all around here. I won't live for long in a log shanty, you may be sure of that. Though I do admit this isn't a bad one," he added, as Abraham gave him a quick, hurt glance—for it had been Abraham, really, who had built that cabin for Hananiah.

Abraham helped him finish the place and then went back belatedly to his own land. Mord was fourteen now and getting to be a great help. He was growing fast, rawboned and tough, almost as tall as his father. And Jo was reaching up there, too. Jo would never be as big as Abraham; Josiah Lincoln took after his mother, everyone said. But he was strong and he could help Mord grub brush and break ground. Even the lazy Tommy could do his share, though it was harder to keep him at a job than it was to do it yourself. Tommy was seven now, and he was like Mord, tough as a hickory-knot, and stubborn as one, too. He stoutly insisted that he would not stay at the fort with Bathsheba and the girls. He wanted to be with the men and boys and horses, working like a man—or lounging around like one, or playing alone by the creek. Abraham let him come. The sooner Tom grew up, the better it would be. Abraham needed strong boys to help. This whole land, if it was to be developed, needed strong men and boys to wrestle with the wilderness and bring out of it towns and farms.

A whole year went by and the new farm still was not ready, nor was the new house. Bathsheba was irked at having to stay so long in the cramped little one-room cabin inside the walls of the fort, where the family had to sleep on straw-ticks on the floor—an earth floor where sometimes she found snakes which had crept under the logs! The cabin was ugly and dark and full of vermin, which all her energetic attacks could not keep out. She longed for a place of her own and wished urgently that Abraham and the boys would hurry a little in getting their new home finished. But Abraham had lost his driving energy which had brought him full of hope and strength from Virginia to settle in Kentucky. None of her urging seemed to do any good. He worked, yes, but he didn't seem to accomplish much. Hananiah still was around; he came visiting often and Abraham knocked off work to sit in the shade and talk, and his cousin always stayed to dinner because he liked Bathsheba's cooking. And there was no work done when the visitor was present. A whole year to clear land and build a house . . .

CHAPTER EIGHTEEN

THERE WAS thunder in the air one day in May, 1786, a feeling of menace in the unseasonable closeness and heat. It was a time of storms and warmth and high winds that raked through the trees and tore off new leaves like feathers, or broke boughs and boles as if they were splinters.

Bathsheba was nervous that morning when Abraham and the boys started out to the clearing half a mile away, for the sunrise was carmine, the sky as if dyed in blood, a color which was reflected on everything for a little while, until clouds grayed the ruddiness, then released the sun, which burned down with greater intensity than springtime should know.

"Don't worry about us," said Abraham cheerfully. "If it storms, we'll get us inside the house. The roof is on and the clapboards are tight enough to shed any amount of water. When we get the logs chinked, it'll be as snug a house as you would ever want to see. Won't be long before we can all move in. Mord and Jo'll get busy on the chinking today, but I've got to grub out more brush so's I can get the rest of the corn in." He cast a practiced eye over the sky. The air was close and hot; he was bathed in perspiration already. "Looks as if it might thicken up and rain a mite, after all," he said. But they went off anyway.

Not until afternoon did there appear in the northwest a low, blue-black cloud mass which climbed silently up the sky. The heat of the day had grown more oppressive and ominous, and there was such a

stillness everywhere, as if the whole land were waiting for something to pounce . . . something . . . as if a great beast lurked
beyond the dark forest, waiting to leap upon a soft and defenseless
land, as Indians did on the lone cabins of the wilderness. Abraham
wished that something would break that deadly calm.

The clouds churned. They climbed like curtains up the sky until
the afternoon sun was suddenly hidden, and then they didn't appear
quite so black, though the sky actually darkened the land until it
seemed almost night.

Tommy whimpered. "Pa, I'm skeered," he whined, and clutched
Abraham's pants leg.

"Nothing to be feared of," his father said absently, patting the
little boy's black hair. "Just a storm coming up. Be over soon and we
can get back to work." They started up to the cabin, where he
could see Mord and Jo standing in the dark doorway, anxiously
watching the sky and waiting for the two to join them in the only
shelter they had.

The clouds were like night. Then Abraham heard a low, ominous
sound of the wind coming far off, away in the distance, roaring like
the falls of the Ohio, long before you came to them, roaring like the
waves he had seen once at Scituate. And off in the far forest he could
see how the maple leaves were turning inside out and shining like
silver as the wind struck and pushed and lifted and churned, and
sent tatters of broken leaves high into the dark air. It was only early
afternoon, but Abraham and his sons could hardly see each other in
the gloom. The boys were quiet and scared, watching, and Abraham
knew that their hearts were pounding hard, as they wondered what
would happen, and would it be a whirlwind to kill them all and
wreck the house. They'd heard of these terrors—how a twisting
wind, dark as night, swooped down and tore trees to bits, and picked
up cabins and threw them like toys down in another place, smashed
to flinders like matchwood; and how folk were hurled high in the
air and came down burst and dead wherever they lay.

Now the wind was coming nearer and they crouched to meet it,
and knew that the animals out in the forest were crouching, too,

and the birds in the trees—numberless creatures in dens and tree
hollows and hideyholes, crouching against that wind. There was a
bright slashing of silver lightning that streaked up and down and up
and down over the blue-black sky; and the thunder was rumbling far
off, down in its throat at first, as if it just threatened; now coming
closer, as if it meant business at last.

The wind hit the cabin so that they could feel it give, could feel
how those oak and walnut logs shivered in their fibers under the
great push, and then let the intruder come ranting through the open
windows and the door and blow out through the cracks which Mord
and Jo hadn't finished chinking with handfuls of wet clay and wood
chips. The wind blew suddenly cold, cold as in early winter, and
the heat seemed suddenly washed out of the sticky-hot day, leaving it
icy-feeling and refreshing to their perspiring skins. And the wind, as
if it was a procession of might, went on its way and again left that
emptiness, that waiting.

But now the wind came again and it was all about them in earnest.
The trees were bending and slashing this way and that, the wind and
the trees roaring. Boughs broke and came down, but so noisy was
the wind and so loud the thunder that those in the cabin couldn't
even hear the sounds of breaking trees. The thunder was all about
them and the lightning was terrible.

"What if it hits the cabin?" said Jo to Mord, loudly so he'd be
heard.

"Guess there's nothin' to do about it, one way or the other," said
Mord, watching the storm, "nothin' but pray, I guess. That's what
Mammy would do, and I guess she's doin' it now."

Then the rain came in a vast white sheet, enwrapping the cabin in
spray and water, dimming the forest, blurring across the fields and
lowlands, filling the little runs with foaming water and making the
creek rise fast.

The storm slackened off after a while. The worst was over. They
could hear the thunder grumbling away into the east, the wind and
lightning with it, and the world lay dripping and soaked and glad to
be alive. A robin sat on a wet bough and sang a rollicking spring song,

then flew down to gather mud for a new nest.

Tommy let go of his father's britches leg at last and went to the muddy doorstep.

"Look, Pa, a rainbow!" he cried. And there it was, a reassuring bright bow of light arching over the blue-black clouds which were retreating into the east.

The brush would be easier to get out now in the softened earth. The air was so cool that working would be a pleasure.

"Get busy on that there chinking, boys," Abraham ordered. "Tom, you come with me. You eternally think you have to pitch mud balls instead of plastering that clay in the cracks. You come along and leave Mord and Jo alone. You're big enough to pull switches. And Mord," Abraham added as he stepped out of the door, "don't you dast to touch that gun of mine!" He pointed to the long Kentucky rifle leaning in the dim corner of the cabin.

"No, Pa, I won't," Mord promised, though Abraham knew he loved that rifle gun and would have liked nothing better than the chance to use it.

Mord watched his father and little brother go down the slippery slope to the corn patch they were clearing, then he returned to his tiresome work of smearing handfuls of wet clay in the hollows between the logs, and packing in wedges of split chips.

Half an hour later Mord almost jumped out of his skin when he heard the short, sharp explosion of a gunshot.

Nobody ever came around here, or hardly ever. Mord and Jo plunged to a window and saw Abraham stretched out on the muddy earth, Tommy crouching near him. A Shawanee brave, his rain-wet feathers drooping, and a silver crescent gleaming against his bronzy bosom, was bending over Abraham's body. Mord turned white and a wild clutch of fear squeezed his heart. He whirled on Jo.

"An Injun's got Pa!" he whispered fiercely. "Skin out the back way and run to the fort for help. Fast as you kin, Jo!" Josiah, pale as a dogwood blossom, climbed out a rear window and raced without a word over the hill, tearing through the mud and wet as fast as his thin legs could take him. The Injun'd got Pa. . . . The Injun'd got Pa. . . . A sob was climbing into his throat but he didn't dare cry now.

Mord wiped his muddy hands on his pants and swooped up Abraham's forbidden rifle gun. He cradled the smooth stock against his cheek, stuck the barrel through a hole he hadn't chinked, aimed steadily at the bright crescent dangling on the Indian's chest, and fired. Mord had never shot anything bigger than squirrels with the old flintlock Abraham let him use, but this bigger game wasn't too big for him. He saw the Indian crumple and fall down on top of Pa, and Tommy tumbled over backward and lay with his knees drawn up and his arms over his face, as if warding off a blow of a tomahawk.

Mordecai caught a glimpse of two more Indians—at least two more, though the woods and thickets could be full of them—hiding in the brush, and he was reloading when men from the fort came at a gallop over the hill.

"Down there!" he gasped, pointing. "There's more of 'em!" There were shots and yells, and when it was over another dead Shawnee was bleeding on the ground, and his companion, struck by a rifle ball, lay kicking convulsively near by until dispatched with a second shot. And that was the day that Mordecai Lincoln ceased to be a boy and became a man.

CHAPTER NINETEEN

Deserted and hopeless with the blank eyes of its unfilled windows looking out on the half-cleared land and on the fields which would never know the green feathers of corn planted by Abraham Lincoln, Esquire, the cabin stood alone.

When the burying was over and Abraham was gone forever, Bathsheba sat with dry eyes and limp hands and wondered what to do next. Dan Boone and Rebecca had come to the services, and Rebecca pityingly had tried to persuade Bathsheba to come with the children to Maysville, whence the Boones were moving, but Bathsheba could not bring herself to do so. Yet what she was to do puzzled her. To complete the half-finished cabin and move into it was impossible. To go back to the other cabin near Green River was intolerable. It was still too remote from the settlements, and it would be immeasurably more dangerous to a lone widow and her brood of young ones, even if they could manage to farm the place alone. They could stay on at Hughes Station, folk told them kindly, trying to ease the bitter pain of the killing, but Bathsheba would not stay any longer than need be. She had already remained at Hughes Station far too long; daily the little cramped cabin seemed to grow more ugly and impossible. Bathsheba wanted a home of her own. She wanted her own land, her own furniture and fixings, a decent place for the silver candlesticks and the silver spoons, a place of safety for herself and her children.

Momentarily she toyed with the idea of going back to Virginia.

Her kin in Charlottesville would give her sanctuary until she should buy a piece of land with the money Hananiah would pay back, now that Abraham was dead and his estate must be settled. She had seen little of Hananiah, however, since the burial.

But she put the thought of Virginia out of her mind, firmly and forever. Abraham had been so determined to make his home in Kentucky, in carving out for himself and his children a piece of wild land and taming it to suit himself and them—she couldn't go back on him now and run away to the safety and sweetness of the Valley of Virginia. Not now, not while Abraham's body lay in the Kentucky earth and one day would become part of that earth itself. But if he just hadn't given Hananiah that money, the only money she had in the world until the farms were sold; and she'd prefer to keep the farms as a dower for the children.

Bathsheba went determinedly, then, to the little strong box to get the note Hananiah had signed. She'd take it to him now while her courage was up and demand payment. But there was no note. Frantically she riffled through the few papers in the box. No note! The light-fingered Hananiah had managed with his usual skill to spirit it away, and there was no evidence to say that he possessed the money belonging to Abraham Lincoln's widow.

Sudden tears boiled up into her eyes and rolled scalding down her cheeks before her impatient fingers wiped them away. She would not pity herself, Bathsheba scolded fiercely, grimly. She would not.

And then calmly she knew what she would do. For years upon end, the Lincolns had sheltered and fed and humored Hananiah, had loaned him money and hadn't demanded payment, had babied and coddled and waited upon him. Hananiah had a piece of land on Beech Fork and a fine cabin, and he had her money. And now he could take care of his kinfolk.

Bathsheba and the five children moved in one day when Hananiah was out. The door was locked, but Mord found a large window which he could open, and they all climbed in, Bathsheba, too, laughing a little with the children at how funny she looked pushing her bundles of bedding and her silver candlesticks and spoons through the window, and then scrambling in herself, with Mord pulling from the inside and Jo pushing from the outside. Bathsheba was smaller than they were; she managed. The horses and cows they tethered at the barn. And so the Lincolns were all there in the cabin when the door opened and a most startled Hananiah walked in. He stopped dumbfoundedly in his tracks. Bathsheba, with satisfaction, could not remember ever having seen him so taken aback, the fluent Hananiah so lacking in words, the debonair Hananiah so utterly stricken with surprise and chagrin.

"How do you do, Cousin," said Bathsheba levelly, standing small before him, her heart pounding in her throat, and her hands, held so lightly before her, at their old nervous trick of digging thumbnails into palms. "We've no home, you know, and so we've come to you. You have so much room, I know you'll be glad of the chance to give us shelter. The boys will help with the work and I'll be your house-keeper, Hananiah, if that will please you. I know you've always paid me the compliment of liking my cookery." She was still too gracious a lady to mention the embarrassing fact of all the countless meals he had eaten at her house.

Hananiah, struggling for composure, swallowed hard.

"Why—why—yes, surely, Cousin Basheby, surely you are most welcome until you have secured a place of your own. Until then, do make yourselves comfortable."

"I'm sorry, Hananiah," she said slowly, patiently, a chill coming into her level voice. "I'm sorry, but until you pay back the money you owe me, now that Abraham is gone, we shall have to stay here in this house and make it our home. I have no money to go anywhere else. It's the only thing left for me to do. The other house isn't finished, and that Green River cabin is too remote. Hananiah, whether you like it or not, here we stay!"

She had him there and she knew it. He knew it, too, and he squirmed inwardly at the fix he'd let himself in for. He really didn't think Bathsheba Lincoln would do a thing like that to him—move bag and baggage and five noisy young ones into his fine new house, when he'd been planning all along to take himself a wife and settle down. He'd never persuade a wife to come in with a parcel of indigent kinfolk. Well, his inner self remarked casually, you know what you can do, don't you? Yes, he knew, but he'd be hanged if he paid back all that money. He'd find a way. Hananiah Lincoln always managed, somehow, in the tightest spots, to find a way.

His handsome face cleared. "Right you are, Cousin, and welcome to stay as long as you like," he said jauntily.

"When can you pay back the money, Hananiah?" Bathsheba pursued relentlessly. Really, he thought, she wasn't quite ladylike to take such an interest in money and talk about it brazenly like that to a gentleman. He brushed his sleeve and picked off a thread.

"I don't know what money you're talking about, Basheby," he answered casually.

Bathsheba looked him straight in the eye.

"I mean," she said, still levelly and coldly, "the forty-five hundred pounds which Abraham loaned you to buy this land and build this house, at three per cent. You know what I'm talking about, and trying to evade it won't help you a bit, Hananiah Lincoln. This piece of land and this house, fine though it is, never in the world cost that much money. And I want what you owe me!"

"You must be mistaken, honey," he said genially, smiling in his old jaunty way. "Abraham didn't loan me any money and I certainly have no intention of giving money to you, whether you are under the delusion that I must or not. Your grief must have turned your head, of a truth. And please do not harp on the matter. It is very unbecoming a lady." And Hananiah virtuously pursed his mouth and went to his bedroom and softly closed the door.

But it could have been a resounding crash of noise, for in it Bathsheba knew the truth. She sat down heavily on the cherry-wood chair which had come by river boat down the Ohio. She suddenly felt old and defeated and helpless and frightened, and very much alone. If only Abraham were here . . . if he were only here to hurl the lie back in Hananiah's flashing white teeth and make him pay what he owed.

"Mammy," said tall Mord quietly, smoothing her hair with his big hands. "Mammy, never mind. Jo and I are big enough to work and we'll see that you're taken care of, you and the girls and Tom, too, till he gets big enough to work out. Never you fear, Mammy. Long's I'm here, I'll see that you're taken care of." There were tears in her eyes when she stood up and kissed him softly on his brown forehead. Yes, Mord was there and she felt inexpressibly comforted. Everything, somehow, some way, would come out right.

Hananiah thought that Bathsheba surely would feel uncomfortable at her position in his household and would go away after a bit. But when a year had passed since Abraham's death and still she stayed and showed no intention of moving, he put it up to her again.

"Cousin Basheby, when do you expect to move out of my house?"

"Never, Hananiah," she smiled at him with composure, sure of herself now, "till you pay me the money you owe us." Let him see how it was to have unwanted guests. He had camped with the Lincolns for a long enough time.

He flung out an expletive which Bathsheba gave no sign of having heard. She returned to the big fireplace to tend a roast of venison hanging on the spit. He followed her.

"Listen to me, Bathsheba Lincoln," he flared, for the first time losing control of his temper. "You are a shameless creature to impose yourself and your brats in my house! This day next week I am going to marry a lady who will not think kindly of me if I bring her into a house full of kinfolk. I'll thank you to get out before then!"

"Not until you pay me the forty-five hundred pounds, Hananiah," she said calmly.

He stamped out of the kitchen and she heard the big front door slam so hard it shook the house. Let him, she thought with satisfaction. Not a step would she stir from this house with her children until she was ready, until she had that money safely in her pocket again, to take care of her and her family.

The wife Hananiah brought home the following week was a pretty little thing with fluffy red hair and bright blue eyes. Bathsheba greeted her soberly and with dignity, and took in with a quick, comprehensive glance the lady's fine clothing and her soft white hands. No need to ask it—the new Mrs. Lincoln never had worked very hard in her life, hadn't split much wood for the stove, probably never had made soap and hackled flax and carded wool, nor milked cows and spun yarn, nor done the thousand-and-one jobs a pioneer woman must do.

"Now in Richmond," Sarah Jeffrey Lincoln would say in her high, thin voice, piddling with her corn pone, "*we* always had white raised bread, and there were always plenty of slaves to do the work. My, Mrs. Lincoln," she'd say in a wondering, complaining sort of way, "I don't see how you work so hard and keep your figure, I really don't!"

Hmmm, thought Bathsheba drily, no danger of you, my fine lady, losing *your* figure through hard work. Rather the other way around, getting soft and fat through doing nothing. Sarah Jeffrey had come down the Ohio to Louisville; she had always managed to avoid work when it presented itself.

It didn't last long. The children annoyed Sarah. Bathsheba annoyed her. Everything annoyed her.

"I will not stay in this house another day!" cried Sarah Jeffrey Lincoln shrilly, haranguing Hananiah while Bathsheba could not help but overhear. "Mrs. Lincoln's always here, always bustling about in that vulgar way she has, and the boys—'Niah, I simply cannot *stand* those boys, that awful Mord in particular. He all but insults me every time he opens his mouth, honey, he really does. And Tommy—truly, he came up for no reason at all yesterday and kicked me—yes, kicked me on the ankle! For no reason at all. They've got to go, every blessed one of them!"

"Now, Sarah, listen, I can't turn them out. They're Cousin Abraham's own wife and young ones . . ."

"Yes, you can, or I'll go out myself and never come back," the woman shrieked.

"Listen, Sally, honey, you don't know the whole business and I can't explain it to you now," he soothed, keeping his voice low, but Bathsheba heard. "But if I turn them out, we'll lose forty-five hundred pounds. *Now* do you understand?"

"Then let's go somewhere else till they get tired and go away," she wailed, pouring tears into his coat front.

And that is what happened. One morning a few days later, Bathsheba found that Mr. and Mrs. Hananiah Lincoln did not come to breakfast, and their room was empty, their clothes gone.

"Let them go," Bathsheba said with satisfaction. "But here we stay!"

CHAPTER TWENTY

Men lived and men died. They fought with the Indians and they fought with the forest. And year by year, as the buffalo and the Indians followed more remote trails westward through the retreating wilderness, the great roads they had carved through the Kentucky country grew brighter. The Buffalo Trace and the Warriors Path, Boone's Trace and the Wilderness Road—over these great trails, beaten out by millions of feet and stained with living blood of Virginians and Carolinians eager for new land in Kentucky, more folk came to settle in the land beyond the Cumberlands. And on and on, always beyond where new settlements grew, beyond the mountains, beyond the Kentucky meadowlands, across the Ohio, across Indiana, over the ancient crossing on the Wabash, across the Illinois prairies to the Mississippi . . . and beyond . . . beyond . . . with the buffalo and the Indians always a little way ahead and, when they could, the Indians turning a little and fighting back.

George Rogers Clark and his militia came to Hughes Station in the autumn following Abraham's murder and asked for donations of money and goods so that he and his men could pursue the Indians and sweep them out of Kentucky. Something had to be done; Kentucky couldn't exist in such imminent fear of Indians. Bathsheba wanted to help, but she had little of any use to soldiers . . . little except the gun. The fine rifle gun of which Abraham had been so proud and which he would not let Jo or Mord touch; the gun he'd cared for so lovingly; the gun which Mord had used to shoot the

Shawanee who had killed his father.

Bathsheba took it down from the mantelpiece and held it, heavy, in her small hands. The cool metal of the barrel struck a chill through her veins as she touched it; the smooth walnut stock, satiny to the touch, held only revulsion to her. It was a fine rifle gun. George Clark might find good use for it.

Bathsheba said nothing about her actions until they were finished and beyond revoking. She saddled a horse by herself and mounted, holding the gun across her lap as she rode, a rapt, far-off look on her serene face. Bathsheba rode to Hughes Station and dismounted, still holding the gun. The big gates were open; other folk were coming with contributions for General Clark and his men. Bathsheba Lincoln held the rifle in her hands and walked to the center of the enclosure of Hughes Station. She was so small that she had to look up at General Clark's kind, ruddy, harassed face, and she knew at that moment that she had done the right thing.

"Sir, I have brought a rifle gun for your men," she said, laying it in his hands and curtsying. "This is the rifle gun which my son used to kill the Shawanee who had just murdered my husband," and thus mildly explaining the potent weapon she had bestowed upon him, she turned away.

"Wait, Madam," said George Rogers Clark, putting out his hand to detain her. "Tell me about this gun. It is a fine, well-cared-for rifle. Tell me . . ."

"There is little to tell, sir," she said softly, looking up at him again and finding courage in his gentle face. "Except that my husband, Abraham Lincoln, carried this rifle gun from Virginia up the Wilderness Road. He shot Indians with it; he defended two parties of travelers. He would never let his sons touch it, but that day . . . that day when the Shawanee crept up and shot him as he worked in the new field, his eldest son, Mordecai, for the first time used this gun and killed the Indian. He will be angry with me for giving it away, but—but I think it should be used to defend other people from savages. It will be more useful thus than hanging over our mantelpiece and being used only sometimes by Mord. But he will be angry. . . ." Her glance strayed to the growing pile of arms and food which had been contributed to the Cause, and she took heart again. "Please take it, sir!" she urged, and smiled at him. He bowed deeply and looked after her admiringly, as her small, trim figure walked quickly to the gates of the stockade and, without help, mounted her horse.

Mordecai was heartbroken when he found out what she had done.

"But, Mammy—that was *my* gun now! Pa wouldn't ever let me use it while he was living, but now I'm his oldest son and I ought to have it! That was *my* gun and you'd no right to give it away!" For the first time in his life he looked in anger at his mother, as if he hated her.

"Mord,—Son, I'm sorry," she began lamely, but taking heart as she remembered General Clark and the heap of contributions, she went on bravely, "The gun will go out to defend us from Indians —not only us, but all the people in Kentucky who need to be defended. It is selfish to keep it. Some day you'll have a better gun, Mord. But now, take pride in having given it to a noble cause! If you think of that, you won't feel like this. Forgive me, Son, but I thought it was best to do it." He did forgive her, after a while, but she knew he was deeply hurt.

It was not until nine years later that the Indians were ousted from Kentucky, but their presence in the land did not prevent thousands of people from coming up the trails. No horrors, no hardships, no heartbreaks seemed to keep them back.

And it happened that in 1784, two years after Abraham Lincoln, Esquire, and his family came with their few household goods and their cow and their best horses and the silver candlesticks from the farm in Virginia, that another Virginia family also came up the Wilderness Road and settled not far from where the Lincolns ultimately lived.

Joseph Hanks' family was simply one of the many groups who came. Like the Virginia Lincolns, there was nothing distinguished about them. They were not like the Boones and the Floyds and the

MORD AND JO PLUNGED TO A WINDOW AND SAW ABRAHAM STRETCHED OUT
ON THE MUDDY EARTH

THE DEED WHICH ATTESTED THAT HE HAD PAID FOUR DOLLARS AND SIXTY-
THREE CENTS...ON HIS TWO HUNDRED ACRES...IN CUMBERLAND COUNTY

Logans, bent on fighting the wilderness. People like the Hankses and Lincolns were the followers, the ones who came in after most of the fighting had been done; they were anxious to build new farms and new homes to replace those they still thought about back in the Valley of Virginia. Few among them were forward-pushing enough to make a name for themselves.

Joseph and Ann Hanks came with eight of their nine, mostly grown-up children. They traveled the usual hard way and experienced the usual difficulties and the same fear of Indians, the same bone-sagging weariness at the end of each long, grinding day. And the baby cried a lot. Her grandmother, Ann Hanks, was worried, though Lucy, little Nancy Hanks' mother, wasn't overly concerned.

"She's just a-cuttin' teeth," Lucy said gravely, and gave the baby a piece of peeled sassafras to chew. Nancy Hanks was less than a year old when she traveled in her mother's arms up the same wilderness path which little Tommy Lincoln had traveled not long before, on his mother's horse.

The Hankses and the Lincolns were neighbors, as neighbors go in a newly opened country. Nobody lived close to anyone else for a while, though in Elizabethtown and Springfield and Lexington and Louisville, people were gathering together in towns that might amount to something, everyone began to say. There were many lone cabins, however, out in the rolling, grassy hills, many houses and families living solitary lives in clearings of the forest and along the streams. The youngest Hankses and the Lincoln children sometimes may have played together when the mothers and grandmothers paid a call on one or another, and sat drinking dittany tea and eating corn pone while the young ones rolled and frolicked out of doors.

Nancy, who had no father, lived in her grandfather's house until she was nearly ten. Then it was that old Joseph, ailing for several years, laid down his weary bones for the last time and died. Ann, mourning, sold her household goods or divided them among her children—she had never accepted Kentucky as Bathsheba Lincoln had—and traveled the long, lone, hard way back to her kinfolk in Virginia.

Three years later, in 1796, when one of Ann's daughters, Betsy, married Thomas Sparrow, they adopted young Nancy. And because, as the years passed, they never had any children of their own, Nancy became their own beloved daughter. A few years later they adopted Polly Hanks's son, Dennis, who was born in 1799.

Nancy Hanks, learning how to be a fine seamstress so that she could earn a living when she was grown, stayed on in the home which had adopted her, and when she was old enough to be aware of boys, she looked sometimes with speculative eyes at Tom Lincoln, with whom she had played boy-games when she was a child.

The years had passed, and Tommy Lincoln was twenty when Nancy Hanks was only fifteen—and having trouble sewing the fine seams which Betsy insisted she learn to do painstakingly well. Tom had looked at a lot of girls. It was funny, he sometimes thought, trying to slick his unruly black hair down with bear grease so it would look neater, how for years he couldn't abide the sight of girls with all their silliness, except his little sister, who might amount to something, after all, because she could climb trees and pitch pebbles almost as well as a boy could. And maybe Mary was pretty good, too. Mary had always looked after him when his mammy was busy. But now he liked to look at other girls and take them to meeting when the circuit rider came around, and to sociables.

He gave no thought to Nancy Hanks, who seemed very young in his eyes, though she was tall for her age and a pretty thing, dark-eyed and rosy-cheeked, gay as a thistle-bird sometimes.

Tom admired Sally Bush over in Elizabethtown, but he didn't get very far with her. Sally was a sparkling lass who could speak her mind sometimes too briskly for a young fellow to enjoy. Sally was strong and she was pretty as an apple blossom, and Tom began to get it in his mind that when he got a little older he might ask her to marry him.

To Bathsheba, grown thinner and more frail-looking, yet still more enduring, it was rather incredible to see her children so big, so grown, so independent. Somehow she'd done it—had managed to rear them all decently, and now it was up to them, mostly. It hadn't been easy, and she never could have done it without

Mordecai's steady mind and his unending help—Mord hiring himself out to every farmer who would have him, Mord farming the
acres around Hananiah's house, Mord giving her the money to pay
the lawyer when at last she sued Hananiah for the forty-five hundred
pounds, which he still managed to lie out of so that she never got a
penny and could not legally possess the house and land. Mord was
the one who could goad the lazy Tom to stir himself when he grew
old enough, prodded him into working out with Mord and Jo, and
at the same time letting Jo tend to his books whenever he got the
chance. Bathsheba would always feel a deep grief about the fair-
haired Josiah. He wanted education so, and she hadn't been able to
let him have it.

"Joey," she had said one day, with worried eyes on his earnest
young face, "I wish you could go to the Seminary over at Lexington
this fall, but I don't see how we're to get the money, I really don't."
And she had seen the strength shine back of that face when he said
quietly:

"I wish I could, too, Mammy, worse than anything in the world,
but I know I can't, just yet. We haven't the money, and if I was in
school, I wouldn't be here to work. Don't worry, Mammy, I'll get
my learnin' someway . . . somehow. There's a teacher over at the
Seminary who'll let me borrow books; that'll help." But it would
always hurt her that Jo couldn't have the education he ought to have.
Might be he could become a great man, a lawyer, perhaps, or a doctor
or a statesman, had he the learning. None of the others could have
education, either: but it was only Josiah who seemed to care whether
he had it or not.

Kentucky was blossoming. The Indian troubles were over.
Quickly, only a few years after the Blue Licks tragedy and the
clearing out of the Indians following the Treaty of Greenville, there
were stores in Lexington and Louisville and Danville which adver-
tised all the fancy commodities anyone would want. There was even
a newspaper in Lexington, and it was in that town that the Jockey
Club held horse races every summer. Tom pined to see a horse race,
and once in a rare while he earned enough extra money to pay his
way. For days after that he could talk nothing but horses.

CHAPTER TWENTY-ONE

THE LAST TEN years of the eighteenth century remained vividly in Bathsheba Lincoln's mind. In these years came the end of many of the ancient struggles of the past, the triumph of the white man and his development of Kentucky and the lands beyond. In 1792, Kentucky cut the connecting tissue which had bound her to Virginia as a county—a county which had paid its taxes beyond the mountains, had had to carry its lawsuits to Richmond or Williamsburg, had had to live by laws made for Virginians which did not always fit nor suit Kentuckians. The Kentuckians framed a constitution at Danville and on the first day of June there was a good deal of shouting and racketing and firing of guns and rejoicing as Kentucky became a state in the growing union of the United States of America.

In that same year Mordecai Lincoln came of age. Mord was twenty-one, and as his father's eldest son it was up to him to settle the estate . . . what there was of it, Bathsheba thought bitterly, thinking again of the money Hananiah owed them and which would have made life so much easier and kinder. But there were at least the two farms, and since by law they would have to be sold so that they could be divided among the heirs, Mord set about putting them up for sale. Because of inflation of land prices, the farms brought far more than Abraham originally had paid for them.

When it was all over and the money was distributed fairly, Mord —Bathsheba's steady mainstay—Mord decided to get married. With his share of the money he bought a piece of land and got it partly cleared and a good cabin built before he asked Mary Mudd to be his wife. Mary was a pleasant girl; Bathsheba liked her. She could see that the two would get on well together. The new farm wasn't far from where Bathsheba still lived on Beech Fork, so that she saw Mord and his wife often, yet her house seemed surprisingly big and empty with one of the brood gone.

In 1795 Tom Lincoln served for a month in the Kentucky Militia under Lieutenant George Ewing but nothing much was happening and the militia kept him for only a month. That same year, off in the Ohio country, however, a good deal was going on, and finally the news came sifting in—how Mad Anthony Wayne had fought the Battle of Fallen Timbers in '94, and the Treaty of Greenville had been signed the following year. This ended the Indian troubles once and for all . . . or enough to let folk go out and settle in Kentucky or the Northwest Territory without living in deathly fear of Indian attack. Boats could travel safely down the Ohio and could bring in freight and people in greater numbers than ever before.

In 1796 the Wilderness Road was cleared and leveled enough to be called a wagon road. Whereupon, Dan Boone, hurt to the core that his offers of help in developing the road he had laid out in 1775 were spurned, suddenly concluded that Kaintucky was too crowded for him.

"Not enough elbow room," he said, tight-lipped and grim, to anyone who asked why he was packing up his wilderness gear, ready for a trip somewhere. "I'm goin' out to Missouri where I kin breathe!" In '98 Daniel Boone stomped out of Kentucky and never came back to it alive.

It was in 1798 that Tom Lincoln went off, too, somewhat against his will, to work for a spell for his Uncle Isaac at the Watauga settlements in Tennessee.

Bathsheba had been getting a little bit desperate about what to do with Tommy. He simply wouldn't work on the farm with Jo; and though he could be a good carpenter, he would not apply himself. He liked to lounge at the village store and get into fights, and with his great strength he usually whipped anyone who took him on. But

Bathsheba didn't like it, and she spoke to Mord about her problem.

"I remember Pa talkin' about Uncle Isaac," said Mord reflectively, while Mary, his wife, dandled their second child on her knee. "He lived on a big farm down in the Watauga country in Tennessee. That's not awful far from Cumberland Gap. Uncle Isaac never had any children and I reckon he'd be glad of some help if we could send Tom down there. Might be good for Tom; help him grow up and be a man. Anyway, we could try it."

"Don't want to," said Tom, preoccupied in watching a dogfight out in the dusty road. "Rather stay here."

"You got to, Tom!" spoke back Mord sharply. "You're naught but a drain on Ma. She can't take care of you *all* your life; you got to learn how to work for a livin' and it looks like you won't get at it here. So you go down to Tennessee; likely you'll fancy it when you get there. And I'll let you take my roan mare, if you'll treat her good."

That changed the color of the argument, as Mord knew it would. Put a horse in the conversation and Tom Lincoln went in that direction.

"You mean I can take her for a year, Mord? You mean it? That's mighty handsome of you—yes, I'll go if I can take Shawnee!" cried Tom, a light in his eyes at last.

The mare made the trip suddenly exciting and to be desired. The family was going to make him take that journey down to Uncle Isaac's—he'd only intended to hold out a suitable length of time, but he knew he'd have to give in to them at last—but the horse made him want to start at once. He got to thinking how much fun it would be to ride off like that down the Wilderness Road on a mount he could call his own . . . for a little while, anyway. Just give him time, though, and he'd own horses and he'd own land.

Bathsheba kissed him good-by and marveled to see how sturdy and fine her twenty-year-old Tommy looked on the roan mare, his saddlebags all packed neatly and his rifle over the saddle, just like a pioneer going off into the old wilderness.

"Be careful, Tommy," she urged, patting Shawnee's satiny rump with her thin little hand, "and don't get into any fights or any trouble. Give our greetings to Uncle Isaac and tell Aunt Martha I'd enjoy a sight of her, if ever they're up in Kentucky. Now mind your manners, and behave yourself," she admonished once more.

"Yes, Ma," said Tom impatiently. "Good-by!" And he was off with a wave and a flourish of his gun. The dogs tore after him in a streamer of enthusiasm, tonguing and barking until they couldn't stand the dust in their mouths, and then came back with tongues lolling and dripping, to collapse in the shade of the porch.

Tom Lincoln, traveling the improved trail of the Wilderness Road, backtracked down Kentucky. He wondered where it was that some of the things had happened his Pa had told about, stories the family had retold till he could never forget them: how they buried the little baby in a hemlock log, and where it was that Jesse Hamilton's horse fell backward into the laurels, the time the Injuns tried to steal the packhorses. Many's the time he had heard the stories; but if Mord and Ma hadn't talked about it sometimes, Tom would have long since forgotten, for the memory of his father was dim.

Now, riding across the ford of the Rockcastle, which low water made an easy thing to do, and climbing the laurel trails—the laurels stood back, now, from the cleared pathway—and seeing, far and blue and massive down the Pine Mountain valley, the staunch bulk of Cumberland Mountain with the Gap as a saddle, Tom recalled more than he thought he knew. Or perhaps it was a remembering of things and events he actually had never known, the inner consciousness of a people who were born to roam, to battle the wilderness and follow, forever and always, strange trails and echoing hills . . . trails and hills which were never too strange, but always held an element of familiarity, as if they had all been seen before.

Tom Lincoln rode Shawnee to the top of the Gap, reining in his mount when he reached the crest. He felt like a conqueror when he got there and looked down into the valley which was part of Virginia and part of Tennessee, with the blue mountains stretching away in tiers and layers. Back of him lay the green sea which was Kentucky. Once, Kentucky had been the land of adventure for the

Lincolns of Virginia. Now a Kentucky Lincoln was coming to Virginia and Tennessee in pursuit of his personal land of adventure.

Tom didn't exactly enjoy his year in Tennessee, and it wasn't exactly adventure. When he thought back on it, it was just pure hard work and he could have had that at home. But at least he earned some money by it, while at home they expected him to work for nothing. So it was that in the spring of 1799, when Tom set out for home on Mord's roan mare, Shawnee, he felt himself much more a man than when he had started out to Tennessee, if for no other reason than that he had money in his pocket, wages he'd earned himself. There was that sum from the sale of his pa's farms, but Mord was taking care of that till Tom came of age. And he'd *be* of age, too, when he finally got home again. He would be really rich with all the money he had and all that was coming to him. He thought with satisfaction that he might buy himself some land as soon as he got back and maybe start clearing and building pretty soon. He was old enough to get married and maybe Sally Bush would have him. But there were a couple of others he'd been sweet on, too—Rhoda Gideon and Cassandra Smith and Fortune Wyatt—they were all nice girls. He'd decide which one later on.

At the smoky, low-ceilinged inn in Bristol he stood around self-consciously for a while after he had eaten his supper, to watch men playing cards. They were silent, intent, skillful men who said little and played intensely. Tom was especially fascinated with the way a tall, darkly handsome, lank fellow with thin white fingers shuffled cards with a careless ease which Tom envied, and dealt cards so lightly they were like butterflies flitting to their proper places.

"Howdy, young man," the card player said carelessly, looking up suddenly to find Tom's eyes fixed upon him. "Like to join the game?"

"No, thanks," Tom said, flattered that he'd been noticed. "My ma never lets me, and I don't aim to start now. But I'd admire to watch if I don't bother you."

"Not at all, not at all," the tall man said, smiling, but with just a trace of puzzlement in his face. When the game was over he came over to Tom and bought him a mug of ale. By the time they'd finished their drinks the stranger had got out of Tom all about the year in Watauga and the fact that he had money and was thinking of buying a piece of land before it went up any more. But Tom, with the inborn caution of wilderness men, had not told the stranger his name, nor had the stranger, with that politeness of the wilderness, asked him. But in a mannerly, roundabout way, the stranger finally got it out of him.

"Son, haven't I seen you somewhere before?" the stranger asked, peering intently at Tom's dark face with the thatch of black hair which would never stay down.

"Not's I know of," said Tom, doing his share of peering by looking keenly at the stranger, who had a vaguely familiar, faintly disturbing look. Something like Mord, he concluded, and that was funny!

"Well, I'm Tom Lincoln of Nelson County, Kentucky," he began. And Hananiah Lincoln's heart gave a defensive leap.

Why, it's little Tommy Lincoln who always loved the horses so! Basheby's littlest boy—Abe's boy—grown big and broad and a man!

With an effort, Hananiah got hold of himself.

"Well, now, that's queer, isn't it?" he said genially. "My name's Lincoln, too—I'm your Cousin Hananiah, second cousin, I guess you'd call me, son. Remember Cousin 'Niah whose horse you always wanted to ride? I recollect I helped you up over the rocks of Cumberland Gap the time you fell and skinned your nose. And I lived at your house for years."

Tom beamed. He'd heard talk years ago about 'Niah but he hadn't listened very closely and he didn't remember much—guess 'Niah hadn't been up to Nelson County in quite some time.

"Now, I know just the land you ought to buy!" cried Hananiah enthusiastically, clapping Tom companionably on the shoulder, so that he felt warm and happy in the company of this fine man who was his blood kin. "If you weren't kinfolk, I wouldn't let you have it, but seeing as how you're my own cousin's boy—"

"Where is it?" asked Tom eagerly. This was just what he needed

—help in knowing what to buy.

"Over in Cumberland County," said the tall man. "It's a newly opened area, just above the Tennessee line, not much settled there yet, but it will be soon, oh, it will be soon, just like the rest of Kentucky, and you'd make a good investment to put your money in it. Now I'd sell this land to you at two hundred dollars even, if you'd be interested."

"Well, now," said Tom in disappointment, fingering the money in his pocket. "I didn't want to spend it all on the land, and I ain't even got two hundred dollars besides. I only got one-fifty, and I got to take some home to Ma. She'd be disappointed if I didn't, and likely Mord would whale into me if I didn't bring none of it home."

"I'll make it a hundred, how about that?" suggested Hananiah agreeably.

"Is it your land?" asked Tom timidly, still holding on to the money in his pocket.

"Well, not exactly," admitted Hananiah, looking over Tom's head, "but since I know the country better than you, and won't be leaving here for some time, you could pay me and I could take care of the deal for you."

"Well, that sounds all right," said Tom cautiously, trying to make his slow mind tell him what to do. But if Cousin 'Niah said it was all right, it must be. He smiled suddenly.

"All right, Cousin 'Niah, I'll do it!"

The next day the notary witnessed Tom's signing of the deed which attested that he had paid four dollars and sixty-three cents as the first payment with interest on his 200 acres of land in Cumberland County. Hananiah promised to pay the remainder later.

Tom looked admiringly at his signature. He had signed it bright and clear in a fairly good hand—that was *all* he could write, but he'd practiced enough to put down his name almost as well as a Seminary man.

Cumberland County, Hananiah said, was off to the west and it was several days' travel in those parts, where it was heavily forested and the trails were poor. It would be better if Tom went on home and came back some day to look over his land at leisure, because just now he'd want to get back to see his mother.

With Hananiah's promises in his ears and the deed to the first land he'd ever owned carried proudly in his pocket, Tom Lincoln went home. The day he arrived, with a great hullabaloo from the dogs, Bathsheba ran to the door to meet her big son. He had a weathered, sturdy, grown-up look which was good to see.

Tom was aglow that evening when he told of how he'd bought a piece of land down in Cumberland County. He was a landowner himself now, that he was!

"Who sold you the land, Son?" Bathsheba asked fondly, though she'd hoped he would bring home more than a mere fifty dollars from his year's work.

"You'd never guess, Ma!" he cried, grinning. "It was Pa's Cousin Hananiah. I'd never have known him, of course, but he knew all about us. He asked for you and hoped you were keeping well, and wondered whether we were still living in this house. He was especially interested in the house, though I don't know why, do you?"

Bathsheba Lincoln didn't know when she had felt more aghast. That man . . . he eternally popped up whenever a Lincoln had some money in his pocket!

"Tom Lincoln!" She dropped her hands helplessly and groped for words, exasperation struggling with her calmness as the absurdity of the situation came over her. "Don't you know what that man did to you—to us—haven't you sense to remember? *Haven't* you heard us talk about it, and *can't* you remember how we came here and crawled like thieves through the window when he was out? No wonder Hananiah was interested in the house! It's legally his. He's a swindler, Tom; he robbed us of all the money Pa saved from selling the farm in Virginia, and now you've let him have *your* hard-earned money. Really, when I think of it, I—I could scream!"

Tom's broad brown face looked disturbed. "Oh, now Ma, don't take on so. I got the deed and I reckon it's all square and proper. See how good I signed my name, and Cousin 'Niah guarantees to finish up the payments for me, since I won't be down there for a spell. Cousin 'Niah's a real nice man; I don't see why you're so down on him."

Everyone always thought that—Hananiah Lincoln is a real nice man—Bathsheba was shrieking inside herself. She knew she'd never get anywhere arguing with Tom; when he got an idea in his head, it was there to stay.

"All right, Son," she said tightly, wrinkles sharp between her blue eyes. "But if I were you I'd go down and investigate that land and make sure it's there. I wouldn't put it past him to sell you a chunk of air or a nice neat length of the Mississippi!"

CHAPTER TWENTY-TWO

THE CENTURY that had brought independence to the United States was drawing inexorably toward its end. It was in 1799 that America knew peace. France declared war against Austria. Napoleon Bonaparte went to Egypt and brought back to France strange curios from ancient tombs—and left a portion of a defeated army buried in the sands. The Dutch fleet was delivered to the English in August, and George Washington died on December 14, while the nation he had fostered mourned his going.

That autumn Crazy Meg, down by Carter's Fork, was predicting disaster. Every time she came to the village with her basket of ginseng and sassafras and mandrake root she set everyone by the ears with her wild talk. Crazy Meg had been beautiful once, Bathsheba remembered, seeing that regal profile which scarcely was spoiled, even though Meg's teeth were all gone and her cheeks were sunken and wrinkled. Meg was tall and thin but there was something splendid in her face which was fitted to her bones so that the good structure showed through. She was still handsome, and there was something infinitely piercing and probing in her pale gray eyes.

"Where did she ever come from?" asked Mary Lincoln, who had come home from the village store with tales of how Crazy Meg had been carrying on. "She's a queer old thing."

"Queer she is, and right enough," said Bathsheba severely. "But she's not to be laughed at by any member of my family, and I want you to remember it! Meg McAllister and her husband came up the

Wilderness Road with Pa back in 1780, the first time he traveled to Kentucky to look for land. Even then, he said, she acted a little queer, always rambling around at the edge of camp each evening and not helping much with the work as the other women did, but eternally looking for plants and herbs to put in her bag. He said she sometimes got off her horse to pick a flower, and when they were all struggling up Cumberland Gap, Mrs. McAllister gathered flowers among the rocks! He said she was very beautiful, too, but none of the men dared look at her, she was so cold and stern; and her husband was a silent man, with a black look for any man he caught staring at his wife, or any woman who snickered at how Meg wandered about. People said the McAllisters were gentry from Scotland, but I don't know. Surely they acted different, Abraham said."

"They'd no right to act high and mighty when they were on the trail together with other people. They should've done their part," said Mary sharply.

"They did," said Bathsheba calmly. "At least Mr. McAllister did. He brought in meat and he helped put up tents and take care of the horses. He did more than his share, Abraham said. And you can't blame her for being queer; they say she had twin sons who were killed by Indians down in Carolina, and then—then she and her husband were at Bryans Station when the Indians attacked, and she watched her man go out and he never came back alive. They wouldn't let her see him; they said he was too dreadful to look at with the top of his head torn away by a tomahawk. But she went clean crazy after that. So don't make fun of her, Mary, because she's a poor pitiful creature."

"But Ma, you ought to *hear* her carry on!" cried Mary in defense. "I don't know whether to laugh at her or be scared, and I don't think other folk know, either."

Bathsheba herself was in the village store the next day when Meg McAllister walked with royal bearing into the dusky room which smelled variously of deer hides, furs, tallow, bacon, cinnamon, coal oil, and sweating men. It was hot for autumn. Bathsheba smiled at Meg and said politely, "Good morning, Mrs. McAllister," and nodded at her.

The tall woman looked down at the small figure of Bathsheba Lincoln. "How do you do, Madam Lincoln," she replied. "I would advise you to go home at once and prepare to meet your doom!" she added with a rising note of fervor in her dignified voice. Bathsheba looked nonplussed and stepped backward a bit.

"Yes, yes, I say to you all," cried Crazy Meg, "and it's got to be true if I say it! The next century will never get here, that it won't! We'll never live to see the nineteenth century. It'll be the end of the world when the century ends, and that I'm saying to you all!" Enoch Lambert was weighing her herbs, to exchange them for bacon and sugar and coffee. He paused to watch her with speculative eyes, just as he had watched her when she was one of the party he had joined on the Wilderness Road long ago. "Mark you well and prepare to meet your Maker!" she shrilled. "Put on your ascension robes and set your affairs in order, for none of you will live to see the new year!"

Stout Callie Smith looked a little frightened and dropped her basket with fresh eggs in it, and in a fluster got down on her plump knees to salvage the unbroken ones. Enoch's fox hound came in and sniffed at the broken eggs.

"Shoo, get away!" cried Callie in vexation, pushing at the sleek black-and-tan hide. The dog wagged his tail so that it thumped against her arm and he lapped her face with a friendly tongue. "Shoo!" she cried again, trying to rescue the eggs, and shoved him hard. He fell against the tall form of Meg McAllister, who stepped backward one step and in stentorian tones, pointing to the door, boomed:

"Out! Out! Out, vile cur!" and the dog slunk out as if he'd been whipped.

The boys snickered and tried to snatch roots from her other basket without her seeing them. But even while she was ranting, Meg knew what was going on behind her back, and reaching around suddenly, she cracked the nearest boy on the head. He yelped and the others scattered, and Crazy Meg was at it again.

"You'll rue the day you lived lives of sin," she cried, her eyes flaring and bits of saliva foaming at the corners of her mouth. "The end of the world is at hand and the Angel Gabriel is getting ready to blow his trumpet and call us to the Judgment Seat. Get ready, all ye sinners, I cry out to you, *repent!*"

Nobody quite believed her, and yet, each in his heart was a little bit disturbed at the prophecy. Millie Bolting and Hephzibah Wyatt both bought a couple of lengths of muslin from Enoch Lambert, keeping it secret from each other, and carried it home to make into an ascension robe—though neither Hephzibah nor Millie knew exactly what an ascension robe looked like.

More than one person listened seriously to Crazy Meg's ranting, and then went home and looked over his accounts and paid some back debts he'd left hanging, just in case. Though if all were consumed in the ending of the world, certain canny souls reasoned, what then would be the use in anyone's having anything paid back? Still, it would ease a man's own conscience and at the Seat of Judgment it would be a good thing to present a clear record.

It was a warm autumn, unseasonably warm, and so dry that the corn withered in the fields long before it was time. Grass on the rolling hills was sere and crisp, and cattle found little greenery to graze.

"It's the beginning of the end," prophesied Meg McAllister at the store one day. "It's too hot and you know it; it's the beginning of a greater heat which is about to consume us all!"

"How's the world a-goin' to *come* to its endin'?" asked Frank McCullough, the Indian fighter with a clean red scar around his head where a Wyandot had tried to scalp him. Frank wasn't afraid of much any more; he'd survived everything fearful that could befall a man in Kentucky. His dark face openly sneered at the tall, thin, wild-eyed woman. "How're we goin' to know when it's startin'?" he added.

"*How're* you to *know?* Hah!" cackled the woman, looking him through and through. "*You'll* know! The days'll be filled with heat and at night you'll *see* the fire! The stars will fall out of their places and the sun will drop down nearer, and nearer, and nearer, like it's doing now to make it so hot for October—oh, yes, you'll know!"

"THE SKY'S AFIRE!" SHE GASPED. "WE'RE—ALL GOING TO BE—CONSUMED..."

IT REARED BACK ON ITS HIND LEGS AND PAWED THE AIR, AND AS IT DID SO
NANCY SLID OFF AND DROPPED INERT ON THE GROUND

It *was* pretty warm, everyone agreed in subdued tones when the old woman had walked down the road, stately and queenly as always, never hurrying, with her big white shawl wrapped around her shoulders, even though the day was hot and sultry, like July.

Tom came home and told Bathsheba and the others about it at supper time. He'd met Frank McCullough, who had told him what Meg had added to her prophecy—about the sun and stars coming down until they ignited the earth. Tom was pretty sober about it.

"She's a crazy old thing," said Nancy virtuously, breaking a piece of corn pone with her slim fingers and putting it into her mouth. "It isn't right she's allowed to roam around like that."

"She's harmless enough, I guess," said Mary judicially. "She's never hurt anyone, has she?" Mary could never see evil in anyone.

"No, but you can't tell about a crazy woman—she might up and kill someone before you'd expect it."

"Don't talk about Mrs. McAllister like that!" Bathsheba spoke sharply. "She's had plenty of trouble to make her the way she is. She's harmless."

"People are afraid of her, though," said Jo, spearing another piece of pork from the platter. "They say she's a witch and will throw a spell on them, if she so fancies. I don't see how she manages to live, though, without a man to do for her, in that old cabin down on Carter's Fork. And now she's so set on this end of the world business, it's making everyone around here as nervous as a herd of deer."

October went and November was passing, and it was still too hot, though folk could tell it was cooling off a bit at night.

On the evening of the fifteenth of November, Bathsheba was sitting with her hands in her lap, thinking and resting, for the candle light hurt her eyes now when she tried to sew or mend at night. The door banged open and Tom, with a clatter, burst into the room.

"Ma!" he cried, his face white, his eyes wild. *"It's the end of the world! It's come!"*

She was on her feet, her hand at her mouth. His alarm was contagious.

"What . . ." she gasped. Jo came pelting down from the loft

and Mary and Nancy ran from their room. "What is it?" they all cried.

"The end of the world . . . she was right. . . . Crazy Meg's right—it *is* the end—the whole sky—it's a-burnin' up! The stars are fallin'!" Tom was panting. His eyes were bright with fear. Bathsheba in a split-second thought he looked like a cornered buck with the dogs at its throat. She fought for calm.

They stumbled after Tom to the doorway, and Mary screamed at what she saw. Nancy sank down and covered her eyes and moaned, over and over. Bathsheba caught hold of the door jamb to steady herself.

Yes, the world looked as if it were coming to a fiery end. Over the dark canopy of the night burst long trails of fire, great flaming streamers of stars tumbling everywhere. They were radiating in all directions from a central point, until the whole sky seemed full of falling fire. In vast silence, the night seemed to be igniting the world to a certain destruction.

The panic the Lincolns felt was in the hearts of everyone that blazing night in November, when the century was drawing to a close and it looked as if humanity itself were approaching its end. From the direction of Wyatt's cabin down the road, the Lincolns could hear shrieks, and they saw lanterns bobbing over along the creek in the direction of Boltings' farm.

The night was a terrible thing to see—beautiful, awe-inspiring, fearful, beyond the realms of earth and its understanding. The Lincolns could not tear themselves away to hide their eyes, all but Nancy, who would not look, but crouched moaning on the doorstep.

Bathsheba was breathing in little panting gasps; tears ran down Mary's face. Tom stared grimly, as if transfixed at the sight of approaching doom. Only Jo seemed to be less afraid, more in command of the situation.

He put his arm around Bathsheba. "They're shooting stars, that's all they are, Ma. Don't be afraid."

Bathsheba nodded mutely. "I'm not afraid, Son," she whispered. "I've gotten over being afraid of anything, I think . . . there's been so much . . . but this—no, it's not fear . . . exactly. . . ." He could feel her trembling.

"They're shooting stars," he repeated. "I read about 'em in a book I borrowed over at the Seminary last year. I don't know what makes 'em fall in such numbers like that—never knew they'd light up the sky so awful—but I'm sure that's what they are. You'd better come in and sit down, Ma."

But Bathsheba Lincoln would not leave the doorway. Her heart was easing a little in its frantic pounding, however, as she saw that no one had been consumed in the celestial fires and that so far none had fallen to the earth. But they were so unutterably silent. She thought that if they made a noise, a sizzling, a banging, they would not be as terrible. They were so like the hand of God Himself in their silence.

The Lincolns in their doorway heard a screaming, a high, piercing, keening sound coming down the road.

It was enough to make the hair rise up on your head to hear it, it was so frightful, so full of desperate terror and despair and madness. Madness—that was it.

"It's Crazy Meg!" cried Jo to Tom.

They ran down to the road—it was light enough to see by with all those falling stars lighting the sky—and tried to stop the apparition which came pelting through the dust, her long gown tattered and her white shawl flying like wings behind, and her white hair streaming as she ran. Her face was pale as milk and drawn with inner terror.

"It's—the end—of the—world!" she gasped, not looking at the two young men. "The sky's afire! We're—all going to be—consumed . . ." And she eluded Jo and Tom and went on and on and they could not stop her.

The night passed, and the morning sun, with a November paleness, came serenely over the wintry hills. The Lincolns had gone to bed very late and Bathsheba was sure she would not be able to sleep, yet she did. And the morning was as placid as any other morning of her life, so that she could hardly believe in what had happened the night before. Nothing had been consumed, nothing was burnt, except the dryness of leaves and cornfields, and that was caused by the hot sun of autumn, not by falling stars at the end of the world.

Jo and Tom went early to see what they could find out in the village and were gone a long time.

"Well," said Jo grimly, when they came back home at last, bursting with news. "Every living soul, it seems, thought it was surely Judgment come at last. Millie Bolting put on her ascension robe and stood on the shed roof, waiting for the angels to take her by the hand and lead her up to Heaven. She got tired along about midnight and sat down because she was getting a mite giddy from looking up at the sky so long. And pretty soon she got drowsy, and next thing she knew she'd rolled clean off that shed roof and landed in the pig pen and broke her arm. They're having a time with her this morning. She's out of her head!"

Bathsheba clucked her tongue. "What a shame," she said. "I'll take her some broth; that might make her feel better."

"And Hephzibah Wyatt put on *her* robe and waited out in the damp all night long, and I guess she feels pretty used up this morning. I hear she wrung all her chickens' necks last night to save 'em the agony of being burned up, and she would have knocked her cow in the head if she'd been strong enough with an ax. The cow is lucky —but Millie doesn't have a chicken to her name!"

"What did you hear about poor Mrs. McAllister?" asked Bathsheba, remembering with an inner shudder the woman's awful shrieks the night before.

"Well, I guess it *was* the end of the world for her," said Jo soberly. "They just found her at the edge of the creek a little while ago, drowned. Fell in and hit her head on a rock, I guess. It's too shallow even to cover her body, but she fell face down and drowned there in six inches of water."

Bathsheba and her children stood a moment in silence, each thinking his or her own thoughts about the death of this woman who had traveled the Wilderness Road and who had lived alone for so long in a land unfriendly to her.

Tom finally broke the silence. "Well," he said cheerfully, with just a tinge of regret, "I guess since it ain't the end of the world, after all, there's nothin' for it but that I got to go over to Elizabethtown today and take that job of work Ruel Johnston offered me!"

With the blazing skies of the Leonid meteor showers of November, 1799, and with the death of George Washington in December, the eighteenth century drew to a close, and folk who could write would now head their letters "1800."

CHAPTER TWENTY-THREE

SALLY BUSH was prettiest when she was angry. Tom Lincoln hardly heard what she was saying, so busy was he admiring the way her cheeks flamed and her black eyes snapped. Her dark hair was thick and rich and she kept it in such pretty curls. Tom always thought it would be fun to slip his finger into one of those curly tendrils and see what it felt like around his finger—and then he'd grin to himself when he thought how she'd slap him good for taking such a liberty.

"Tom Lincoln, I'll not go out with you till you clean up!" She was saying briskly in that clear voice of hers, but he was faintly aware that her voice had a sharp edge. "You're a sight to behold, and you can't lay it to anybody but yourself. Look at you—tatters in your trousers' knees, as if you'd been down on your marrowbones praying for salvation, when I know right well you haven't, not you! Look at your hands—filthy as if you'd been grubbing weeds with your fingernails, and hadn't bothered to wash for weeks, let alone clear the mud out from under the nails. You're a pure disgrace, and you needn't expect a decent girl to go anywhere with you. You go home and wash that hair of yours, too—it's greasy and black as an Indian's —and get spruced up some, and then I'll see about going to meeting or to the social with you. And not till then, Tom Lincoln!" And Sally Bush, after this long speech, flounced down off Lambert's grocery store step with her basket, ready to go home.

"Sally," said Tom in a moon-calf voice he hardly knew was his own. "Sally, will you marry me?"

Sally Bush turned around at that and stared at his face. Was the
fellow crazy? Didn't he know what she was talking about all that
time? If she wasn't one to walk out on a summer evening with him,
why would she up and *marry* him?

"Tom Lincoln, I think you're daft!" she cried helplessly, trying not
to laugh, those eyes of hers all but talking. "You'd be the last man
I'd ever want to marry, and you must be crazy for thinking so—or
drunk, though you don't look it. Didn't you hear a word I was saying
a moment ago? About you're not being neat enough and clean enough
for a decent girl to go out with? And it's nobody's fault but your
own, and you know it! Mary's been at you ever since you were a
little tyke, as she's told me many a time, and yet you were always
the one who had to go dirty because you grubbed in the mud like
a hog soon's she got you cleaned up. You can't blame your mother,
either; Mrs. Lincoln's a clean, neat, pretty woman, and none of the
others look like you. You're just a wild Indian and till you get around
to neating yourself up a little, no girl will look twice at you. Marry
you! Why, Tom Lincoln, I . . ." At that she ran out of words, and
while Tom stood there with his big hands hanging limp at his sides
and his rough black hair jutting over his forehead and standing up
every which-way on his head, and his pants knees showing skin un-
derneath, and his gray eyes following her with admiration and love,
Sally Bush, laughing inside herself, went off down the path to her
father's house. When she was out of earshot, she let go and whooped
with laughter. That Tom Lincoln!

Tom went home and peered at himself in his mother's looking glass
which Jo had brought her from Lexington.

"Ma," he called to where Bathsheba was sewing a little shirt for
one of Mord's young ones. "Ma, I don't think I look so all-fired bad,
do you?"

"Whatever are you talking about, Tommy?" she said absently,
holding the little garment up to measure the seams. Her eyes weren't
so reliable now and she wanted to be careful that this was right. "I
s'pose you do look all right. Who said you didn't?"

"Sally—you know, Sally Bush. She's pretty, ain't she, Ma?" And

Tom Lincoln's broad, dark face glowed when he thought of Sally. "Well, she said I wasn't spruce enough to go to meetin' with her, and she wouldn't marry me, neither!"

"My soul, did you ask Sally Bush to *marry* you, Tommy?" cried Bathsheba, startled enough to lay down her sewing and peer over at her child, who was so suddenly grown up.

"Yes, Ma, I did, but she wouldn't have me. Not if I was the last man in Kentucky, she said." Tom looked a little sheepish. "But *I* don't think I look so bad, do you, Ma? And it ain't every man my age owns a horse and two sections of land, is it now?"

Bathsheba frowned. She looked sternly at her youngest son, who was so unlike the others—not steady and calm like Mord, ready to take any responsibility that came along; not like Josiah, who was eager to learn things; not like Mary, who was grown-up when she was a young one because of the cares that were put upon her so early; not like Nancy, who was a bright butterfly of a girl, smart and dancing and pretty. Tom was different. He wasn't as tall as Mord or Abraham, but he was sturdy and so terribly strong, and his chest was big and powerful. Tom could be a good carpenter—he was handy with tools—if he had a mind to, but he was still lazy. The way it looked to her, she sighed, Tom was born lazy and had never got over it.

"Thomas Lincoln, listen to me!" his mother said crisply, and bit off her thread with a decisive snap of her teeth. "Sally is right. You *are* dirty, you *are* shiftless, and the sooner you know it the better, so's you can ask a decent woman to marry you and be an example to your children. Now go out to the well and you scrub yourself; heat some water and wash that hair of yours—you look filthy as any Shawnee I ever saw—and get some clean pants. Hand me those torn ones. I'll patch 'em for work, but don't you ever again dare ask a young lady to go sparking when you wear clothes like that. Now scoot!"

"Yes, Ma," said Tom meekly.

Tom Lincoln did spruce up some, the girls around Beech Fork and Elizabethtown remarked, but Sally Bush always stayed clear of him. The day she married Dan Johnston, Tom felt terrible. He felt empty inside, curiously without any real feeling at all, only that lost space in his middle. He got on his horse and rode off into the countryside, on the March-mudded roads, down around Green River where the old cabin was that his Pa'd built. Tom rode past Hughes Station and went out to see the place where Pa'd been shot, and it seemed so long ago he could only remember it as if in a dream. He knew that he had been there, but he didn't know whether he really remembered it or not, the others had talked of it so much. He was feeling so mournful that anything sad and gloomy did him good, and he lingered a long time beside graveyards and felt a kindly sympathy for all those with broken hearts who lay there.

The brief but deep spell of desolation somehow lifted from Thomas Lincoln's soul as the days of March showed the bright signs of the coming of spring, which arrived early that year. Tom felt it burgeoning as if a yeasty sort of stuff were making him grow and spread himself. After Sally Bush married, and when he came home from his solitary ride, saddle-weary and as mud-spattered as his own horse, he found that he had lost some of the thing with which all his life he had felt weighted. He couldn't have explained what it was—Tom Lincoln wasn't free with words; they didn't come easily to his mouth—but he felt a new vigor and a new resolve. His mother had harped for years on his applying himself to a job and making something of himself. Now he set to work in earnest to become a good carpenter like his father; maybe even better than his father.

Tom's cronies around Lambert's store didn't see him very much after that. He was working for Ruel Johnston in Elizabethtown again and turning out creditable pieces of cabinetry. He learned to love the feel of smoothly planed wood, learned to recognize the kinds by their smell, by the subtle or strong scent of the wood itself —the nutty smell of walnut; the sweet, maple-sugary scent of raw maple; the rank odor of oak, a different kind for every oak; the good, clean, resinous smell of Kentucky pine. And it was a pure delight when he could take lengths of fine wood and turn them into beds and chairs and cabinets which people would buy. Tom had found himself. There was a new confidence in his level gray eyes, a firmer, more determined line to his mouth. Thomas Lincoln, Esquire, was a good carpenter and cabinet-maker and his mother was proud of him. Never, she thought many a time with satisfaction, never did a woman have five such fine and deserving children as she had . . . she and Abraham.

Bathsheba was now living with Nancy and her husband, Bill Brumfield, on a big farm down a little way from Beech Fork. She had finally left Hananiah's borrowed house, to which she had no legal right. But neither could he eject her from it until she was ready to go. Her children were grown. All but Tom were married and had left her. Now Tom himself was living in Elizabethtown. When Bathsheba Lincoln took her few possessions and locked Hananiah's door for the last time, there was a meditative look in her fading blue eyes, and a curious little quirk in the corner of her mouth. Well, Cousin Hananiah, she was thinking, the quirk deepening, I wonder where you are and how long it will be before you know that your house is vacant at last. It was kind of you to let us stay—oh, very kind. But I'd still prefer to have my forty-five hundred pounds, thank you! Knowing you, though, Cousin 'Niah, I should think that *you* no longer have that money, either, and that might be some satisfaction. Good-by, Cousin."

At Nancy's house, Bathsheba sewed and knit for the babies and did her share of the work, and sometimes Tom rode out to see her.

It was on a Sunday when he had said all his good-bys and was setting off on the Elizabethtown road when he heard a racket behind him and wheeled his horse to see.

Down the road, dusty even now in the warm sunshine of May, came a wildly galloping gray horse with a figure clinging in desperation to reins and mane. A runaway! The animal was clearly addled by something which had startled it, and was pelting along, wide-eyed, nostrils flaring and foam flying back from its lips. Tom saw it was Nancy Hanks riding. He watched with a calculating eye, and as the horse neared him, he spurred his own mount into action. For a few moments the two horses and their riders raced parallel. The foam from the runaway's mouth splashed back on Tom and his own horse, and then his big hand got the bridle of the runaway and his great strength pulled back so hard that the gray was brought up sharply.

It reared back on its hind legs and pawed the air, and as it did so Nancy slid off and dropped inert on the ground. If the runaway's pawing forefeet came down just there, the quiet figure would be crushed.

Tom yanked sharply to one side, and the gray's forefeet plunged down in a harmless spot, and then Tom was off his own horse and down on his knees in the dust.

"Nancy, honey—Nancy, wake up, are you all right?" Tenderly he picked her up out of the dust and carried her to the grassy embankment where violets made a purple carpet, and laid her down gently and wondered what he could do and how badly she was hurt. Off and on for years he had seen and talked to Nancy Hanks, but he thought that now he saw her for the first time. Looking at her like that on the bank of violets, Tom felt his heart thudding in a way he'd never remembered before. Passively, her horse grazed on the sweet spring grass.

Nancy opened her dark eyes and looked straight up into Tom Lincoln's worried face.

"Oh, Tom," she murmured, a little color coming back into her lips. She put her hand to her eyes as if to shut out the memory of her wild ride. "I—I—my horse got scared back there—a bear came out of the brush and crossed the road right in front of us, and she near threw me. And then, for a while—I thought I'd never get off alive, Tom. My feet had slipped out of the stirrups. . . . You always did know how to handle horses, didn't you, Tom?" And she smiled wanly and tried to sit up.

He smoothed back her tumbled hair without thinking how bold he was, and seeing her like that, weak and white and laid out almost like a corpse among the spring flowers, he felt a curious wrenching twinge inside himself. How pretty she was, how young and pretty and weak and in need of someone like him to take care of her forever and ever. Nancy, Nancy . . . he was crying inside himself . . . Nancy, you're mine . . . you belong to me. . . .

"Come, I'll help you up," was all he said. He took her two smooth hands in his and got her to her feet. She swayed against him and he held her tenderly in his arms and laid his lips on her shining dark hair. "Do you think you can ride?" was all he asked her.

"I don't—know," she murmured. "I think I'm afraid, Tom—if my horse sees that bear again, I don't know what she'll do."

"Never mind," soothed Tom. "You ride with me. My mare'll take us both, easy, you're so light, and I'll lead yours till we get back. You bound for the Sparrows'?"

"Yes, Tom," she said, a little more color in her face as he lifted her to the saddle and then swung himself up behind her, with his arms around her slender waist so she wouldn't fall. "I finished a job of sewing for the Berrys and promised Aunt Betsy to come home soon as I did, before I started on Fortune Wyatt's wedding clothes. Aunt gets so lonesome when I'm away, with only Dennis and Uncle Tom for company."

Tom Lincoln rode his horse slowly and carefully as if she carried a precious load, and led Nancy Hanks' gray until they got to the Sparrow cabin. He helped Nancy down and she winced when her feet touched the ground.

"Oh—my foot!" she cried. "I must have turned it!" So he helped her into the house, and explained to Betsy Sparrow what had happened.

"The poor child!" cried Betsy, her spare body all angles as she tried to help. "Do lie down, child—you're all over dust—here, I'll take off your slippers." Betsy knelt down to take off Nancy's dusty shoes, and exclaimed at the bruise swelling the slim ankle.

"Ouch!" cried Nancy involuntarily when her aunt touched it. "That hurts!"

Tom was beside Mrs. Sparrow then, each getting in the other's way and resenting each other's presence. Nancy's ankle was certainly swelling and it was turning purplish with a bruise. Tom hurt to see her in pain. Betsy stood up and bustled about to get hot cloths to bathe

the ankle.

"She'll be all right, Tom," Betsy said briskly, pushing Tom determinedly toward the door. "You go on home, young man, and I'll take care of her. Dennis, go out to the gate with Tom and see he has a drink from the well before he goes."

Tom found himself at the door, Dennis Hanks grinning like a monkey beside him. Tom turned sadly to look back at Nancy, laid out so weakly and in pain on the bed. She smiled at him and waved her hand.

"I'll come back tomorrow, Nancy," he said gently, and to her alone. But Betsy Sparrow heard, and glared at him as she tested the temperature of the hot water.

"You in love of Nance, ain't you?" The gamin Dennis grinned, peering up at Tom's set face.

Yes, that was it. That was the stirring he felt, the pain he knew at sight of her pain, the wanting to hold her and protect her and keep her from being hurt or unhappy ever again.

Suddenly he smiled back at Dennis. "Might be!" was all he said.

Tom Lincoln came back to the Sparrows' cabin the next day and stayed so long that Betsy grimly had to invite him for supper. Nancy's ankle was better, but she couldn't stand on it yet. Tom carried her to her chair at the table, though Dennis guffawed into his grimy hands and Tom Sparrow smiled, and Betsy looked grimmer than ever. Her thin, lined, Puritan face was bleak, her greenish eyes lit with the stark fear of losing her loved Nancy. This Tom Lincoln, he was going too far . . . before she knew it he'd have taken Nancy away from her forever and ever. Betsy Sparrow, who had had so little in her life, so few material possessions, so few people to love and to love her, clutched Nancy to her bosom whenever the thought of giving her up reared its ugly head.

"Have some pone, Tom," Betsy said sternly through thin lips. Her hands suddenly were shaking, and in irritation at her weakness, she thrust them out of sight under the table until they were quieter. But Tom hadn't noticed. He was too busy eating, too busy looking at Nancy Hanks, sitting so sweetly across the table from him.

Tom neglected his work that week. It had been neglected enough, Ruel Johnston pointed out one day, when Tom had had to take a week off to serve on a jury, and before that he'd had to help guard prisoners because he had been sworn in as a deputy. But although he was at work in Elizabethtown this present week, Ruel Johnston said that he might as well be off in China, for all the good he was doing.

Mainly, Tom was spending so much time riding back and forth between the Sparrows' house and Elizabethtown that he had to quit work early in the evening and was tired in the morning; it was easy to relax over his workbench and just dream a bit.

Nancy could walk now, but Betsy wouldn't hear of her going to the Wyatts' to sew for another week at least. It was as if Betsy Sparrow saw what was coming and wanted to hold on with clutching hands to the girl who was all but a blood daughter to her, and the dearest, brightest thing in her meager, hard-working, unrewarded life in the wilderness. Thomas Sparrow was stout and amiable and easy-going, and whatever Betsy wanted was all right with him, but he couldn't do anything about keeping Nancy away from Tom Lincoln. They'd miss Nancy, of course, when she went off and was married, but that was what happened to girls in anyone's family; or if they didn't get married, it was something of a disgrace to know your daughter didn't please the sight of any man and was saddled on you for good. He couldn't see Betsy's fright; women were silly things sometimes, Tom Sparrow solemnly agreed with himself. After all, the girl was twenty-three, and that was getting along in years —most females in the back country were married long before they were twenty and had three or four young ones long before they were as old as Nancy. He didn't see why she had been so choosy— she'd turned down several offers, he knew, and goodness only knew how many more he hadn't been told about.

But Nancy Hanks had been in no hurry. She didn't want to marry just any man who asked her. She couldn't have said who or what she was waiting for, but she knew she hadn't found the man yet. Nancy Hanks liked most people; she could see their goodness and not their evil, could see the best in a man and not his worst. With her big, beautiful, trusting eyes, she could look up at a man and make him think he was a pretty fine specimen of manhood, and then he'd likely go out and prove to himself and to her that he really was like that. Her laugh was kindly and never malicious. Women felt drawn toward her, too. Her strong, slender hands with the talented, tapering fingers could bake and sew and mend, and could soothe an aching head or an aching heart with equal ease. The flame in Nancy Hanks kindled a like flame in all those she gazed upon.

Tom came to call on a sweet May night when the black locust trees in the grove were all in bloom with chains of white flowers, so richly perfuming the air that it lay heavily in the dusk, poignant with the memories of every other springtime in America.

Tom and Nancy walked out into the scented dusk and climbed the hill where the locusts stood dripping with blossoms, and watched the hawk moths whirring silently from flower to flower. Tom held Nancy's slim hand in his big hard one. He could fairly taste the perfume on his lips as he bent and laid them on Nancy's in a long, deep kiss that was like an embrace.

"Nancy, honey, will you marry me?" he murmured, holding her close in the May night.

There was a long pause. Then she pulled her head back and looked at his face.

"Yes, Tom, I will—and thank you kindly."

"When, Nancy, when?" he cried. "When?"

"Oh, June, maybe," she said, holding her voice steady so he wouldn't see how much she loved him or how thankful she was to know that he loved her, too. "June's a nice month for a marrying," she went on conversationally. "I'll talk to Aunt Betsy about it and tell you the day, and you can talk to Parson Head about arrangements. Oh, Tom—Tom—do you really love me?" her voice broke.

"*Love* you?" murmured Tom. "Nancy, I love you so much that I'd—I'd do anything if it was what you wanted and it would make you happy. I ain't rich and likely never will be, but however I can,

Nancy, I'll try to make you happy and never let you want for anything I can provide."

And so in June, 1806, Thomas Lincoln, twenty-eight, married Nancy Hanks, twenty-three, and the Baptist minister, Reverend Jesse Head, clearing his throat a mite, said the words that made Nancy Mrs. Lincoln. Bathsheba wept a little, as she had wept at the marryings of all her young ones, more especially since Tommy was the last and there wouldn't be any more marryings until the grandchildren were grown. Bathsheba loved weddings, but the oldest grandchildren—Mord's four—would be a while coming to the preacher to have the words said over them.

It was comfortable having grandchildren, Bathsheba was thinking, her gray hair arranged in a puff under her bonnet, and her best black Sunday dress, which Jo had got for her in Lexington, draped neatly around her knees, as she watched the ceremony. She hoped Tom and Nancy had a lot of children.

It made her feel good to have them around her; grandchildren gave her a sense of continuity, of a reason-to-be, the why-and-wherefore of her own life and Abraham's. If they'd had no children, and no grandchildren, and all the generations yet to come, there would have been no reason for their terrible struggles in the wilderness, no reason to accept the death of her husband at the hand of a savage, no reason for her to have remained in the wilderness to make the life for her family which he had planned with her. The children were reason enough, and the grandchildren were still more reason; she could look off into eternity with her fading eyes and see the long lines of grandchildren unto unknown generations, each fulfilling his destiny in a way which was influenced by Abraham and Bathsheba Lincoln in Kentucky. Mayhap some of them would be great men, and if they were, then they would owe some of their greatness to the grandfather they never knew, Abraham Lincoln, Esquire, of Virginia—and somewhat to her, too, because she had mothered his five children and helped care for *their* children as they came along. Yes, the grandchildren gave reason and meaning to sacrifice which for a little while she could not understand but could only with bitterness accept.

The grandchildren were increasing, too, and when they were old enough she could tell them the story about how she and Abraham came up the Wilderness Road, so long ago, and about the Indians and bears and buffalo and such like. And they'd come, as they were coming even now, soon as they could crawl and talk, calling her "Granny Basheby" in their sweet baby tones. It was nice hearing the name again—Basheby. Not since she'd left Virginia had she been called that by anyone but Abraham and Hananiah. And now it was "Granny Basheby" from Mord's, Jo's, Mary's, and Nancy's children, and maybe there'd be some of Tom's, too, pretty soon, to call her that and climb on to her thin knees and sit on her cupped lap so her bony hands could play with their hair and play patty-cake with their small soft hands.

Bathsheba Lincoln sat and thought. She was little and spare, and she was all bones and gristle, as she often said, but she was enduring. She was fifty-six now, and there was nothing the matter with her, she said, when folk told her kindly she ought to eat more fat pork and put butter on her corn bread so's she could get some flesh on her poor bones. Nothing the matter with her, and she'd likely outlive them all. Her own grandmother had lived past ninety. The women in Bathsheba's family could look for long lives unless the Indians got them first. And the Indians were no bother now, thank the Lord. Tom and Nancy could go off to wherever they would live, and make their home without the fear of massacre which had so darkly colored Bathsheba Lincoln's early days in Kentucky.

The wedding was over, and the infare began. Everyone in the neighborhood trooped to the Berry cabin, where the fiddler played for dancing, and there was food a-plenty for everyone.

CHAPTER TWENTY-FOUR

THERE WAS a big business in coffins in Kentucky. A good carpenter who could turn out a neat, tight, oak box was in demand, and Tom Lincoln had plenty of work, even after he left Ruel Johnston's employ when they could not get along. Tom knew he was a good carpenter, but his temper wore too thin when his employer demanded things which Tom either couldn't or wouldn't do. He was happier working for himself; then when he felt like resting he could rest— for days if he wanted to—and no one was nagging at him to get busy. Late summer, though, was a busy time for a carpenter in Kentucky; lots of people died then. It used to be Indians people were afraid of, and which caused their deaths; now it was typhoid and dysentery which carried folk off, and the milk-sick and chills-and-fever, black vomit and cholera. Summer was a bad time for babies, too, yet winter or summer, the man who could make a good coffin was in demand. Tom could get six dollars for a man's coffin and a dollar less for a woman's, unless she was a big, hefty-built female, and then her box cost the same as a man's. A coffin for a young one was only three dollars. Tom hated to make coffins for children. It was so pitiful to see such little boxes and know the heartbreak they held. Nancy would never come and watch him while he was making a coffin of any kind; it made her feel sad and almost doomed herself to watch him work on such a thing. He would much rather stick to furniture building, though, and it was then that Nancy, when her work was finished in the little two-room house in Elizabethtown, would come and sit in the shavings to watch him and talk while he worked. He always felt he did better on anything he tackled if Nancy was there with him.

All that summer and autumn Tom worked and he got a little money ahead. But he wasn't satisfied with the way they were living. Town was no place for a man to live who'd always spent his time out in the open. Too cramped, too muddy or dusty and noisy, even in a place as little as Elizabethtown in the rolling hills. Soon as the baby was born early next spring, they'd have to move out somewhere, he figured, maybe to that Sinking Spring farm he had bought out south of Elizabethtown several years ago. Yes, that was the place for them to move to. He liked its name, and the queer way the spring bubbled out of the limestone layers down in a hollow of the hills, and then went off again mysteriously underground. He thought about the farm all that winter in Elizabethtown, and in the thinking the farm grew brighter and finer in his mind than it ever had been before or since.

"What shall we name the baby when it comes?" Nancy said idly one day that winter. She'd finished all the sewing she needed to outfit any child, and her hands were idle sometimes now. She wished she could go out to sew for people as she had before she was married. It was a way to earn money to lay by, but Tom wouldn't hear of it.

"Well," said Tom companionably, pausing in the tangle of wood curls and chips where he was making a chair. "We'll call him Abraham because Pa was named that."

"But your brother Mord's oldest boy is named Abraham," protested Nancy. "Won't it be confusing if there's two Abraham Lincolns hereabouts?"

" 'Twon't matter," said Tom stubbornly, his mind set.

"What if it's a girl, Tom?" added Nancy, smiling, her cheek dimples showing.

"Won't be," said Tom positively. You could never argue with Tom.

But on February 10, 1807, the midwife brought a little red-faced girl-child to show Tom, who was busily ruining a half-made table because he couldn't keep his mind on his work, and Isaac Bond wanted that table soon now. Tom would just have to make it over, that was sure, for he kept on gouging and hacking till he should be ashamed of what he was doing. But with what was going on in the other room, he couldn't help himself.

He could hardly believe that the child was a girl.

"You sure?" he muttered, poking a finger at the blanket.

"Sure I'm sure." The woman chuckled. "Ain't no doubt about it. What you goin' to name her?"

"Well, now," said Tom, and scratched his head.

"We can call her Sarah," said Nancy's spent voice from the bed in the other room. "Sarah was the wife of Abraham in the Bible. That'll be a nice name for our daughter, Tom. Isn't she beautiful?"

"Sarah Lincoln. Sarah Lincoln—Sally—well, yes, that'll do," agreed Tom equably, his face clearing. He went in and kissed Nancy, and covered her snugly and warmly, the baby beside her, and then went back to work. He decided he'd have to start on a new table, after all, for Isaac Bond. When a man had a new daughter, he could be excused for working poorly, but he couldn't expect Isaac Bond to condone a ruined table.

Impatient though he was to get out on a farm again, Tom Lincoln stayed with his family in Elizabethtown. Work was good; he had all the carpentering he could do. But he was eternally getting into lawsuits with men he worked for, and Nancy, busy with Sarah, wished sadly that Tom could keep from flaring up in a temper when someone crossed him. Lawsuits were costly, especially when you lost.

There was that dreadful suit which Denton Geohegan brought against Tom late in 1807.

"But Geohegan *said* he'd pay me not only for hewing out those timbers for his mill, but for helping cut and tote them, too, and he only paid me for hewing! I won't stand for it, Nan, I won't, I tell you! I'll take it to court and get my money. This was one of the biggest contracts I ever had, and I won't stand to be cheated!"

"Are you sure that's what the contract said, Tom?" asked Nancy wearily, comforting Sally, who had fallen against a chair where she was trying to pull herself up. Sally couldn't walk yet, but she was getting near it, thought Nancy with pride.

"Of course I'm sure!" he blustered, and he took his case to court.

It was a long suit. Tom won. But Denton Geohegan was stubborn and he still would not pay Tom what was due him, and went to jail instead.

"That's the fair limit!" Tom exploded. "I tell you, Nan, I won't stay in town another day longer! Nothing but dishonesty and lawsuits, and folk not paying you what they promise! Even that land I bought in Cumberland County didn't have a clear title, like Cousin Hananiah said it did, and I lost it *and* the money!"

The Lincolns left Elizabethtown. Tom borrowed a big wagon from Mord and brought it to Elizabethtown and loaded all their belongings in it, and started out into the rolling Kentucky hills. George Brownfield had offered him a job working on his farm near Buffalo, so Tom, though he didn't enjoy farm work, took the job and he, Nancy, and little Sarah lived in a rude cabin in a grove of wild crab-apple trees. Sarah played with the little hard green apples which fell off the spiny trees. But working on a farm for another man didn't please Tom, either. It was as bad as that year when he worked for Uncle Isaac at Watauga. In the autumn, when the work was done, the Lincolns loaded their belongings into a wagon they borrowed from George Brownfield and trundled over the rutted road south to the Sinking Spring farm which Tom had owned and paid taxes on since 1803. Time he got the use out of it, he thought with satisfaction.

It was bright, dry, autumn weather. The Lincolns camped merrily in the lee of a big, cedar-crested hill, close to the spring, while Tom busied himself putting up a rough cabin. He was in a hurry to get it up before the autumn rains set in. He admitted to himself that it was no fancy job of house building, that little one-roomed, half-round log cabin perched on the level part of a hill before it reached the crest. It would be a good spot for a house, though, he judged, because it would face east to get the bright morning sun, and would be sheltered from the north and west by all the cedar trees and beeches, and by the rise of the hills themselves in that direction. Down the gentle slope below the cabin there was the spring, bubbling away with a subterranean gurgle, out of the limestone, across a ledge, dropping off and into a bottomless pit of great darkness and mystery. Nancy was terrified of the spring with its shadowy depths, into which the water fell.

"Tom, it's a hideous place!" she cried, holding on to Sally, who was walking now and was into everything. "How'll I *ever* keep Sally out of it, I'd like to know? If she should fall into that hole, we'd never get her out; it goes down to the middle of the earth, I have no doubt. You can't even hear the water stop falling after it goes over that ledge. I'm scared, Tom. A young one Sally's age hasn't the sense to stay away, and I can't be with her all the time."

"I'll build a good stout fence around the spring," Tom promised, looking a little perplexed at Nancy's acid-toned argument. He could see her point, but he didn't see why she was so upset about it. Ought to be easy enough to keep a little girl-child like Sally out of the spring. Maybe it was because Nancy was going to have another young-one late in the winter; sometimes things like that made women-folk nervous and irritable. That was unlike Nancy, though; she was always so patient and equable. But Tom took time from building the cabin to put up a stout stockade fence all around the sinking spring so that Sally couldn't get in, even if she tried. And of course she did try. The sight of the fence lured her on, and Nancy raced one day to rescue Sally from the top of the fence, where she hung suspended by her homespun gown.

Pale and furious, Nancy went to where Tom was putting on the roof.

"Tom Lincoln," she said sternly, "if you don't find a way to keep Sally out of that spring, I'm going to take her back to Elizabethtown and we'll stay there till you can make it safe for her!"

So Tom stopped work on the cabin and tore out the stockade, and built a higher one, that a man couldn't have climbed over, with a gate so he or Nancy could go in to fetch water when it was needed, and a leather thong to hook over the top picket where Sally couldn't reach it, to lock the gate against her inquisitive fingers.

Winter came on early that year, and what with fixing the fence over, Tom had all he could do to get the roof shakes on before snows came. There wasn't even a door to the cabin, and into the opening where he had intended to hang a good stout door, the winds swirled and carried gusts of dried leaves which settled into the corners. There was no plank floor, no puncheon floor, only hard-packed earth, and there were so many gaps between the bottom logs and the floor that all manner of little wild creatures came venturing in out of the cold. Nancy was always finding a wood mouse in the corn bin, or a late chipmunk, its cheeks stuffed with dried corn, scampering off for dear life through a crack, to hide its loot and then come venturing back for more. If it had been warmer, there would have been snakes coming in, she knew, but it was too late now, she thought thankfully; they were all holed in for the winter. That open door, too, was an invitation for every living thing in the woods and fields to come in and make itself at home. And when, on late autumn nights, the voices of wolves howling to the sailing cold disk of the moon came to her where she lay on her leaf bed, covered with a bearskin blanket, Nancy shivered, but not with cold. She would put her hand out and touch Sally where she lay asleep close by, to make sure she was safe.

Tom finally got around to hanging a big bearskin in the doorway. It was fastened with pegs at the top, and it was tightened at the bottom with rocks which held it firmly, so that cold winds stayed out, and varmints could not come in so easily.

It was a cold winter, for Kentucky. Heavy frosts came early and corn stalks hung grim and bare and rattled in a wind so that they streamed straight out like ragged banners in the gales from the north. The spring water at the bottom of the hill never froze, but a vapor of frost mist rose eternally from it. That winter it was always Tom who went down the slippery slope and over the icy rocks to draw water Nancy needed in the house. He was afraid she might slip and fall.

The dark cedars bent their plumes in the wind, and the ancient white oak, which everyone around there called the Boundary Oak, marking the southwest corner of Tom's land, rattled its thousand branches. It was a cold, long winter. But it brightened somewhat for Nancy in the rude, uncomfortable cabin when Betsy and Tom Sparrow moved into an old cabin down the town road, so they could be nearer to the young woman who was the life and joy in Betsy Sparrow's narrow life. Betsy came almost every day to visit Nancy as the winter wore on, and always she brought something—a pan of corn-bread, a piece of roast venison, some fresh eggs. Nancy was grateful. Tom wasn't working this winter and they hadn't much money left from his summer's jobs.

"Her time'll come soon now," Betsy warned Tom one day in early February when a fresh light snow powdered the hills and the cedars. "You be sure to hurry and get me!"

"Yes, Aunt," promised Tom. "And I aim to get Polly Walters, too. They say she's the best midwife around here, and I want Nancy to have the best I can get for her."

"You won't need no midwife if *I'm* consulted in the matter!" snapped Betsy. "I know everything any granny-woman ever knew; you won't have no need for that Mis Walters, I tell you!"

"Well," said Tom, not looking at Betsy Sparrow's blazing, jealous eyes, "I reckon I'll get her just the same."

Nancy, smiling to herself so her dimples tucked themselves into her cheeks, could have told Aunt Betsy that she was wasting her breath to argue with Tom when he had his mind set on something. Nancy had learned that long ago.

It was a Sunday morning—the twelfth of February, 1809—when Nancy woke Tom and sent him off, blinking sleep out of his eyes, in the frosty, chill light of early day, to get Polly Walters, who lived three miles down the town road. He stumbled in the darkness, trying to find his clothes, fell over Sally's cradle, barked his shin and cried out in anguish, while Nancy lay back under her bearskin blanket and laughed at him between her pains.

"Now don't break your neck riding, Tom," she called after him as he went out the door and fastened down the bearskin so the wind wouldn't come through. It was whipping up keenly again out of the north and he figured it might snow again. Nancy could hear the receding hoofbeats going down the frozen hill to the road, and then she was alone with Sally, who had not yet wakened. Nancy lay quietly, as if she lived that moment in a great globe of shining glass, from which she could see everything as from a far-off distance and could look into the future and back into the past, as if the present had no meaning, and she floated suspended in the globe. Then the pains hit her again and she came back to where she was, but when they were past she felt again as if she were floating, thinking, dreaming, seeing far, far . . .

Polly Walters was there, then, with Tom trying to be useful and only getting in the way, until Polly cheerfully sent him out to see to the horses and feed the cow.

Then Polly Walters called to Tom to come in, and he saw Nancy, worn-out looking but smiling as always when she looked at him, and there was the little new one in the crook of her arm.

He couldn't form the words he felt. He simply knelt down beside Nancy and the baby and leaned his head on her arm. With her free hand she stroked his rough black hair.

"We have a son this time, Tom," she said softly. "And we know what his name is, right enough, don't we?" Tom looked up at her then.

"We'll call him Abraham, like you wanted to the first time—Abraham Lincoln."

CHAPTER TWENTY-FIVE

MORE THAN a year went by after the new Lincoln baby was born, and it was spring, 1810. Breaking ground in the bottoms below the cabin, Tom Lincoln paused more than once on that fine, fresh March day to watch the lines and Vs of wild geese heading north and to listen to their splendid cries.

Those goose-calls, that fresh, mysterious scent in the air, that new color on the maples, that good tillable feel in the damp earth his plow was turning—all of it mingled in an exciting magic so that he could not work. He left the plow in the furrow, while the horse stood patiently waiting and the blackbirds walked over the moist clods to pick out worms, and he went over and sat down under a wild plum tree whose pearl-buds were beginning to burst into fragrant bloom. He didn't understand that unrest inside him; he couldn't think what in the world was the matter with him. Instead of getting properly at the spring work while the weather was so fine, here he sat smelling plum blossoms and watching geese flying north. He could not know of that restlessness which had touched so many of the Lincolns . . . taking them out of New England long ago . . . out of Pennsylvania . . . out of Virginia . . . over the Cumberland Gap and up the Wilderness Road . . . over the Buffalo Trace, and where else? Where else? Surely Kentucky was not the end of the road for the Lincolns. A Lincoln had to move on eventually.

Tom Lincoln lay back and wondered lazily about how land was over across the Ohio. If he had much more trouble with lawsuits over his Sinking Spring farm, maybe he'd see what it was like over in Indiana some day. The Buffalo Trace which his Pa had followed could lead him to Indiana just as it had led Pa to Kentucky, and it went on to Illinois, he had heard, if he wanted to follow it that far. Well, maybe, some day, he mused, but not for a while.

A day like this, though, a fellow simply couldn't get to work on plowing and clearing. He had to *go* somewhere. Then a thought hit him and he sat up. He got to his feet and pelted up the hill to the cabin, where he still hadn't found time to hang a door in the doorway.

"Nancy!" he bellowed, and she came out in a hurry, the baby in her arms and Sally hanging to her skirts. Nancy looked tired.

"What's the matter, Tom?" she asked, alarmed.

"Nothin's the matter!" he cried, beaming. "We're goin' on a trip, that's what we're goin' to do, you and Sally and little Abe and me, we're goin' on a trip!"

"What on earth you talking about, Tom Lincoln?" said Nancy crossly. "Stop that pulling on me, Sally . . . all right, Abe, get down if you want," and she put the squirming little boy, thirteen months old now, on the earth floor. He busied himself with a handful of wood chips.

"Well, it's like this." Tom grinned, calming down some. "We haven't been to see Ma for years. She ain't never seen Abraham, and ain't had a sight of Sally since she was a baby younger'n he is. Now I say we ought to put up a little lunch-dinner and take those two young ones, and go see Ma while she's still livin'. We could stay overnight at Mary's house and get there tomorrow. Come on, Nancy, say you will!"

Nancy knew better than to object to a plan when Tom was like that, so set on it, his eyes shining with excitement because he hadn't been away in such a long time.

"All right," she agreed pleasantly. "You want to go today?"

"Sure, today, soon's we can get ready!"

And so it was that the plow was left in the furrow where the black-birds, glistening in the sunshine, still walked solemnly about picking up worms, and the horse was saddled for Nancy and the baby, while

Tom rode his other horse, with Sally in front of him. They all set off to the northeast, hitting into an old buffalo trace, then into more traveled roads.

Bathsheba Lincoln was sitting by herself in the half-dusk of the Brumfields' big kitchen when she heard horses and voices, and strained to think who they might be. She could usually place voices: those of the children, of the people they had married, of their children, of the neighbors down along Beech Fork. She had even remembered the deep, stirring tones of Adam Marlow before she saw him, that time he came to see her. His hair had grown white and his bearing was more stately. He was a preacher up at Harrodsburg, which was what they called Jim Harrod's town now. But she had remembered his resonant voice. She'd know Dan Boone's voice, too, if ever he came back from Missouri, and Jemima's and Rebecca's, also.

She listened intently. That voice, surely she ought to know it. She had just risen to her feet when the door burst open and Tom rushed in and flung his big arms around her frail shoulders.

"Tommy!" she cried. "Why, it's Tommy! Oh, Son, I've missed you so!" She turned her head. "Is Nancy with you? And the baby?"

"They're all here—*both* babies, Ma!" Tom shouted. This was the kind of thing he loved, all the loud confusion and joy of a homecoming, with kinfolk crowding around and everyone talking at once, and tears coming in his mother's eyes because she was so glad he was home again. Mary and her family had come along with them that morning, and Jo had waved to them as they passed, and had come, too. No doubt Mord and his family would be over in a little while; they'd all be together again.

"What do you mean, *both* babies?" asked Bathsheba, regaining her composure and straightening her cap, which he had knocked askew. "You mean to tell me you've had another child and nobody came to tell me? Fie on you, Thomas Lincoln! Where is this child?"

Nancy, beaming, came in, leaving Sally with Nancy Brumfield's young ones, who were entertaining her so thoroughly that the shy little girl didn't miss her mother.

"Here he is, Ma." Nancy Lincoln smiled at Bathsheba, and put the little boy on the floor in front of his grandmother. He was lean and tall for his age; his eyes were big and gray and looked up at her with the searching gaze of a very young child who isn't certain about his surroundings.

"He can walk already," said Nancy proudly. "Show your Granny how you can walk, Abe, that's a good boy!"

Bathsheba put her hand to her heart and threw Nancy a quick look, then turned her eyes to the little boy, who was still standing quietly.

"Did you say—Abe?" quavered Bathsheba, a whole procession of memories flashing across her mind, a whole lifetime of memories conjured up by that one name. Abe. "Did you name him Abraham?" she asked quietly.

"Yes, we did," Nancy explained gently, putting an understanding hand on the old woman's thin shoulder. "We were going to name Sally that, you know, only she was a girl, so we saved the name. Even though one of Mord's young ones is named that, we didn't think you'd mind. Tom always has been so proud of his pa and all he did to help settle this part of the country, though he doesn't recollect much about him. But it's a good name, and I hope little Abe does it credit." She smiled down at her son.

Bathsheba was scarcely listening. She was looking at the boy.

"Yes." She said it softly, as if she were talking to herself or to someone who was not in the room. "Yes, he really does look like you, Abraham. Those big gray eyes, that sweet thin mouth, the line of of his jaw, even though it's only a baby's jaw, it's still like yours. He'll be tall, too, you can tell it even now." She looked up at Nancy.

"Yes, he's rightly named Abraham Lincoln," Bathsheba said proudly, and her eyes went off into the past again, seeing a tall, gray-eyed man in dusty leather clothing coming back up a road in Virginia after a year away in the wilderness . . . a tall, determined man somehow getting his family over the rocks of Cumberland Gap, all the way to Boonesborough and beyond . . . a lean-jawed man listening to the story of the massacre at Blue Licks . . . seeing once again that limp form brought home, dead, from the field he had been clearing . . .

"I trust he'll do honor to Kentucky!" ended Bathsheba formally.

Then she stooped suddenly and held out her blue-veined hands to the little boy.

"Come to Granny, baby, come to Granny Basheby!"

And with a sudden smile on his earnest little face, Abraham Lincoln ran to her longing arms.

VIRGINIA S. EIFERT

was born and grew up in Springfield, Illinois. Near here runs the Sangamon River, down which Abraham Lincoln once traveled via three rivers south to New Orleans. The endless fascination of these woods and waters of middle America prompted the writing of her distinguished book, THREE RIVERS SOUTH: *A Story of Young Abe Lincoln,* which preceded THE BUFFALO TRACE.

Mrs. Eifert's writing career has been chiefly in the field of non-fiction, principally in the field of nature. *Nature Magazine, Natural History Magazine, Canadian Nature,* and youth magazines have published much of her work, but the bulk of her writing and illustrating has been issued by the Illinois State Museum, at which institution she has been editor since 1939. In addition to articles in the monthly magazine, *The Living Museum,* and five booklets in the Museum's *Story of Illinois* series, Mrs. Eifert is author of two nature books, BIRDS IN YOUR BACKYARD and ILLINOIS WILD FLOWERS.

Photography, painting, and a love for the out-of-doors, begun as hobbies, have grown into a life work which is carried on simultaneously with the role of wife, mother, and homemaker. As a family—Herman, Virginia, and their young son Larry—spend their leisure hours in exploring the woods and byways not only of the Lincoln Country but of much of America.

www.ingramcontent.com/pod-product-compliance
Lightning Source LLC
Chambersburg PA
CBHW030519020726
47494CB00004B/1158